C.S. BILLS

BEYOND
BELIEF

CLAN OF THE ICE MOUNTAINS

Copyright

BEYOND BELIEF

Book Four:
Clan of the Ice Mountains

C.S. Bills

Highest Hope Publishing LLC.

Table of Contents

Acknowledgments
A Word from the Author
Dedication
Chapter 1
Chapter 2
Chapter 3
Chapter 4
Chapter 5
Chapter 6
Chapter 7
Chapter 8
Chapter 9
Chapter 10
Chapter 11
Chapter 12
Chapter 13
Chapter 14
Chapter 15
Chapter 16
Chapter 17
Chapter 18
Chapter 19
Chapter 20
Chapter 21
Chapter 22
Chapter 23
Chapter 24
Chapter 25
Epilogue

Acknowledgements

Thanks again to Bethany Eicher, my invaluable editor and mentor. It has been an awesome adventure working with you!

A Word from the Author

You can find me on amazon.com. Visit my Amazon author page to see my other books, and use the comment section to ask a question or leave a comment. I'd love to hear from you!

Dedication

To Chloe Min and Miriam Wren:
Blessed additions to our Clan!

Chapter 1

Attu stood at the end of a rocky finger of land extending far out into the bay. A stiff breeze blew through his fur trimmed parka hood, and his eyes stung. All around him the ice groaned as large hunks of it pushed against each other like male nuknuks during the breeding season.

Soon Broken Rock Bay will be a solid Expanse strong enough to walk on.

Attu turned back and looked at the six hills a couple of spear throws from the shoreline. He and Rika had built a sturdy shelter there just two moons ago. And now, under the protection of the largest hill, wrapped in the love and attention of all the women of the Clan, Rika was giving birth to their first child, and Attu had been banished from camp until she did.

Attu's spirit called to him to run as fast as he could back to the shelter and Rika, but he knew the women of the Clan would stop him long before he got to her side.

Suka will come with the news. Soon.

Attuanin, please keep Rika and my new son or daughter safe!

Women sometimes died in childbirth… and Rika was the Clan's healer.

What if something goes wrong and no one else knows what to do to save her?

Rika's child was not the first to be born in this new place, far to the north of the Raven Clan they'd fled and the camp of their new friends, the Nukeena. While Attu battled the killer whales fishes' desire to attack and eat them all, his Clan had paddled their skin boats around the peninsula and into this bay, through the narrow openings between the teeth-like boulders standing guard over the bay's mouth. The Clan had built their shelters and explored most of the area surrounding their new home when, as the Elder women gone Between had promised Attu's Clan, it was time to receive Attuanin's gift. The babies started coming.

Yural had been first to give birth. Rika thought the poolik was coming too early, but Yural assured her both Attu and Meavu had been born before Elder Nuanu thought Yural's time had come. And Yural had delivered a healthy boy.

"A son to hunt for me in my old age," Ubantu said, and the rest of the Clan had laughed. Ubantu was as strong as a tuskie, and Attu had never seen his father so healthy. Life on the water had made them all vigorous.

When it had been Farnook's turn and Suka was banned from camp, he circled just outside it, calling again and again for a report on his woman until even Attu, who understood Suka's concern, grew tired of his pacing.

"You are like an old ice bear, looking for easy game," Attu said. "Go hunt something. We'll come get you when it's over."

But Suka had just scowled at Attu and kept circling.

Farnook was small, and the baby had come with difficulty. After a day and night of labor, a girl child was born. She was tiny, and her resemblance to Farnook, with her darker skin and delicate features, had Suka entranced from the moment he laid eyes on her. Rika told Attu she didn't know who'd been more exhausted afterward. She'd left the three of them sleeping, Farnook and the babe both exhausted from delivery, and Suka from pacing the entire time his woman labored.

Several other pooliks followed, and soon the air was filled with infant cries day and night. The entire camp smelled of wetness coverings. Keanu, Nuka, and Meavu, who was due with her own poolik in two more moons, rushed from one shelter to another helping to care for the new mothers and their babies. Suanu, with her son, Brovik, riding in her hood, assisted as much as she could, and Veshria helped also, often shadowd by her young daughter Tishria, who was eager to run and fetch for the women as they worked. Attu was thankful Veshria had rallied after the stillbirth of her last child, taking her place again among the women. Veshria seemed more at peace now.

The new fathers walked around with perpetual smiles. United under their new Clan tattoo, the People of the Waters rejoiced in the gift of so many new children.

And now it was Attu's turn to pace, to wait, and to be banned from camp until word was sent of their new child.

"I wish Rika was my only worry right now," Attu whispered. Nagging thoughts had been eating at him ever since he'd returned to camp.

The hunters had explored north and south along the coast and into the caves, but not past their hills and the next range of hills to the east. The landscape was barren there except for low-growing plants. Most thought it held only small game animals and birds, and the men were too busy hunting seals and fishing to take time to walk the area. That morning, Attu had decided he would take a day to do it. It was close to camp, and Rika was due to deliver their child any day.

"You won't go too far," Rika had urged.

"No, I'll be back before dark," Attu had reassured her. And he'd kept his word, returning even earlier than she'd expected. Climbing up over the last hill before their settlement, he had seen Suka running to meet him.

"Rika is laboring," he said, and the two dashed back to the settlement.

Why didn't you tell me? Attu mind spoke to Rika as they neared his shelter.

I want to follow tradition in this. Now mind the women.

Suka and Attu reached Attu's shelter, only to have the women shoo them both away. The men walked slowly back toward the beach.

Rika, Attu had tried again.

No response.

Rika? Rika!

I mean it. This is women's work, and I'll be fine. I don't want you in my thoughts right now. I need to concentrate on delivering this baby. You can't help me, and it would only pain you to know how much this will hurt.

Rika!

Nothing.

"Rika won't let me mind speak with her." Attu heard the desperation in his voice, but he couldn't help himself.

For once Suka didn't joke with Attu, but looked with understanding at his cousin.

"Why didn't she tell me she would block me out when her time came?"

"Because she knew you'd try to argue her out of her decision."

Attu swore.

"Sorry. I've got to grab the net I need to repair." Suka turned and started loping back along the path they'd worn between the shelters and the beach.

"Suka, I need…" But the path curved sharply among some boulders, and Suka was already out of sight.

Attu walked toward the open water at the southern tip of the bay. His thoughts were in turmoil and Attu instinctively sought the water, near his name spirit, Attuanin. Attuanin had spoken to him when Attu's mind was in the killer whale fish, and his name spirit's wisdom had strengthened Attu.

He stood on the rocky tip of the bay now and let the wind blow in his face. But its freshness didn't clear his thoughts. "Still I stand here, worried about both Rika and what I saw today," Attu mumbled to himself. He stood for a long while, looking out over the bay, his mind filled with anxiety. He hated feeling like this. So helpless.

The sound of footsteps on rocks caused Attu to look back toward camp. His father, Ubantu, was walking toward him. The sun was on the edge of the horizon. More time had passed than Attu had realized, so lost had he been in his own thoughts.

"The baby?" Attu rushed to his father.

"Not yet, my son. Have patience. Your mother assures me all is going well. She sent me to tell you."

"Good." Attu took a moment to let his father's words sink in. Rika was doing well. But as his worry about Rika abated for the moment, the other worry surfaced again. "Father, I saw something today while I was out exploring."

"What?"

"I came up over one of the hills, farther to the south than we've passed through before, and in the distance I saw a dark man-shape standing on the top of a low hill. It startled me so much I couldn't breathe. I fell to the ground, hoping the man hadn't seen my outline against the sky like I was seeing his."

"A man? Just one?" Ubantu faced his son.

"I asked myself, 'Where did he come from? Why is he standing there, alone and unmoving?' But I looked closer and realized it was not a man at all, but rocks arranged to look like a hunter."

Ubantu popped his lips. "Made of rocks?"

"Yes. Large rocks. I walked across the flat area and up the hill to its crest, where the rocks were piled. When I got close to it, it became obvious that the man-shape had been constructed."

"Who did this thing? And why?" Ubantu asked.

"That's what I want to know. And where are they now?"

"Did the rocks look like someone moved them there recently?"

"No. They'd been there for a while. A small plant was growing out of the crevice between two of them. On the north side of the rocks, moss and lichens clung to the surface."

"But whoever built it could still be in the area, even though we haven't seen anyone since we arrived." Ubantu's thick brows creased.

"Or they could come through seasonally, following some game."

"Attu! Attu!" Suka ran up the peninsula, dodging the large rocks on the beach in the growing darkness.

"Rika! Is she all right?" Attu asked, as Suka bent over, his hands on his knees to catch his breath.

"She's fine!" Suka straightened and beamed at the two of them. "You have a son!" he exclaimed.

"A son!" Attu said. "I-"

"And a daughter." Suka grinned. "Both strong and healthy."

"Two babies?" Attu sat down hard on a nearby rock as Ubantu and Suka took turns pounding him on the back.

"Two?" Attu repeated. "A boy and a girl?"

Ubantu and Suka roared with laughter and slapped their thighs at Attu's incredulous look.

Attu grinned up at his father and cousin, an ear-splitting smile that made the two other men laugh again. Realizing he was still sitting on the rock, Attu leaped up. "What are we waiting for? Come on!" Attu ran back to camp, Suka and his father right behind him.

"I'm fine," Rika said, as Attu asked her for the tenth time if she needed anything. "I'm doing well, just tired." Rika smiled, lifting her hand to Attu's face briefly before resting it back on the baby nestled at her side.

Meavu balanced the other newborn on her protruding stomach as her eyes danced between her brother and Rika.

"They are small," Attu said. "Are you sure they're all right?" He sat down on the furs beside Rika and touched the fuzzy dark hair of his son.

"Each is as large as Farnook's daughter, and she is doing well," Rika said. She yawned. "And now we know why I grew large so fast and why it felt like the baby within me never went to the Between of sleep, but was forever kicking…" She closed her eyes.

"Because four little feet were kicking," Attu finished her thought, grinning at his woman. "And four little hands were pushing."

But Rika had fallen asleep.

"Here, hold your daughter," Meavu said. "Elder Nuka will be here soon, and Rika needs to sleep. I'm getting some sleep, too."

"But I-" Attu protested. Meavu tucked a small bundle into his arms, and before he could stop her she patted his shoulder and left the shelter.

Attu looked down at his new daughter. She gazed back at him. Still wrinkled, she looked like a wise old woman, not a poolik. Attu touched her cheek and she turned toward his fingers, her lips moving, seeking milk.

"Now *that* I can't provide for you," Attu whispered. He slid his fingers over her hair: thick, dark, curly tresses, longer than he'd seen on any of the other babies. She was beautiful.

Beside Rika, Attu's new son whimpered, opening his mouth and uttering a small, mewling cry.

"Oh no," Attu said. "Your mother needs to sleep." He scooped the infant up with his free arm, balancing them both toes to toes in the crooks of his arms. "Attuanin, you have greatly blessed me," Attu whispered as two sets of eyes -- dark like the glossy rock in the hills -- shone up at him out of two almost identical faces.

Attu sat back against a shelter pole and jiggled his new son and daughter on his knees. His son mewled again, and Attu adjusted his wrappings. It was hard to do, and Attu put both babies into his left arm, side by side, as he adjusted the wrappings with his right hand. As soon as the babies were touching, his son stopped crying. His daughter's hand escaped the wrappings and found her brother's ear. His son squirmed and wriggled his hand free. The babies continued searching for each other.

Attu unwrapped both pooliks quickly, for the night air was becoming chilly inside the shelter, even with a good fire. He laid the babies side by side, and then wrapped them up together. Both stopped squirming and turned slightly, as if to get a good look at the person they'd been sharing that warm, dark space with for so many moons before they were born. Satisfied they had found each other again, both babies' eyes closed, and as Attu watched, they fell asleep. He tucked them back in with their mother and turned to warm up some fish stew Rika had made earlier. He was hungry, and Rika would be too, once she awoke.

"They like being near each other?" Elder Nuka asked, as she entered the shelter.

"My son was beginning to fuss, but near his sister, he seems content." Attu looked to the Elder. He wasn't sure he'd done the right thing by wrapping the two together, even though it was working.

"May it be so forever," Elder Nuka said. "For twin spirits are woven together, and like a rope of more than one strand, together they are more powerful than each alone. That twin spirits are born to our leader and our healer, Nuviks strong in the Gifts, is a good omen for our people."

Elder Nuka wiped her cheeks roughly, turning away from Attu to hide her tears. She bustled around the shelter, putting things back in order from the birth and shooing Attu out before he had a chance to eat.

"I'll call you when Rika awakes," she assured him. "Go. Hear the congratulations of the rest of the Clan. Keanu has prepared fish over the camp's main fire, and Suka is telling stories."

"You should have seen Attu's face when I told him he was the father of twins!"

Suka was regaling the rest of the men as Attu rounded the shelter nearest where the hunters had gathered around the fire.

The men popped their lips in approval as Suka mimicked Attu's look of astonishment before falling sideways back onto his furs.

"Oh, Suka. You make everything so much better in the retelling than it actually was when it happened," Attu said as he slid into an open spot and someone handed him a bowl of hot food. He took a bite then choked on it as the men slapped him on the back and congratulated him on the birth of his twins.

"We shouldn't be surprised," Suka began again. "Attu almost always comes out on top in any contest. He would be the one whose woman bore two babies at once. You know Attu. He's so desperate to win at everything. He probably persuaded Attuanin to let him win at fatherhood as well."

Attu looked to his cousin and frowned. *Everyone knows it's Suka who always needs to win whenever there's a competition between us, and it's Suka who makes everything into a contest in the first place.*

Suka kept still, letting the moment hang -- everyone looking at him -- before he burst into laughter and ended with a mischievous grin and a wink at Attu. Realizing Suka was pulling a joke on himself, the men joined in.

Attu settled back into the furs around the fire. He was tired. The waiting and worrying had worn him out more than a three-day trek across the Expanse hauling a full-grown nuknuk.

The last thing Attu remembered was someone pulling a warm fur over him.

"Will you be all right?" Attu asked, hovering over Rika as she fed their daughter. Their son had already fallen asleep after his meal and was nestled on Rika's lap next to his sister. Rika looked tired, but alert. She seemed in no pain. Attu had waited another day, just to be sure they were all fine, but the men were pestering him to show them the rock man. Still, Attu was reluctant to leave Rika and the pooliks.

"I'll stay with you."

"No. You need to go. I'll be fine. Elder Nuka will be here soon to watch them while I sleep. Everyone has been so helpful." Rika smiled at the snorting noises their daughter was making as she ate. "The other women know how exhausting it is to have one poolik, so everyone is thinking of me, with two." Rika grinned up at him. "I don't think I would be getting this much help if I'd just had one." She motioned with her head to the food all prepared and stacked behind them, ready to heat over the fire, the pile of fresh wetness coverings, and the wood their people had brought.

"Usually I'm the one helping others," Rika said. She seemed overwhelmed by the practical help the Clan had showered on her the day before, coming in to see the twins and each leaving something she could use. Women had offered to watch the pooliks while Rika slept, even though most of them had newborns of their own to care for or were ready to deliver any day.

Attu knew it was more than just Rika having twins. She kept watch over everyone and thought nothing of rising in the night to go to any shelter where someone felt ill. She'd delivered every baby safely so far and was helping each new mother whenever the need arose. But Rika wouldn't take gifts for doing her healer's work. Giving to the twins was a way the Clan could say thank you.

"I'm proud of you for accepting help," Attu said. "I know it's not easy for you."

"It's easier when it's for our son and daughter." Rika looked down at her pooliks. Love radiated from her. Never had Rika looked more beautiful to Attu than she did now. As Attu stood watching them, the urge to protect his family welled up in his spirit.

"Go," Rika said, pretending to scowl. "I don't need you in my shelter again today, hovering over your sleeping children and getting in my way, looking like a lovesick nuknuk." She smiled at Attu, but the smile disappeared as she added, "Go, and figure out if that rock man means a threat to us or not."

Chapter 2

After two days of searching -- short excursions between fishing and caring for their families -- Attu and his hunters found four more rock men, all placed on the tops of hills, alternating on one side and the other of the range.

"I can't believe these were so close to us and we didn't see them before," Ubantu said as the men stood at the top of one of the nearer hills, looking at the rock men.

"They show up best when we're below, on the barren land between the hills, and no one bothered to walk down there until Attu. Not enough game to make it worthwhile," Rusik said.

"Each is positioned so when you look up, you see it silhouetted against the sky, like I did when I saw the first one. I think that's important."

"Could they be here for some spiritual reason?" Soantek asked.

"They might be spiritual territory markers, like the Ravens' totem poles," Tingiyok said, "but I don't feel any power coming from them, do you?" He turned to Attu.

"None. What do you think, Father?"

"I thought they might be grave markers, but these hills are too rocky to dig into and we've found no rock piles like we made on the Expanse to bury our dead." Ubantu looked out over the hills, his face thoughtful.

Rovek placed himself in front of the rock man they'd been examining, imitating its stance, his arms wide. He looked across the land toward where they knew the other rock men were placed. He studied the area as the others pulled out some dried seal strips and squatted out of the wind just below the crest of the hill, eating the tough hunks of meat, softening them with mouthfuls of water before chewing.

"When we hunted the tuskies," Rovek began, as if he were thinking aloud, "we had hunters on both sides of them. We came in on one side and drove them over the cliff." He pointed to a gap between two hills. Each had a rock man at its crest. "Between those two hills, there is a way for game to get through and end up at the river on the other side." Rovek's voice grew more certain as he continued. "Hunters wouldn't want the game to get through that pass because the river and plains are flat and open all the way to the mountains. They'd never catch big animals running on that plain."

"I see it now." Attu pointed north. "If they could keep the animals moving north, they would end up going through the gap between those last two hills and into that small lake. See how the land rises up all around it?"

"The perfect place to trap whatever it is they're hunting," Rusik said.

"I think the rock men were built so that from the valley between the hills, animals look up and see the outline of a man. A very large fat man!" Rovek said. Attu and the other hunters laughed with Rovek. The rock men were more than twice as wide as a Nuvik, and about a head taller.

"A panicking animal sees the first rock man and moves away from its one chance of escape onto the plains," Rovek continued, "right into the hunters' trap. The other rock men keep it going north between those last two hills. If you don't have as many men as we had to hunt the tuskies, it must work to use the rock men. They force the game to move into that lake, where it can be killed."

Tingiyok joined in. "The lake is shallow quite far out. The tall grassy plants with the long brown tops only grow in water less than thigh deep, and in that lake, the plants grow almost a spear throw from shore."

"The boys have to use the skin boats in the lake," Attu said. "The women want the fluff in the tops of those plants to use inside wetness coverings, but the boys can't just wade in and get it."

"No, they tried and Kossu got stuck in the mud," Rusik said. "It took Ganik, Chonik, and me to pull him out, and he was only knee deep in the water. The mud was ankle deep and held him like a toothfish."

"So the animals get stuck or at least flounder in the mud there, making them easy prey," Soantek said. "I think Rovek's right. These rock men are for funneling the game to the lake."

"So whoever they are, the people who built the rock men and hunt the animals are clever." Ubantu looked out over the hills. "If they're hunting paddle antlers, they'll be back next spring when the grass greens and the herds move north again."

"Could they be the same men you saw in your vision?" Tingiyok asked. Others wondered aloud as well.

"They could return sooner, then," Ubantu said, looking to Attu.

As realization hit him, Attu felt the blood leave his face. Ubantu caught his eye and nodded, his own face etched with worry.

"What is it?" Rovek asked.

"Children. Rika said 'children' in the vision. I thought that meant we had more time, at least this winter. But now that she's had twins…" Attu let his words fade as he saw the others' dawning comprehension.

"One good snowfall," Tingiyok said. "That's all the attackers need."

The nights were growing long and becoming a time of conversation by the fire like they'd been on the Expanse around the nuknuk lamps. Usually, the women came and went as needed, gathering around the flames, chatting among themselves as they fed pooliks and changed wetness coverings. But tonight everyone was quiet, tense.

"Those hunters might not come at all," Rusik said. "The rock men have been on the hills for a long time. The animals might have changed their route north. Tuskies do. The hunters would follow them."

"But what if the people who built those rock men don't follow the animals in the winter? What if they roam large areas with those bear-like animals pulling sleds, like Attu saw in his vision?" Rovek asked. "The rock men builders could also be the ones who attack us, couldn't they?"

"Whether the people who built the rock men are the ones who will attack us or not, now that we've realized the attack could come this winter, we don't have much time," Rusik said. "What do we need to do to get ready?"

The men started talking at once, their women joining in. One of the men started shouting at another, but his woman cut him off.

"Don't wake the sleeping pooliks," she hissed at him.

The others grew quiet.

Attu stood. Those gathered looked his way as Attu held out his hands, then sat again, crossing his legs and looking toward the others. They rearranged themselves to begin the discussion.

Ubantu put his hand out to speak. "We need to explore the caves that the Nukeena found when they came to the bay the first time."

Soantek nodded.

"And we need to get them supplied with food, water, and furs," one of the women said after Attu acknowledged her signal to speak.

"It could snow soon," Tingiyok added.

"Or it could be another moon or so," Rusik said, trying to sound hopeful.

Keanu sat beside Attu. "I'll begin flying daily again. Starting tomorrow." Keanu assured him. "No one will sneak up on us."

The rest of the evening was spent with the women making plans to outfit the caves with everything necessary for a prolonged stay, and the men planning how best to defend the women and children once they were hidden.

"We'll start preparing at first light," Attu said. All around him, most of his people nodded their approval. Attu saw that Veshria was scowling and appeared to be arguing with Rusik. "I don't believe him," she said. She looked up and saw Attu watching her. Veshria turned away and dropped her voice. Another woman joined them and then another hunter. Rusik kept glancing toward Attu when he thought Attu wasn't looking.

Attu wrapped his fur around himself, feeling suddenly chilled. He knew that some of his people didn't believe his vision would come true. No matter how many times Attu and others with Gifts had Seen true, some just couldn't believe them. There would be much to do in preparing the caves, on top of the already increased hunting and caregiving of the pooliks. They would see it as unnecessary work.

Rika sat beside him, handing him his son and cradling his daughter in her lap. "I get so angry when Veshria stirs up trouble. She's just like Moolnik was."

"Some of our people agree with her," Attu said. "But that won't stop us from getting ready, anyway." Attu pulled the soft furs more closely around his son. "When most of us start stocking the caves, those few will join in. They won't risk their lives on being right."

Attu dreamed that night about small bears with long curling tails, pulling men on sleds through the snow toward their shelters. Dread filled him as he mind spoke to Rika in his dream. *Gather everyone and flee to the caves.*

But this time, Rika didn't answer him, didn't tell him she would keep their children safe. Instead, all he heard was a lonely wind rustling through the pine trees. He called in his mind. He shouted aloud. But no one answered. Instead, his voice became the wind, mindlessly blowing through the trees and warning no one.

"I didn't realize the caves were this extensive," Attu said as the men marked the various openings and places large enough for people to gather.

"We need to keep torches just inside each entrance," Suka said.

The caves were dry, and the walls were hard stone, grey in the light of the torches. It was cool inside, but not nearly as cold as outside. The walls sloped in sharply when they reached about twice the height of a snow house, and the larger open areas were bigger than a group snow house. The caves should have felt spacious, yet Attu felt his chest tightening as he walked deeper into them.

"We need to build fire circles of stone where we know the smoke can get through those small holes." Ubantu pointed to one of the areas where some light was making its way down to the floor through the rocks above. "And we need to build test fires to make sure we won't be smoked out."

"And to make sure the smoke can't be seen easily from outside," Mantouk added.

They continued marking. "Block off this tunnel," Tingiyok said, returning from his exploration of a side passage. "It goes into a maze of openings that I couldn't find an end to. It's a good thing I kept track of my turnings as I went."

Rovek moved some loose rocks across the opening and placed a stick with a marker on it, much as they'd done on the Expanse to show thin ice.

"So we use the south-facing entrance to move everything in and leave the other entrances hidden." Attu turned to leave. "Suka, you're the best at it. Take some men next day and disguise the other entrances so you have to know just where they are to see them. We need to do that before it snows."

They stepped out into the daylight again. "I hope we don't have to stay in them long," Ubantu said. "Or better yet, I hope by the spirits we don't need to use them at all." He took in a deep breath. Attu thought he looked a bit queasy.

Attu flashed his father a look of understanding.

"But I'm glad they're here," Ubantu added. "If the strangers try to come in after us, they'll only be able to come in one at a time, and we can kill each one as he enters."

"I'll make sure we have plenty of weapons stored near the entrance." Attu walked back to camp with the other men as they made plans to cut more torches and have another group head back to do the test fires the next day.

Chapter 3

"It's so warm." Tingiyok pulled off his over shirt and tied it around his waist. He'd already taken his parka off and wrapped it in his pack.

Attu was only wearing his sleeveless under-vest, and he was still sweating in his foot miks. He jabbed at a stone with his spear. "I was so sure the ice would be hard by now." He shielded his eyes from the sun as he looked out over the bay.

They'd prepared the caves as best they could in case snow came suddenly, but then the weather had changed. It went from freezing to mild, and the women had been forced to remove the small amount of fresh meat they'd been able to store in the caves. Only dried meat and berries had been left behind for food, along with water pouches and old furs for warmth. The men had stored extra weapons and a lot of stacked wood throughout their hiding place. Their preparations as complete as they could make them, it was   time to hunt again.

Attu was glad it had grown warm because warmth meant no snow, so no strangers attacking, but it was also making their hunting difficult. "And it doesn't help to see all those nuknuks floating on ice chunks, sunning themselves as if it were the middle of summer," Ubantu said.

"I had no idea that a warm wind could break up ice so quickly." Attu pointed out over the expanse of open water. "And the large chunks of ice left are moving with it. I wouldn't want to be caught between those in a skin boat."

Attu shuddered as he remembered how larger chunks of ice had struck the one he'd been stranded on with Rika, Elder Nuanu, and Moolnik. It had been a miracle of Attuanin that the giant whale fish had propelled them to the shore with a great flap of its tail before the ice they'd been trapped on had crumbled to pieces.

The hunters walked back toward camp. "I've never been out among ice chunks," Ubantu said, "but if this weather keeps up, I think we'll need to try to take nuknuks by skin boat."

"I think we can do it, if we're careful," Tingiyok said. "But it will be tricky. Nuknuks are so much bigger than seals."

"I'd feel a lot better about hunting them on solid ice, that's for sure," Ubantu said.

"But with all these mouths to feed, we need more than fish," Attu said, "and almost all the seals left when the nuknuks came." He took in a deep breath before speaking the truth of his own fear. "We should be able to maneuver around the ice chunks without them hitting us, but I think it will be dangerous. I'm afraid to try it."

"I, for one, am looking forward to it." Tingiyok smiled at them all. "Even though I, too, am afraid."

One of the other hunters looked to Tingiyok and Attu in disgust.

Tingiyok stared at the man until he looked away.

Ubantu nodded at Tingiyok, Attu, and the others. "No one can maneuver a boat as well as Tingiyok. If he is afraid, then it is wise for us all to be." He looked at the disgusted hunter, who dropped his eyes. "We will go if we must. We are strong Nuvik hunters. We will face our fear, and we will be successful."

Attu let his father see the gratitude in his eyes.

Attu sat in their shelter, holding his son while his daughter slept. The poolik was wide-awake, wiggling and looking first this way then that.

"I bring no evil," Tingiyok called.

"Come in, have a seat," Rika answered and moved to the door flap before Attu could stand.

Tingiyok sat in the place for visitors, farthest from the door, as the warm wind whistled around the shelter. He reached for Attu's son, and Attu handed the squirming poolik over to the Elder. Tingiyok gazed at the poolik, who had grabbed the Elder's finger. "He's a strong one." Tingiyok grinned at the little one, his mouth wide, his few teeth gleaming in the light of the small fire. Attu's son looked back at Tingiyok, fascinated.

"He likes you," Rika said.

"I sense it," Tingiyok said. "It's strange to listen to all these pooliks' minds. No words, fuzzy images, much emotion. And they're all as loud as you were with your thoughts, Attu, after you flew with the falcon in the dream, but before you learned to hold your increased power in your mind."

Attu's face burned, but he said nothing. He knew Tingiyok's words were true.

"It helps me so much," Rika said. "I can tell which poolik is stirring by their thoughts, and I'm learning to understand their jumble of emotions and mind images. I often know what my son or daughter wants before they cry to get it."

"But when they cry-" Attu began.

"No need to say more." Tingiyok put up his hand. "The first time it happened, I was holding Suka's daughter. She went from cooing to screaming, and I almost dropped her!"

They all laughed. Suka's daughter cried louder than any of the other pooliks.

"While we're waiting for this strong wind to die down, I'm taking Ganik, Kossu, and Chonik out into the grasslands to the east, by the rock men," Tingiyok said. "Rusik and Mantouk have asked me to begin training the two younger ones to set snares, and Kossu wants to come along. Do you?"

"Their fathers asked you?" Rika sat beside them, picking up some small sewing.

"Seers don't train their own boys to hunt. We believe the boy's father may not be tough enough on his own son. And without the proper skills and ability to persevere in the hunt when things get difficult, the rest of the Clan will suffer."

Tingiyok handed the poolik to Rika. "We're ready to leave. Will you join us?"

Attu glanced at Rika. She nodded. "All is well here. Go."

Attu joined Kossu as he walked from his shelter to where the others waited at the edge of camp. Kossu grinned at Attu as they moved out toward the hills north and east of camp. Kossu, the oldest of Rusik's sons, was nearing the time of his hunter's ceremony and needed no instruction. Attu suspected Veshria had sent him to make sure Ganik behaved himself, but Attu also knew that going with the younger boys was a chance for Kossu to spend time with Attu and Tingiyok and to let them see his skills.

"Kossu has already set several rabbit snares off the path to the lake. Should we check those first?" Chonik asked.

"It's a good place to start," Tingiyok said. They headed north through the flat land toward the lake.

Chonik was a short sturdy boy, the son of Mantouk and his woman, Trika, two other Seers who'd joined Attu's Clan. He was about Ganik's age but seemed to have more common sense, except when he was following Ganik. Chonik followed Ganik without question, no matter how crazy the boy's schemes.

"Kossu is best with the snares, and Chonik with finding the long roots to use for the snares. But I'm best at spotting where to put them. I'm good at finding the animals' paths and footprints."

"Ganik, it's wrong to brag," Kossu said, tousling his younger brother's hair.

"Aww, you know it's true," Ganik whined.

"Your brother is right," Tingiyok said. "The true hunter never brags about his own skills and is careful not to say too much about another's. The spirits are always listening, and they do not reward the hunter whose pride is puffed up like the nuknuk bull at mating time."

The boys laughed at this.

Attu watched Kossu expertly set a snare. *Soon he will be ready for his hunter's ceremony. Who will become his woman? There is none here available.*

A cry pierced the air.

"What was that?" Ganik shouted.

"Hush!" Kossu clamped a hand over Ganik's mouth.

"It came from over there," Tingiyok said. "Stay behind us."

Attu and Tingiyok took the lead, running low to the ground. The boys followed. Attu glanced back to see Ganik keeping pace, quiet now, but scowling from his brother's scolding. Ahead, the noise grew louder.

Coming up over a small rise, Attu signaled a halt and dropped to the ground. Below them, a moose was bawling, flinging its antlers back and forth. On its side hung an animal like Attu had seen in his vision. It was large, although not compared to the moose. It looked like a bear, but smaller and with a longer snout. It was trying to rip at the moose with its teeth and front feet.

"Look there," Tingiyok whispered. Near the edge of what appeared to be a small cave, another of the bear-like animals, much smaller than the one still fighting the moose, was lying torn and bloody, its eyes wide in death.

"Its mate?" Kossu whispered, slipping up beside the older hunters.

"Maybe," Attu said.

The moose pushed off with its hind legs and landed with a jolt on its front ones. The bear-like animal lost its grip and fell to the ground. The moose lowered its head and caught its attacker with the full force of its huge antlers. It ground the animal into the dirt, twisting and pushing its spiky points into the animal like spears. The animal screamed in pain. The hairs on Attu's neck rose. Chonik gasped and covered his ears as the animal continued to cry out.

Muscles straining in its neck and shoulders, the moose lifted its attacker, now impaled on its antlers, and twisting its whole body, the moose threw the animal several spear lengths, where it crunched to the rocky ground, lifeless.

Ganik started to rise, but Tingiyok pulled him down. "This moose is still in the blood lust of killing. If it sees you, you will be the next to feel the force of those powerful antlers."

"We don't try to kill it?" Ganik said. "The meat. You said we need-"

"We need to stay alive," Attu said. "We wait here until it leaves."

The moose walked over to where the larger of the two bear-like animals lay, pawing at it as if to make sure it was dead. Then, without a backward glance, it trotted away toward the river.

Attu waited until the moose was out of sight behind the next hill before he signaled the others to investigate the dead animals.

"I've never seen anything like them," Tingiyok said. "Are they like the animals in your vision, Attu?"

Attu examined the larger one. "This one looks a lot like the animals I saw pulling the sleds in my vision, but it's larger and its fur is lighter." He walked over to the smaller one. "This one is about the size of the animals I saw. But its fur is darker on its back, with all these markings of different colors on its sides and white underneath. I've never seen an animal like that, black and brown and white all on one body. Have you?"

Tingiyok shook his head.

"Ganik. Chonik. Where are you?" Kossu called. He looked around. "They were just here beside me."

"In here," a voice answered from what Attu had suspected to be a small cave.

"Get out of there!" Kossu hollered, running toward the cave with Attu and Tingiyok on his heels. "You don't know if there are more…"

His words faded as the two boys came out of the cave. Chonik carried a large furry bundle that was trying to claw its way up his chest. Ganik was struggling to hang on to two more.

"Look what we found. No, come back!" Ganik cried as one of the animals leaped free of his arms and ran to the smaller of the two dead animals and pushed at its side. When it got no response from its mother, the little creature licked her face, lying with its belly on the ground, whimpering and swinging its long tail back and forth so rapidly it blurred.

The sound of its crying tugged at Attu.

The whining animal turned at Tingiyok's approach. Its fur stood up and it growled. Its whole body shook as it stood its ground over its mother.

"A braver kip I have never seen," Tingiyok said. He grinned.

"Kip?" Attu looked at the animal. It didn't look much like a baby nuknuk to him.

"Might as well call them kips, since we don't know what they are."

Tingiyok held his hand out to the kip. Attu was surprised when the animal didn't bite the Elder, but stopped growling and sniffed Tingiyok's hand, instead. Tingiyok reached out further, and the animal let him pick it up by the scruff of its neck, like nuknuk mothers picked up their babies. Tingiyok cradled it in his arms, and the kip sniffed at one of Tingiyok's pockets, where he had some dried meat.

"Good nose," Tingiyok said. "I think this one is more hungry than afraid." He gave it a small bite of meat. The kip gobbled it up. "The mother must have been gone for some time on the hunt."

Chonik, Ganik, and Kossu sat on the ground in a circle with the other kips in the middle. Ganik was feeding his dried sunset fish strip to one of them, the largest one, light-colored like its father. The other was much smaller and preferred Chonik and Kossu in turn.

"What do we do with them?" Kossu asked. "They will die without their mother and father."

"But it would be the Nuvik way not to disturb the balance of the spirits," Tingiyok said. "Some predator will come along soon…"

"No! No!" Ganik and Chonik cried out together.

"Leave the kips for now," Tingiyok said. He put the kip he was holding down and moved to where many tracks went up over the hill. "We are here for your training. Tell me what you see."

Ganik and Chonik reluctantly set the other two kips down and walked over to where Tingiyok was pointing.

"Lots of tracks," Ganik said. He scowled at Tingiyok, angry at having to put down the kip he'd been holding. Kossu gave him a look, and Ganik dropped his eyes.

"When the moose came up over the hill, it was running," Chonik said, pointing to the wide-spaced hoof prints.

"Good," Tingiyok said.

"And both adults were chasing it," Ganik said, not to be outdone by Chonik.

"What else?" Tingiyok asked. The boys studied the tracks but said nothing. Tingiyok turned to Kossu.

"The path the moose took was the most direct and easiest, given the terrain it was running on," Kossu said after a moment. "I think it was an accident that the fight ended here by the animals' shelter, although…" he shook his head, changing his mind. "It would be the smart thing to do to drive the moose back here, where once it was dead, the kips could feed on the meat too, without going too far from their shelter. And the parents wouldn't have to guard both the meat and their shelter, or drag hunks of the meat a long distance to their cave, attracting other predators." He looked to Tingiyok.

"I agree. Which tells us more about these animals. They are very smart. It should have worked. But the moose was just too big for the two of them, too powerful."

As Attu was listening to Tingiyok teach the boys, he considered how the women would react if he brought the kips back to camp. He knew for certain that Rika would be afraid the kips might hurt their pooliks. And she would probably be right.

The adults had tried to take down a full-grown moose. The kips had sharp teeth. They could kill a baby.

But the men who drove the bear-like animals had to keep them in their camps, didn't they? And somehow the animals had to be trained to pull the sleds, to go where the men wanted them to go. It all seemed so strange to Attu. *Except,* he thought, *perhaps not so strange after all. If I can work in an animal's mind to have it do my bidding, why couldn't an animal be taught like a poolik, with treats, with kind words and things it desired, to do what a person wanted it to do?*

One by one, the kips ran up to the boys, sniffing at their clothing for more meat.

Tingiyok and Attu stepped away, nodding to the boys that they could resume playing with the kips. "They're learning already," Tingiyok said after Attu had shared his thoughts. "I think we can teach these kips. You can mind blend with them. And then, when the men come, we will know how to get their animals to do what we want. Do you think your mind-blending could overcome whatever training the animals had from their men, if we needed it to?"

"I don't know. If our people are threatened, I might have to enter the animals' minds against their wills…" Attu didn't like the idea, but if necessary he would do it. "It would be better if we knew what would work best to influence them with their consent."

"I believe it is no accident that we found these kips today." Tingiyok watched as Kossu put down the kip he was holding, then walked a spear-length away from it and turned, holding out meat. The kip ran toward him, jumping up on him, trying to reach the food.

"Perhaps this is part of Attuanin's plan," Attu agreed. "Knowing how to influence the animals should give us an advantage and might keep us all safe."

Attu hadn't really understood exactly what he and Keanu and Soantek were going to do with the animals, but in the vision they'd prepared to mind blend with them. And as Attu thought about it, it made sense. If they could turn the attackers' animals away, they would have more time to prepare a defense.

"Maybe we could make the animals run over thin ice and fall in, drowning the attacking men."

"That would drown the animals, too."

"That doesn't seem right." Attu found his mind pulling away from his initial idea. He wondered at his feelings toward these creatures.

"I feel the same way," Tingiyok said.

"Even though they might grow up to be as dangerous as their father and mother were? You saw how that male was clinging to the moose. And yet…" Attu wondered about the vision, about what that future danger might include. He turned his thoughts inward for a moment, seeking a sign from the spirits that they should keep the animals. But he sensed nothing. He looked to Tingiyok.

"I believe we should keep them," the Elder said.

"We will take the kips back with us," Attu announced. The two younger boys began the ululation cry at Attu's words but stopped -- their mouths agape -- when the largest kip sat, lifted his nose to the sky, and made a noise much like the boys' cry, long and wavering. And loud.

"He is already part of our Clan," Chonik said, his face solemn. "He knows the celebration cry."

And so he does, Attu thought. *What a strange confirmation we are making the right decision in keeping the kips. Thank you, Attuanin.*

Ganik threw back his head again, and soon all three kips were sitting like the first one, crying out with the two younger boys, every little face to the sky.

Chapter 4

"I do not want that animal in here with our children," Rika said.

She'd refused to hold the smaller, dark-colored kip Attu had chosen. He'd thought if she'd just looked into its eyes, felt its warm softness… but Rika would have none of it.

"It might bite our children. What were you thinking, Attu, bringing live animals into our shelter?"

Attu left with the kip. He knew Rika was right. *Maybe Tingiyok will take it.*

Tingiyok was thrilled to take the small dark female. The large male had gone with Ganik and Kossu. They had no pooliks in their shelter either, so it was ideal. Attu didn't think he'd have been able to take the kip from Ganik anyway. The boy had clung to it all the way back to camp, and it seemed equally fond of the boy. It was all so strange to Attu.

"Animals are food," Ubantu said as he walked with Attu and the last female kip to Keanu and Soantek's shelter.

"I know. You don't capture their young and bring them into your shelter to be part of your Clan. You don't feed them and let them play with your children." Attu wrestled with his conflicted thoughts. "To do so would be the ultimate foolishness. Everyone else would know you were crazy. Yet in my vision, I saw these animals pulling the sleds. They'd obviously been taught to pull and must live with the men who were riding behind them."

Attu and Ubantu gave the greeting at the entrance to Keanu and Soantek's shelter. Keanu invited them in, and they all sat. Keanu reached for the female kip and held it gently, stroking its ears and neck. The kip nuzzled into her and closed its eyes.

"What amazing creatures," Soantek said, gazing at the now sleeping kip. "It's like this little one knows it is safe with us. How?"

"I don't know."

"You are worried the adult animals escaped from the men we saw in your vision and those men might be nearby?" Keanu turned anxious eyes on Attu.

"Animals run from humans. But these kips didn't. It makes me wonder."

"And we've never seen any before," Ubantu said.

"I've been thinking about the possibilities," Keanu said. "You said the male was much larger than the female. Could it be some of these creatures were taken by the men and trained to pull sleds, but some are also much larger and live on their own as predators?"

"I would like to think these kips' parents were wild ones of their kind because then we wouldn't have to be worried about the men with the sleds being close by." Attu glanced out the open shelter flap at the bare ground around their camp. "But it could grow cold and snow any day now. What do you think we should do?"

"Keanu has been flying with birds each day to make sure no one is approaching our camp. She can see for great distances from the air," Soantek said.

"I don't think they're close by, yet." Keanu stroked the sleeping kip, her face thoughtful. "Do you want us to start working with this kip, mind blending with it?"

"Yes. I was hoping you'd be able to. Rika won't let one stay with us."

Soantek and Keanu exchanged glances. They looked doubtful. Attu's heart sank.

Keanu scratched the kip again and it stretched. She looked to Soantek.

"I know we need to learn as much as we can about them before some of their kind bring a new enemy to us," Soantek agreed. "But with Keanu flying every day and me hunting," he shrugged, "I don't know if we'll be able to care for the kip, too. But we'll try."

Attu left the shelter with Ubantu, feeling frustrated that he couldn't keep one of the kips for himself, even though he knew it wasn't a good idea with the pooliks.

Ubantu put a hand on Attu's shoulder before turning back to his own shelter. Attu walked to his.

Maybe we can rig an enclosure of some kind in the shelter, to keep the kip away from the babies. Attu decided to ask Rika one more time to reconsider keeping one of the kips. But as he walked into the shelter, Rika was struggling to feed their son while their daughter fussed. As the door flapped closed behind him, Attu's daughter began to cry.

"She just finished eating. I don't know what's wrong," Rika said. She looked exhausted, a new mother overcome with the task of caring for twins. Attu realized he couldn't ask his woman to take a kip. Even if she were willing and they could keep it away from the pooliks, it would be too much for Rika when he was gone. Attu had to hunt. And he had to lead, which took him away from the shelter often.

Attu picked his daughter up and soothed her as best he could. Since bringing home the kips, he'd been able to think of little else. Attu was now convinced Attuanin had sent them to that spot with the curious Ganik, so the boy would find the kips. Knowing about these animals must be crucial for them.

Keanu and Soantek must have the time and patience to work with them. Attu held his spirit necklace as he rocked his daughter in his arms. *When an attack comes, I'll need to lead the men. So it makes sense that Keanu and Soantek work with the animals and not me. I just can't do it all.*

His daughter stopped crying and looked at Attu, her eyes large and dark in her face. Attu knew he had to trust his people to do their part in preparing. He had family responsibilities now, as well as the leadership of the Clan. No matter how much he wanted to be the one to spend time mind blending with the animals, Attu knew he needed to let Keanu and Soantek do most of the exploration into these kips' minds.

"Here, let me take him," Attu said, as Rika finished feeding their son. "You get some rest."

Rika smiled gratefully at Attu and lay back on the furs. She was asleep in moments.

"And now that the weather is warm again, I had to go back and haul all our meat out of the caves. This is the second time. Where are those men Attu said are supposed to attack us?" Attu walked around the corner of Veshria's shelter to see her picking up a large piece of meat from the sledge they'd brought back from the caves. Trika and Tishria carried another. Veshria and Trika had become friends, and just like Ganik and Chonik, Trika seemed to go along with whatever Veshria said.

"Attu said the men would come when it was cold and snowing. He thought the weather would have changed by now," Trika said. Attu was glad to hear the quieter woman object to Veshria's comment.

"That's what I was saying." Veshria's voice became shrill. "You need to listen, Trika. Here, help me with this big piece." She glanced up and saw Attu, flashing an annoyed look at him before turning back to her work. Trika saw Attu, and her face reddened before she turned away.

Attu said nothing, but he felt his temper flare. It was as if the warm weather were a bad thing and somehow all his fault. The women should be glad it was warm. Warm weather meant no snow. They were safe for now.

"Don't let Veshria get to you," Suka said, moving up to walk beside Attu.

Attu jumped. He hadn't heard his cousin approach. He took in a deep breath, working to release his anger. "I know," he said. "Veshria just annoys me sometimes."

"She annoys everyone. Besides, the Clan knows your visions come true. I know. And that's what matters." Suka grinned at Attu. Attu noticed his cousin was carrying his fishing spear. He motioned to it, his eyebrows raised in a question.

"With the bay still unfrozen, Mantouk said he thinks there will be fish feeding near the mouth of the river. Come with us?"

"Yes. Let me grab my fishing spear." Attu walked back toward his shelter with Suka.

"It's just that I wish there were no threat of attack," Attu said, feeling the need to share with Suka. "I'd like to deny it's going to happen right along with Veshria. But then where would we be when those men come?"

The two walked the rest of the way to the river in silence.

"I'm sorry, Attu, but Brovik wouldn't let go of the kip. She's with Suanu and Bashoo now, and I don't think we'll get her back." Keanu shrugged and turned back to her cooking. "I'll still spend time with them and work with her. I know it's important."

"But it won't be as good as having the kip in your shelter all the time," Attu said. He'd gone to check on Keanu and the kip two days after they'd brought the kips back to camp, only to find she no longer had it. "Rika won't even consider me keeping one. I was counting on you, because you and Soantek are the only other ones who can mind blend with animals."

"We told you it might be too hard to fly daily, have Soantek hunt, and care for the kip. You know I can't be responsible for the kip when I'm mind blending. I think this is for the best. Go see for yourself. Brovik won't let the kip out of his sight."

Keanu is right, Attu thought as he sat by Suanu's outdoor cooking fire and watched Brovik play with the kip. It was as if the kip were another poolik or Brovik was another kip the way the two of them wrestled, pushing at each other and collapsing over and over again in a pile. Brovik squealed with delight as the kip licked his face. The kip nipped Brovik's ear with her sharp little teeth, and the toddler slapped her away, but did not cry. He grabbed the kip by something she was wearing around her neck and brought the kip's face nose to nose with his own. The kip quieted, which surprised Attu. He'd thought the kip would pull away. In a moment it was over, and the two were wrestling again, but this time, the kip did not bite at Brovik's ear. She bit at his clothing, instead.

"See, they're working it out," Suanu said. She was sitting near her fire, stirring her cooking skins. It was getting near the evening mealtime, and Attu knew he needed to get back to his own fire. But Attu had to be sure Suanu understood how important this kip was for the Clan, not just as a plaything for Brovik.

"What is the kip wearing around its neck?" Attu asked.

"It's a poolik belt. I made it small enough for her. I'm thinking about adding a piece of rope."

Attu laughed and nodded. "They are quick. It would give you a chance to catch her."

"Before she gets into my dried meat cache again and starts gobbling it down as fast as she can."

"She did?"

"Yes. But I told her 'no' in a firm voice the next time she headed for the meat, and she backed away. It was strange, Attu. When I looked into her eyes, I could tell she understood me. But when my back was turned later, she tried it again. She was too slippery to catch and got a few more scraps of meat before I got her out of the cache."

"And that's when you thought of the poolik belt?"

"Yes. Brovik is wearing a poolik belt so I can grab him before he gets too close to something he should not be touching. I figured it would work for the kip, too. I'll tell the others. Veshria likes how their kip is keeping Ganik occupied, but he's a big one, and if he heads for trouble she won't be able to catch him."

The kip and Brovik had stopped playing. Brovik glanced at the fire nearby and took a step toward it.

"Brovik," Suanu called, reaching out her arms and smiling. The fire forgotten, Brovik's fingers curled in the kip's fur, and they both headed toward Suanu. Brovik looked like the kip was dragging him, but he didn't seem to mind.

"I don't think it will be hard to teach them," Suanu said. "See how the kip follows Brovik? They're both learning to come to me when I call them."

"Suanu, I must tell you, when Keanu told me you'd be raising the kip, I was disappointed."

"I know, Attu, but we all understand how serious this is. And you know I believe in your visions." Suanu paused and looked toward the fire, her eyes growing misty. Attu knew she was thinking of Kinak.

"And besides that," Suanu said, turning her eyes on him again, "think what this animal, once grown, might be able to do for us besides pulling a sled."

"What?" Attu realized he'd been thinking of nothing other than his vision. But they already knew how to mind blend with animals, whether they knew them or not. Perhaps there was something more here.

"The kips might be able to be taught to guard the camp or hunt with the hunters, finding game with their superior senses of smell and hearing," Suanu said. "That's what I've been thinking all day as I've watched these two play together and nap together. These kips could change the whole way of life of our Clan." Suanu looked at Attu, her face serious. "I'm not saying that working with the kips to mind blend won't help us against the coming enemies. I don't have Gifts, so I don't understand all that. But I believe the spirits want us to have these kips. I believe they will make our Clan stronger than it is now."

Attu sat with Keanu and Soantek near where Ganik and Tishria were playing with the large male kip.

"Brovik's kip has been easy to mind blend with. She comes when I call her in my mind and is learning to sit for a treat, all with mind blending. She seems eager to please, not bothered with having me in her mind at all. But I haven't had a chance to try it with Ganik's kip."

Keanu pushed her thoughts gently at the kip, and her eyes unfocused. After a few moments, she blinked, returning to herself.

"What happened?" Attu asked.

"I met no resistance," Keanu said. "Just like with the female. This kip is feeling excited, playing, and I felt its keen sense of smell first. To him, we all smell very strongly," she added, wrinkling her nose. "Ganik, especially. That boy needs a good washing."

"Obviously," Soantek said as they watched the two playing. Ganik was filthy, seal grease plastered in his dirty hair, and his hands and face grubby. He looked like a toddler instead of a boy old enough to have started his training as a hunter. The whole camp had heard Veshria threaten Ganik many times with a dunk in the freezing river when she made him wash and then he returned to his shelter later looking like he'd fallen into a greasy mud pit.

"But the kip likes the smell," Keanu added. She chuckled. "You try it now, Attu."

"Let me try something else." Attu entered the kip's mind, gently, as Attuanin had taught him to do, a question, an asking for permission to enter. The kip didn't push back at all, but welcomed Attu into his mind with a fleeting image of one of the other kips, the female Suanu and Bashoo were keeping. It was as if the kip was asking a question. *Is it you?*

Attu sent an image of himself to the kip. The mind of the kip went still. Attu sensed something like surprise and saw through the kip's eyes an image of himself, squatting nearby. The colors the kip saw were different than Attu saw. Attu felt himself, as the kip, swiveling his ears to hear this creature who'd entered his mind. He sniffed, and an overpowering array of smells hit Attu. He pulled back out of reflex, and was surprised when the animal pushed its own mind forward inquisitively. At the same time, the animal moved toward him.

"Yes, it's me." He sent an image of the kip eating meat from Attu's hand.

The kip took another step, then another, and as he neared Attu's side, Attu came back to himself. The kip stopped and watched Attu with caution as Attu reached into his pocket and brought out a bite of meat. Attu held it out and the kip relaxed. His tail brushed back and forth, and he took the meat, swallowing it in one gulp.

Attu reached out his hand, and the kip allowed himself to be stroked, leaning into Attu and looking at his face. Attu felt pleasure emanating from the kip as he looked into Attu's eyes.

Ganik ran over to where they were sitting. The kip turned from Attu to nuzzle the boy. "He's my kip," Ganik said, frowning.

"We were just stroking him," Attu said.

"Come on," Ganik called, and slapped his thigh as he ran away from the adults and back toward his sister. The kip ran after Ganik. Attu felt a wave of delight wash over him and then something else. He felt both the kip's pleasure in being called to follow the boy with the strong smell, and the pleasure he was getting from *chasing* the boy with the strong smell.

Attu pulled his thoughts back.

"Did either of you sense any of that?"

Soantek and Keanu both nodded. "The last part," Soantek said. "It's as if the kip has the Gift of mind speak, or its equivalent in an animal. I've never felt that with any other animal."

Keanu said, "I wasn't blended with the kip at all, and I felt its pleasure at eating the meat." She paused, "And in the chase. Part of that animal would like to catch Ganik and eat him."

"But the other part, the desire to follow, to be part of Ganik's Clan, or whatever the image I saw was, all the kips running together with Ganik, that part is stronger," Soantek added.

"An animal that can mind speak. I wonder if all of their kind can do that, or if it's a Gift just this kip has?" Attu wondered.

"I'll find out," Keanu said. "And if they all can, then maybe the ones belonging to the attackers can, as well. Just think, if we could know their spontaneous thoughts without mind blending, it might prove very useful to us."

"The weather is growing colder again. Why isn't the bay freezing more quickly?" Tingiyok voiced the hunters' frustration.

Most of the men had joined Attu and Tingiyok to check out the water before nightfall. Attu had wanted to talk to Tingiyok privately about his kip. Since Tingiyok could mind speak with people but couldn't mind blend with animals, Attu was hoping Tingiyok could confirm the kips' ability to share their feelings and thoughts like mind speak.

But no one seemed to be in a hurry to get back to the shelters.

And no wonder, Attu thought. Farnook's and Yural's pooliks had been sick, and everyone was worried about them, as well as about their own, wondering if the sickness would carry to the rest of the babies. And everyone was tired from being woken by the young ones crying off and on through the night. Mothers tried to keep their pooliks calm, but in the camp's close quarters, one baby often set another to crying as well, and soon the whole camp was nothing but crying pooliks. When that happened, the kips howled, too.

"I need to get away from camp," Suka said. "Our daughter is doing better now. I need to go hunting again. I'm as grumpy as a tired poolik. Farnook needs her man out of the shelter."

The others laughed.

"But we can't hunt on ice that won't form. And there's no moose around here right now. No moose, no deer, not even a rabbit," Tingiyok said.

"So, nuknuks by skin boat tomorrow, or do we fish, then prepare to move into the caves until it snows and we can build snow houses?" Ubantu asked.

"We'll need the warmth of the caves if we get no good snow in the next few days," Rusik said. He looked to the others.

"Keanu has seen no one coming," Soantek said. "I say hunt first. What do you think, Attu?"

"I agree. Hunt first. Soantek, do you think we're ready to safely hunt the nuknuk on the open water?" Attu asked, turning toward the racks of skin boats sheltered in the trees nearest the beach.

"We've got the rigging set so we can secure the nuknuks we spear to one of the boats with an outrigger, like Suka's, and paddle them to shore like the Nukeena did with the whales," Soantek said.

"But nuknuks don't always die from the first spear, or even the second," Rovek said. "What if they don't die, even if we spear them several times from several boats like you think will work?"

"That's the dangerous part," Soantek said. "A nuknuk could easily flip a skin boat. We'll just have to be careful."

Suka pulled Attu aside as they neared the fire. "As much as I want to go after the nuknuks, I've got a bad feeling about this." Suka searched Attu's eyes for understanding.

"Me too," Attu agreed, "but I can't tell if it's just because this is all new to us or because we think it's more dangerous than hunting on the Expanse. That was dangerous, too. I think we need to try it. What if the bay never freezes?"

"Then we'll eventually need to head farther north, I guess," Suka said. "We need to be where we can hunt on the ice."

"I'm sure every hunter is thinking like you," Attu said. "But I'm praying this is just an unusually warm winter sent by Attuanin to keep our enemies away, and not how this bay is every winter."

"It's strange. Having it be warmer than we thought seems a good thing because that means the strange men won't come yet, but at the same time, we need cold and snow." Suka took one last look out over the bay. "I need to check on Farnook and our daughter." He grasped Attu's shoulder, then turned and headed back to his shelter.

"Attu?" Tingiyok called. "Wait. The strangest happened today, and I wanted to tell you about it."

"You heard your kip's thoughts," Attu said.

"How did you know?" Tingiyok frowned at Attu. "I've said nothing to anyone about it. It just happened this morning."

"Because the same thing happened with the kip Ganik has when Keanu, Soantek, and I worked with him today."

"But you can mind blend with animals," Tingiyok said. "I can't. I-"

"We think the kips can mind speak somehow, like people with the Gift. If you heard your kip's thoughts, then it must be true."

Tingiyok let out a long whistle. "I thought maybe I'd just been imagining it. That's why I didn't come tell you right away. But then it happened again, just now. It's almost too much to believe. Animals that can mind speak to people." Tingiyok's eyes filled with wonder.

Chapter 5

Darkness came early during this season. The men paddled back toward shore. Attu had speared a nuknuk, and it was lashed to the side of his boat, held out by two poles so its body stabilized Attu's craft. The seals had returned with the warmer weather, and several others had speared them. It had been a good day's hunt.

"This lashing is working well," Attu said to Soantek, who was paddling next to him on the opposite side of the nuknuk. "My skin boat is slogging through the water, but it's staying steady."

"You wouldn't want to navigate any tricky passages through those ice chunks with it, but there's a clear path to shore." Soantek looked ahead.

"Thanks for your help with that second spear throw; your spear killed it."

"I didn't want the nuknuk flipping your boat."

"You should be the one to take this game," Attu said.

"No, first spear takes the game," Soantek said. "You'd speared it before I even saw it. I'm still thinking like a whale hunter and not looking for the more subtle signs of smaller game surfacing."

Smaller? Attu looked at the huge nuknuk lashed to his boat. *I guess to a whale hunter, a nuknuk is nothing.* He grinned. "With your skill at spear throwing, you will surpass us all once you gain more experience. Soon you'll be waiting over the ice hole, not looking out into open water from a skin boat. It's easier to concentrate on the signs, then."

"And easier to keep your balance on firm ice. No rocking boat under your feet."

"Watch out!" Tingiyok shouted.

Attu looked ahead. Several ice chunks had drifted with the wind, and the path to shore had suddenly closed.

Rovek swore as an ice chunk swirled toward him in the increasing wind. Waves began churning among the ice chunks, and the men struggled to keep their crafts from hitting the ice chunks or flipping in the waves.

Attu had never seen the ocean change this fast. His boat rocked so hard Attu knew without the weight of the dead nuknuk steadying him, he would be in danger of flipping over.

Ubantu struggled to keep his skin boat upright as the gale increased. A huge wave hit the back of Tingiyok's craft and it rose in the air and then dropped, skewing sideways. Tingiyok paddled forward furiously, which saved him from getting too much water in his boat, although Attu could see Tingiyok was now sitting in freezing water. The Elder took a pouch held open by bone sewn into the top and bailed the water from his boat.

The men hurried toward shore, dodging the careening ice chunks, their boats clustered around Tingiyok's to make sure he could make it in his waterlogged craft as they struggled to find enough open water to navigate in. Ice crashed against the beach, piling up and blocking much of the shore. Ubantu led the way through the ice, and with one last push, they paddled furiously to land, jumping out of their skin boats into the freezing water and lifting them free of the deadly ice as it chased after them, pushed by the wind and waves.

Suka and Rusik helped Attu pull the nuknuk free of his boat, and the two men hauled the animal out of the water as Attu carried his boat up the beach and collapsed beside the others, far up the shore and away from the crashing ice.

The weather grew colder and the bay froze. A dusting of snow gave the men a chance to track, so a group of them went inland to try again for larger game. They came back with two moose. The Clan celebrated with a feast, and Attu could see the other hunters were as happy as he was not to have to venture out in the skin boats again.

"Where is Attu? I need him." Attu heard Keanu as she approached their shelter. He was holding his fussy daughter, trying to keep her quiet while her brother slept. Rika had stepped out of the shelter to relieve herself before feeding the pooliks their late morning milk.

"He's watching our children," Rika whispered back as she opened the door flap.

"Tell him to-"

"I'm coming," Attu said and handed his daughter to Rika as he stepped out. She hurried back in, closing the door flap against the biting wind.

"A large group of people with animals like the paddle antlers are heading this way from the north," Keanu said. "I just saw them."

"Do they have sleds with the bear-like animals pulling them? How far from us are they? How long before they get here?" Attu's heart pounded in his chest like a Nuvik drum. "Are they-"

Keanu held up her hand to stop his flurry of questions. "These are not the same men. No sleds like we saw in your vision. They are moving with a large number of the paddle antlers. They have the bear-like animals, but they aren't pulling sleds. The animals were circling the paddle antlers, keeping them together, but not attacking them. I've never seen anything like it before. And even stranger, some of the paddle antlers were pulling hides and what looked like supplies behind them, like the way you pulled the meat from the tuskies back from the hunt. Men and woman were leading them with ropes."

"People? Leading paddle antlers?"

"See for yourself." Keanu shared the memory of what she had seen with Attu.

"They don't seem to be organized for attacking other Clans," Attu said, pulling back from Keanu's thoughts. "All those women and children and animals would surely hamper them if they wanted to fight. I can't see them leaving the women and children without losing control of the animals as well. But there's really no way to tell for sure."

"At the pace they're traveling, they'll be here in two days."

"We need to hide from them until they pass," Veshria remarked at the fire that evening.

"Keanu said they didn't look dangerous. They are traveling with their women and children."

Veshria snorted and looked ready to say something when Rusik put his arm on hers. She sighed and said nothing.

"I think Veshria's right," Suka said. "The Ravens had women and children, and look how dangerous they were. I don't think we should take the chance. Just hide and let them go by."

"We can't hide whenever other people come," Mantouk said, his voice scornful. "We are not cowards."

The men argued among themselves, but Attu was careful they did so in the Nuvik way, one at a time, with the others respectful and listening. Attu sat to one side, listening also, but he did not give an opinion. He noticed Rovek deep in conversation with Kossu, and after a while, Rovek moved his hand out to speak.

"Kossu and I have been talking about these strangers moving with a herd of paddle antlers and using the bear-like animals to somehow keep them together. If they are also using some to pull supplies, then obviously they've somehow tamed these paddle antlers to do their bidding, too. The way they are coming, they'll travel south across the range where the rock men are. What if the rock men have been put there by this Clan to keep their animals from stampeding toward the river? What if they travel this way, south, every year?"

"That makes sense," Mantouk said. "I'd like to know if the rock men are theirs, or if there are other Clans responsible for them. Shouldn't we try to find out?"

"Can we hide the women and children and send a few hunters out? Maybe stay up on one of the hills where we could have the advantage if they try to fight or chase us?" Soantek asked.

"I don't want any of our men taking such a risk," Yural said. "They might get killed." She held her son tighter, looking to Ubantu for agreement. But he said nothing.

"We've got to know about others who travel through our land, don't we?" Tingiyok asked. "Know if they are friends or enemies?"

"This is our home now," Farnook added. "We must stand strong here, or we could be overrun and destroyed, like my people were when the Ravens came. These people aren't like Attu saw in his vision, but that doesn't mean anything. They still might be dangerous. Or they might be friendly, like the Nukeena. Either way, we need to know."

"We were many men with no women, yet still friendly," Bashoo said, looking at Suanu and Brovik. His face grew tender.

What should we do, Attuanin? Attu prayed as the others talked.

The discussion continued for a while longer. Most of Attu's people seemed conflicted, wanting to know about these people, but also not willing to risk exposure of the Clan. There was no clear leaning either way.

"I sensed no evil from them, not like the Ravens," Attu said, finally deciding to speak. "These people might know something about the men with the bear-like animals pulling sleds, or other dangers that we know nothing of, dangers these people may have faced or are facing right now. And although I felt no evil coming from them, I did sense fear in them."

"I did, too," Keanu said. "Something is wrong. That is why they are moving so fast, even with the women and children."

"Do you think it's worth the risk?" Ubantu asked.

"With our women and children hidden in the caves, I do," Attu said. "What do you think?"

Tingiyok nodded his agreement. Yural had grown thoughtful after her first dissension. She met Attu's eyes now and nodded her agreement. Mantouk said yes. Rovek was next, and then Ubantu. Soon it became clear that most of the men and women thought that to find out about the rock men and other potential threats was worth the risk, even if these people turned out to be enemies. And some, like Farnook, felt that they must stand their ground and proclaim this bay and the surrounding area as taken to any who came into it.

"We will meet them while protecting ourselves us as much as possible," Attu said. "I think I have a way we can do that."

Attu and his men stood on the ridge of the last hill, looking down at the valley between the hills and the river plain.

"Keanu said they are moving this way and we'll be able to see them soon," Soantek said.

"You said it felt as if they were rushing," Ubantu said. "But you saw no one chasing them?"

"No."

"Look. There they are." Rovek pointed to a small dust cloud rising from the north.

"Move to your places." Attu reached for his spear. The men moved off the ridge and down.

Rovek and Suka flanked Attu as they reached the center of the narrowest part of the valley between the hills. The others hid behind rocks and small hills on either side of them. One of the bear-like animals was running ahead of the strangers. It saw Attu and rushed at him, teeth bared. Attu pushed his mind out to the animal, and its ears flattened as it jumped back in surprise at Attu's mental touch. The animal pulled its mind away, and Attu let it go.

The animal turned and ran back toward the men moving in front of the herd. The few strangers in the lead saw them, but before the strangers could stop the oncoming herd, Attu, Rovek, and Suka were surrounded by paddle antlers and more of the bear-like animals, milling about in noisy confusion.

"What do we do?" Suka shouted.

"Stand still. Don't move," Attu said.

Rovek's eyes were wide, and Attu could feel him shaking. A paddle antler tossed its head a hand's width from Rovek's face. Rovek flinched but held his ground.

Women and children hid behind the paddle antlers that were pulling sledges. One of the women held a knife. Then one of the men yelled something, and Rovek looked to Attu in surprise. "Did that man just shout out a warning to the others in Nuvik?"

"I heard it, too," Suka said. "It sounded like he said there were armed men ahead."

Are you all right? Tingiyok mind spoke, his inner voice tense with fear.

Yes. Stay hidden.

Attu and the others watched as a few of the men began driving more of the paddle antlers around them. Before Attu could move to free himself and his men, the entire herd had completely encircled them, effectively trapping them in place as a larger group of strangers approached them, weapons raised.

Stay where you are, Attu mind spoke to Tingiyok as the man's thoughts, normally well guarded, flooded Attu's mind with his desire to come to their rescue.

"What now?" Suka asked.

Attu motioned, and the three men positioned themselves back to back, facing out.

The strangers drew closer and a chill ran down Attu's spine.

"They look like Nuviks," Suka said. "Like Farnook."

Attu agreed. These people were smaller of stature and darker skinned than Attu's Clan, but with Nuvik facial features. One of the men, apparently their leader, stepped forward, his staff ready at his side. He searched their faces, looking as surprised as Attu at the resemblance between them.

Something in Attu's spirit rose up, and he motioned for Rovek and Suka to imitate him. Their eyes widened, but they moved to face the strangers with him and grinned broadly as Attu grinned, thumping their spears across their chests three times. "We bring no evil," they said.

The lead man's mouth dropped open in shock. He recovered, however, and thumped his own spear across his chest three times. "I am Toonuk."

"I am Attu. We are Nuvik. People of the Waters, once Ice Mountain Clan."

The man pronounced his words oddly, but Attu could understand him. "We are Nuvik, too." The man grinned again. "Tuktu Clan."

"They're Nuviks?" Rovek popped his lips, then jumped back as all around him, the men, women, and children of these paddle antler people popped their lips in response.

"Throw me in a nuknuk breathing hole," Suka said, staring in awe at the strangers. "I don't believe it."

"Brothers," Attu said and stepped forward to grasp the arm of the leader of the Tuktu.

Chapter 6

Toonuk walked into Attu's camp well before their agreed upon time to meet. He had one of the large bear-like animals at his side, and Attu's people moved away from them both as Toonuk saw Attu, raised his hand in greeting, and sat near Attu at his cooking fire.

Toonuk's bear-like animal lay at his side, and Toonuk draped a hand over the animal's back, running his fingers casually through its lustrous fur. Attu watched the two in fascination.

Brovik was nearby with his kip, and when they saw Toonuk and his animal they both froze, staring. Ganik walked by, his kip pulling first toward Brovik and his kip until it spotted Toonuk's animal and stopped, the hair on its back rising. It growled. Ganik looked to where the kip was staring and stopped to stare, also.

"Bring him here," Toonuk said. Ganik looked to Attu. Attu nodded, and the boy walked forward slowly as his kip continued to growl. Toonuk's animal stood up and stared back at the kip. It took a step toward them.

Attu moved to stand.

"It will be all right. Moon Shadow will not harm the pup." Toonuk motioned for Ganik to come closer.

As the two animals came toward each other, Attu pushed his mind out to the kip. He saw confusion in the animal's mind, anxiety mingled with excitement. *He wants this adult one to be a leader. He wants or feels some need of his protection.*

The adult and kip came face to face. Then Ganik's kip dropped low to the ground, its muzzle reaching up to the adult, licking it, whining, and wiggling an impossibly flexible body.

The adult stood his ground, accepting the kip's groveling, then, to Attu's surprise, it dropped low in return, rear end in the air, and made playful yipping sounds.

A flash of movement, and Brovik's kip pushed in, dragging her rope, groveling and yipping, licking and wiggling alongside her brother. Brovik squealed and chased after his kip, but Suanu grabbed him and picked Brovik up as the boy struggled.

Toonuk released the female kip from her rope. "Go. Run," Toonuk said, and the large male bounded off, the kips chasing him.

Ganik cried out while Brovik still squealed in his mother's arms.

"Do not worry, little ones. Moon Shadow will bring them back once they are worn out," Toonuk reassured Ganik, then looked to Brovik, smiling at Suanu. Ganik frowned, but said nothing. He turned away, his shoulders drooping.

"He does not believe me," Toonuk said, his face thoughtful. "Or perhaps he doesn't like being called little?"

Ganik made a sound in his throat.

"Ah," Toonuk said, nodding. He turned to Attu. "I know I am here before our agreed upon time, but I wanted to talk with you before everyone gathered. We have much to discuss."

Attu nodded and waited for the leader to continue.

"We have been harassed on our journey south by a band of Tuktu thieves."

"Thieves?" Attu's heart started pounding. "Where?" He half-stood on instinct, as if an evil Tuktu might even now be lurking at the edges of their camp.

"There is no immediate danger." Toonuk motioned for Attu to sit again. "We're quite sure the men left our trail several days ago to go east where they can find the wood to build sleds for the winter. It is past the time of snow, and they took a big risk to continue following us as long as they did."

"They were following you?" Attu clenched the handle of the knife he'd been sharpening.

"It's very unusual to be this far into the cold time without the ranges of hills and the flat land to the east being covered in snow as high as a man's thighs, drifting much higher in places," Toonuk said, ignoring Attu's question as he continued to explain. "If the snow hits before they have sleds built, those thieves will be stranded. Then the murderers will starve to death."

"Murderers?" Attu's heart pounded.

"Yes. They are Tuktu outcasts, thieves and murderers, taking what they want and killing whoever stands in their way." Toonuk spat off to the side. "I wish they would get stranded. We'd all rejoice and thank the spirits if they died."

"But they are Tuktu? And yet they steal from you and kill your people?"

"Yes. I wanted you to know of the danger. It is a complicated story of how these raiding bands of thieves came to prey off our Clans. We can speak more of it tonight, when all your people can hear. But for now we believe we are safe, so you are as well."

"Why not tell me now? There may be more we need to do to be better prepared in case they attack." Attu knew his people had prepared as best they could for the attack of the men he'd seen in his vision, but now that Attu knew there was a real enemy, perhaps nearby, and not just the one from his vision, he needed to learn whatever Toonuk knew as soon as possible, so he could protect his people.

"I didn't mean to cause you alarm, but just to explain why we cannot stay more than one night," Toonuk said. "We've been held up already for almost a moon and must get farther south before it snows and travel becomes harder. We'll talk tonight." The Tuktu leader rose to go, whistling to call his animal to his side.

Frustrated, Attu stood also. "But-"

Toonuk whistled again, cutting Attu off. His large animal ran through the camp toward where the two men stood. One woman screamed and grabbed her small child up into her arms as the bear-like blur of fur dashed through an open area in the camp, followed by the two kips barking madly and trying to keep up.

Toonuk turned to Attu in surprise. "Why is that woman afraid of my dog?"

"Dog?" Attu asked. "Your what?"

"That is what we call these animals like my Moon Shadow and your pups, although your male seems larger than our pups are at his age. What do you call them?"

"We have no real name for them. We have been calling them kips."

Toonuk's eyebrows rose as he stared at Attu. "Like nuknuk young. Why do you call them that?"

Attu quickly shared the story of their find, and when he got to the part about the smaller female, Toonuk stopped him. "Black, brown, and white, all on the same animal?"

"Yes. Wait." Attu ran into his shelter and brought out the female's hide.

Toonuk looked as if he had been struck. His face paled, and he stepped back from Attu as if on reflex. "You skinned Light and Shadow? Like food?" Toonuk whispered. "Tell me you did not eat her..." his voice trailed away and he looked about to vomit. Then his face grew hard. "I want her hide. I want to bury her, at least what is left of her. Decently." Toonuk touched the hide, then pulled his hand back, brushing it against his clothing as if to rid it of some invisible dirt. "Wrap Light and Shadow's hide in another animal's hide. Now!"

Attu complied, confused at the Tuktu's reaction and his anger. He picked up the hide he'd had resting on his lap while working on his knife, wrapped the dog's hide in it, and handed it back to Toonuk.

"I will go. My people will go. We will trouble you no longer."

"Wait," Attu said, but the Tuktu leader ignored him. With Moon Shadow at his side, he stalked out of the camp, refusing to listen as Attu tried to get him to stop, so he could explain.

"We must go to their camp. We must make them listen," Ubantu said. Attu had rushed to tell his father what had happened.

"Toonuk was livid," Attu said.

"I will go with you," Elder Tingiyok said. "We cannot let these people leave us as enemies. And we must know more about these Tuktu thieves. I will blame our ignorance. Perhaps he will listen to an old man."

Attu felt naked without his weapons as he walked between Ubantu and Tingiyok, his stomach clenched in knots. "How could I have been so stupid?"

"You didn't know. None of us did." Tingiyok answered.

"It's not too late to make this right," Ubantu said. "Pray these Tuktu still practice our way of asking for forgiveness."

As the three walked through the camp, the Tuktu looked away. No one spoke.

Toonuk was standing near one of the sledges as they approached.

Attu stood before Toonuk and felt the eyes of the Tuktu on him. He lowered his head and beat his chest with his bare hand three times. "Please accept my deepest apologies, Toonuk. These dogs, as you call them, are new to my people. We did not kill your female, the moose did. We kept what fur we could of the female because its coloration was so unusual. Both animals had been torn up badly. We buried what was left of their bodies. It is our way. We showed them respect in death. Surely you know this to be true, being a Nuvik. But no matter what our reasons, we now know that saving Light and Shadow's fur was wrong in your eyes. Please forgive us."

"You kept her pups, even though you didn't know what they were." Toonuk lowered his hands from the pack he was adjusting on the sledge. "Why?"

Tingiyok stepped forward. "I was there and saw the dogs killed. We brought back the young because it seemed the right thing to do. Nuvik do not hunt the young of animals unless our families are starving. And the boys seemed so eager to keep the pups. When the pups knew the ululation cry, we thought it was a sign from the spirits to keep them." Tingiyok rushed to explain how the kips had howled with the boys. He said nothing of Attu's vision.

Toonuk continued adjusting the pack. "I thought because you are Nuvik, you should be told about the thieves, but some of my men say that if you don't understand the way of dogs, how can you understand what we're facing with the men who have betrayed our people? Perhaps you, too, are murderers and thieves."

"We do not want you to think we are evil. We don't want you for enemies, but as friends, as brothers," Ubantu said, stepping forward beside his son and Tingiyok. "Please forgive our ignorance about your female and how to respect her in death. I see now you may consider your dogs to be part of your Clan. Is this so?"

"Yes. They are a vital part of our lives." Toonuk faced them now, his face grim. "And you treated them like any wild animal."

"We have no tuktu, like your people," Attu said. "When we first saw you, we couldn't believe you were keeping them together, somehow, and that you would do this instead of just hunting them. We saw the dogs working with you, and we were amazed. Until we brought the pups into our camp, we had never had an animal among us that wasn't game for food, hunted and killed and ready to be eaten. Please try to understand we meant you no disrespect. All of this is new to us."

Toonuk's face seemed to soften a bit. "Our dogs live in our shelters, eat our food, keep us warm in winter, and warn us of danger. They herd our tuktu, and we could not survive without them. So we honor them in death as if they were people, although we know they are not. They are like almost-people to us."

The three Nuviks nodded. They stood side-by-side, heads lowered, and waited for Toonuk's decision.

"All right," Toonuk finally said, "I will explain to the others, and we will come at dusk. It has been many generations since my people came off the ice. We are clearly not the same people anymore. Still, we are related. It is my duty to tell you what you need to know."

The women and children of both Clans had moved to the nearby large shelter after they'd shared the evening meal. Rika sat among them with her twins. At some signal Attu missed, the Tuktu men moved to one side of the outdoor fire and sat together, looking to their leader. Attu walked to the other side of the fire, and his men gathered to sit near him.

One of the Tuktu herders made a harsh comment about what had happened with the dog's fur, loud enough for Attu and his men to hear. Attu ignored the man and sat quietly, waiting for Toonuk to begin. He studied the Tuktu men, dressed in the hides of the tuktu they herded, many with skins draped over their other clothing, the edges cut into fringe.

Toonuk sat near the fire in front of his men, watching Attu's people, his eyes missing nothing, his staff at his side. Attu thought he would speak, once all had quieted, but Toonuk said nothing. Instead, he looked to the Elder sitting beside him.

Elder Spartik's face was stony, and Attu couldn't tell what he was thinking. The other Tuktu had shown him respect, giving him the best place at the fire and first meat when they ate. But when Toonuk had introduced him, it was clear Spartik was more than an Elder. His men's shirt was decorated differently, and he carried a pouch and rattle on a strap tied around his waist, along with his knife. Perhaps he was a healer or a spiritual leader. Whoever he was, Spartik was a man who deserved much honor. Attu wondered if by keeping Light and Shadow's fur, his people had committed an act that Spartik would not forgive, no matter what Toonuk said.

Spartik's gnarled fingers rested on his long staff, and Attu thought of Ashukat, the leader of the Seer Clan, now gone Between for more than a turn of the seasons. Although the two men looked nothing alike, Spartik had the same expression Attu had seen on Ashukat's face, of a man who has seen much. *Is he wise like Ashukat was? Or just an angry old man?*

"I am Spartik," the Elder began. "The dog you found killed was mine. I buried her fur and said the proper words, as any child of our people would have known to do."

"Again, we are sorry for our ignorance," Attu met Spartik's eyes, then looked down, choosing to respect the Elder in spite of being called stupid.

"We will speak more of this later," Spartik said. He looked smug. "Now, Toonuk must tell you of the danger we are in."

So, first you put us in our place, and then you tell us what we need to know. Attu was angry at the Tuktu's treatment of his Clan so far, especially since they had been met with friendliness and the offer of food, but he knew that this posturing of their leaders wasn't as important as knowing why they were all in danger. Attu felt a rush of fear at Spartik's words. Beside him, he felt his hunters tense. They leaned in to hear Toonuk better.

"I have pushed my people to head south over terrain we recently traveled because the tuktu are willing to move faster when there's no good grazing for them. For the last half moon we haven't seen anyone, and we are quite sure they turned east and are following the river to the trees at the base of the mountains to make their winter sleds, but for the first half moon, we were stalked by a band of thieves who attacked our herd."

"These men followed us for days." Spartik sat forward on the furs the Nuvik women had provided for the gathering. His gnarled hands gripped his staff.

"And they are Tuktu?" Tingiyok asked. "Your own people?"

"Not our people!" one of the Tuktu hunters shouted. "How dare you say-"

"Quiet," Toonuk said, turning to glare at the man who'd spoken.

"I am sorry again for my ignorance," Tingiyok said. "You told Attu earlier they were Tuktu. I don't understand."

"Don't you have men who leave your Clan? Men who can find no woman? Or men who will not follow their leader and Elders?" Toonuk glanced again at the Tuktu hunter who had shouted. The man looked embarrassed now. Then Toonuk turned his eyes on Attu. "You are young for a leader. Did you kill the old leader and take his place? Is this how you hold leadership?"

Attu sat back, shocked at the man's comment. All around him, Attu's hunters grumbled.

"I was leader before Attu," Ubantu spoke up, putting up a hand to quiet the men. "Attu was chosen to lead by the spirits. That is our way. He killed no one to lead his people."

"Well, some of our men have risen up in our Clans and tried to kill their leaders. Some have succeeded and now lead Tuktu Clans of their own," Spartik said. "Some have been killed. And some have become thieves. No woman will have them willingly, and they are too lazy to catch wild animals of their own to herd. They live by stealing our animals, and sometimes our women." Spartik looked at Attu's people with skepticism. "Surely you do not all get along all the time. There is fighting among you." He glared at Ubantu, daring him to disagree.

"Perhaps once in a lifetime," Ubantu said, giving Spartik a look of both strength and assuredness. Ubantu broadened his look to include all of the Tuktu hunters, and Attu was proud of the calm strength his father showed in the face of Spartik's challenge. "Among our people," Ubantu continued, "a man might leave the Clan to search for a woman among other Clans, or to explore and hunt alone for a time, but not for long. On the Expanse, a man can't live long without a woman keeping the fire for him when he returns, making his clothing, his food. And a man needs his Clan to share meat with him when he comes home with no game. We must be strong together, or none survive."

A few of the Tuktu hunters looked interested in Ubantu's explanation, but most stared at him rudely, as if he were stupid.

"How long have you been off the ice?" one of the Tuktu hunters asked.

"Just a few turnings of the seasons," Ubantu said.

Several Tuktu popped their lips. One man made a guttural sound of derision. "That Nuvik doesn't even know to call one cycle of seasons its proper name. A year." He laughed, and several other Tuktu hunters joined in.

Spartik flashed the men a withering look, and they grew quiet again. The man who had spoken looked away.

"Enough of this," Spartik said. Attu couldn't tell if he meant Ubantu or his own men's rudeness, but Ubantu sat back, working to keep the anger from his face.

"We have such men. Several bands of them. They are men who show no respect to their leaders, who refuse to herd the tuktu and follow tradition. They either leave or we make them go. In the past, there were just a few. They would hunt the wild tuktu, and it wasn't a problem for us. But a few years ago, there was a Tuktu herder who began stirring up trouble among the

Clans. He gathered many men to himself, and they began stealing from the other Clans. They've since broken into four groups that we know of. And they are dangerous."

Four? Attu looked to his father. Ubantu put his hand to his forehead, the hunter's signal to wait, to listen. Attu could see the fear in his father's eyes.

Rovek moved as if to speak, but Attu placed his hand on the young hunter's shoulder. Rovek stayed quiet.

"We came across this band when we were herding farther north. We'd set up camp and been there for about a moon -- the area was rich in grass -- when some of the thieves snuck into our herds and killed two of our tuktu. Our dogs barked, and I took some men to see what was wrong. The thieves saw us and ran off without the animals they had killed."

"But we knew they'd come back." Toonuk said, picking up Spartik's story. "We set up extra guards, and the next night the thieves attacked again. One of our men was killed. This time we saw their weapons and knew we must flee."

Around them, the Tuktu men popped their lips.

"May the spirit of my brother light up the heavens to lead the way for all of us," Toonuk said. Everyone grew quiet at his words. "My brother Padnik was guarding the herd with the rest of us. The women were working to take down the camp as fast as they could, so we could move out at first light.

"Padnik didn't even have the chance to fight. One moment he was standing near another hunter, the next he was on his back dying. Spartik was near the edge of the camp and heard a noise in the bushes. He saw the dark shape of one of them looking toward the herd. Spartik snuck up behind the thief and hit him on the head with his staff, killing him. It was then we saw the weapon he'd been carrying and figured out what had happened."

Toonuk motioned to one of the other hunters. "I brought the weapon with me because it is so strange. I knew you wouldn't be able to understand my explanation of it unless you saw it."

Several Tuktu hunters sneered at Toonuk's comment, looking to Attu and his men as if they would be incapable of understanding even with the weapon right in front of them. Attu said nothing as the Tuktu hunter handed Toonuk a large bundle wrapped in skins. He undid the ties and pulled out a long staff carved to be flat, and several slim, straight pieces of wood about the length of a man's arm. On one end of the slim pieces were dark stones, sharpened to deadly points. On the other was an arrangement of feathers.

Attu and the others leaned in to get a better look. "But how can this be-"

"Wait," Toonuk said. He hooked a sinew string into a notch at one end of the length of the longer piece of wood and flexed it to hook the sinew into a notch on the other end. He rested one of the slim pieces of wood crossways on the first piece, hooking the feathered end onto the sinew string. "This is an arrow," he said.

Toonuk stood and turned toward the beach where no one was standing. He drew back the string, and the wood bent to an impossible angle before he raised the weapon into the air and released the string. The arrow flew all the way across the beach, travelling an incredible distance before falling and hitting the sand near the water line. It hit point first and stood up in the sand.

Shock made Attu's blood run cold.

"That is why we left," Toonuk said. "We placed my brother's body on a sledge, not even waiting for him to have the proper burial, and we headed south as fast as we could. We thought the men were following us, but then it snowed lightly one night and one of our guards saw footprints heading east, into the trees nearer the mountains."

"Why didn't they attack again?" Mantouk asked, his eyes never leaving the weapon Toonuk still held. Attu saw the look of desire in the hunter's eyes, and also fear.

"We're hoping they've given up on attacking us, due to our larger numbers and their need to build sleds before the snow," Toonuk continued. "We have to head much farther south before we head east to our winter camp near the fire mountains. I didn't want to lead them closer to our winter camp, but we also couldn't stay this far north. We're later than usual, and I'm worried it will snow soon. The winter snowstorms should have started a moon ago. Spartik believes the spirits are delaying them for us. But even that time is running out."

Attu looked to his father. Ubantu had grown very still, as if he were waiting beside the nuknuk hole. Attu felt the hair on the back of his neck rise as he realized what Ubantu was thinking. Toonuk could be wrong. There could be Tuktu thieves nearby. Ubantu looked around, as if at any moment, a shaft with a sharp stone tip might fly out of the night and pierce someone through the chest.

"We have tried to make this weapon," Spartik said, "but every wood we've tried, when bent, does not bow, but breaks." He pointed to a deep cut above his brow. "One of our attempts exploded in my face, nearly blinding me."

"May I?" Suka asked, stepping forward. Tingiyok joined him. Of all Attu's hunters, these men were the best at skin boat making, bending the bone or wood while wet and using sinew to keep it in place as a frame for the skins. "I do not recognize this wood. We've travelled from far south of here and have not seen wood like this." He handed the bowed wood to Tingiyok. Attu and Ubantu and several others moved to join them, taking turns touching the wood, marveling over how it would bend when the sinew string was pulled, then whip back into its original shape when the string was released.

Toonuk took the bowed wood back. "When you release the sinew string, it releases the bow in the wood." Toonuk removed the string from one end of the wood, demonstrating how it relaxed. "But see, it has been carved to have some bend, even without the string pulling it."

"Our boys make small spears we call arrows to hunt rabbits in the long grass," Spartik said. "They make many of them since they are easy to make and are often lost. They are simple things, long enough to be balanced in the hand and thrown, with sharpened wood points. But I have no idea how the thieves thought to do such an amazing thing as to create this bow to shoot arrows with such force as to pierce a man." Toonuk's hand traced the curve of the wooden weapon with his finger.

"And you haven't been able to make a bow?" Attu had taken the bow from Toonuk, studying it, measuring its length against his body, noticing how the center portion was wrapped with leather to give the user's hand a better grip and how the notches were made on each end. He studied the braided sinew that made up the bowstring, then looked to Toonuk.

Toonuk shook his head.

"We need these," Ubantu said.

"Our survival may very well depend on having them," Tingiyok agreed.

Attu reluctantly handed the bow back to Toonuk. "You must keep trying. We will, too."

Around him hunters and herders voiced their agreement.

"We have some other questions about these thieves," Tingiyok said, glancing at Attu.

Attu met his gaze and realized what they still needed to know. "Yes. We are wondering if they also have dogs."

"Of course," Toonuk said. He sounded annoyed. Then a look of understanding replaced his first reaction. "Oh, I forgot about your ignorance of dogs. You are the first people we've met who haven't had them. I understand that you haven't seen wolves; the wild cousin of the dog, because over the years we've killed most of them. They attack our herds. But it's strange you know nothing of dogs."

"Does every Clan use dogs to pull sleds in winter?" Attu asked, trying to ignore being called ignorant, again, and trying to hide his shock that apparently, dogs were common to everyone else and wolves, like the large male that was killed, used roam where his Clan now lived.

"Most use dogs to pull sleds. Some Tuktu herders don't. We use a few of the tuktu we train from the time they are fawns," Toolnuk said. "But the thieves use dogs. They've trained them to pull like the tuktu, and dogs are much faster and easier to maneuver. That way the thieves can attack quickly and escape."

Spartik made a noise in his throat and started walking away.

"We must be leaving at first light, and it grows late." Toonuk looked after Spartik with concern and turned to follow the Elder.

But Spartik had stopped. He looked around the group, and his eyes rested on Yural. She returned his gaze. He nodded and spoke to the whole group. "Be on guard of these thieves," Spartik said. "They may come back from the east at any time. If they discover you are here, they will attack you. Protect your women and children. I pray with your spiritual leader that we can find the bow wood and that both our Clans will be able to make bows of our own to defend ourselves if the thieves come again."

Spartik turned back to Toonuk, and the two men appeared to be arguing as they walked out of Attu's camp with the rest of their people. Attu followed them, wanting to catch up to the leaders to ask a few more questions, but as he drew close, Attu realized the men were arguing about him. Spartik turned and glared at Attu so fiercely that Attu just raised his hand in the farewell sign and moved off to the side toward one of the shelters, as if he'd been meaning to go that way in the first place.

Chapter 7

Attu stood with Toonuk and several others at the top of one of the six hills to the east. The Tuktu were almost ready to leave, and Attu had come to bid the leader a safe journey. Toonuk motioned Attu away from the others.

"I have one more warning before we leave you. Light and Shadow ran off with a wolf," the leader remarked. He turned and looked over the horizon. "That is why they were on their own and the male was so much larger than the female. Half-wolf, half-dog pups usually turn wild when they're grown. The male will be large and the most dangerous. You will have to kill him, as you would one of your men who has gone rogue like an angry male tuktu."

Attu said nothing.

"You would be best to kill the pups now, before the children grow any more fond of them."

Attu nodded as if in agreement. "You are welcome in our camp next spring, if you choose to come," he said, changing the subject. "Thank you for your warning." Attu hit his chest with his spear three times, to honor the Tuktu leader. Toonuk did the same with his staff, then turned and walked down the hill toward his people.

"I did not want to invite them back, but it was the right thing to do." Attu walked back to camp with the others. "They are our only source of information about the thieves."

"I flew at first light and saw no one," Keanu said as the group walked back. "I will fly again tomorrow." She left the group, walking over to where some other women stood at the edge of camp.

"They should have waited another day to travel," Rovek said, joining Attu and Suka as they continued toward their shelters. "It took them too long to get ready, and now it's too late to start out. They won't get far before dark."

"I heard Toonuk and Spartik arguing as they were leaving last night. Spartik was furious with Toonuk for stopping at all and for warning us," Attu said. "I don't like that man."

"I've been thinking about how they shared the bow and arrow weapon with us, even though we'd just met. I would never share knowledge of such a weapon with people I didn't even know." Suka looked perplexed by the Tuktu.

"I don't think they consider us much of a threat," Attu said. "I know they were once Nuvik, but they don't seem to respect anything that links us to them."

"It was wrong for their men to laugh at Ubantu," Suka added.

"I know." Attu turned toward his shelter. "I think they believe we won't be able to make bows and arrows, since they haven't been able to. But I'm glad Toonuk warned us of the thieves."

"I don't trust these Tuktu," Suka said. "When I understood they keep the tuktu alive and care for them, moving to where the grass grows, I thought they'd be a gentle people. But they seemed to be angry with us or ridiculing us most of the time they were with us."

"I've been thinking about that," Attu said. "The Tuktu herd the animals, keep them safe, watch them grow, and when the tuktu are adults and strong, they single out the ones they need for food and kill and eat them. The animals have no choice to come to them by the spirits. It's like mind blending to draw animals to the hunter. It feels wrong."

"The tuktu are safer living with the herders than they would be in the wild," Suka said. "As long as they follow the herders and do what they want them to do."

"Until they are grown…" Attu made a slitting motion across his throat.

Suka nodded his agreement and turned into his shelter.

Attu walked the short distance to his own shelter, thinking about Toonuk's explanation of the Tuktu thieves and his words about the half-wolf pups. *I bet the young, strong tuktu bucks see the knife first in Toonuk's Clan.*

Attu placed extra guards around the camp, and the men and women worked the rest of the day storing more water and meat in the caves. Ganik, Chonik, and the other children dragged pine branches, running in random patterns between the caves and the Clan's camp, adding to the churned earth the tuktu had left.

"If the thieves come back from the east through the pass by the river, following the Tuktu, they'll think this was just the Tuktu's camp," Ubantu said, turning to Attu. "They won't see a path back to ours."

"I hope you're right. It's the best we can do."

"I'll tell the others to stay away from the caves now," Yural said. "But if it doesn't snow and still stays this cold, we'll need to move into them soon."

It was near dawn as Attu held his son in their shelter. His boy had just gone to sleep again. Attu met Rika's tired gaze as she held their daughter, who was yawning but finally quiet as well.

"Do you think a spirit of sickness is trying to enter them?" Attu asked. "I've never seen our children so fussy."

"They have no fever, no stomach sickness, and both are eating well," Rika said. "I don't know what is happening to them. It feels as if they are having bad dreams in the Between of sleep that keep waking them."

"I sense peace in their minds now," Attu said, "or possibly it's exhaustion from being awake for so long."

"Or maybe you're just sensing ours," Rika yawned, rested back against the furs, and closed her eyes.

A moment or two passed, and in the light and crackling of the fire, Attu felt his mind finally drifting into the Between of sleep.

Outside their shelter, the camp erupted in yells. Meavu ripped open their shelter flap. "The thieves are coming for the Tuktu. I saw it. We don't have much time."

"Where are they?" Attu reached for his foot miks. "Can we reach the Tuktu in time to help them?"

"They're sneaking up from the east and south. The Tuktu didn't get very far. Their camp is just a short run south of the bay, and the thieves are closing in on them. You must hurry."

"Go," Rika said. Her eyes held both her love for him and her fear. "I'll get the women and children into the caves."

Attu grabbed his parka and weapons and ran from the shelter.

"Are we too late?" Ubantu asked. They'd only been running for a short while, but up ahead a large cloud of dust was rising as the herd of tuktu came into view, moving north toward them.

"Look!" Mantouk popped his lips. "The Tuktu have surrounded the thieves with their herd, just like they did with us."

"And their dogs are driving the herd between the hills. They'll go right past our camp."

"Is that a Tuktu boy riding on one of the animals?" Rovek shook his head. "Why are they coming back this way? Why would they push them back north, toward us?"

"Not toward us. Into a trap," Attu said. "And we can help."

From the hill closest to the lake, Attu and the others watched in amazement at how the Tuktu kept the thieves in the middle of the moving herd. More than two hundred tuktu surrounded thirty or so men, and the Tuktu were moving the animals at a steady pace, fast, but not running. The thieves were fighting to keep from being crushed under the animals' feet, pushing at the animals with their spears and screaming at them, but the tuktu kept moving. A few arrows flew into the middle of the herd.

"How can they hit anything?" Suka asked. "They can barely keep from being trampled."

"If one of the tuktu gets shot and bolts, maybe the others would follow, like the tuskies do. Then the thieves might have a chance to get away." Attu watched as one of the thieves, shooting wildly into the animals, hit a Tuktu boy riding low on his tuktu's back near the edge of the herd. The boy toppled off into a flash of antlers and hooves.

Attu felt sick.

Another thief shot, and the arrow struck deeply into a tuktu's side. The animal screamed and bolted, but before others could follow it, a dog cut off its path, nipping at its legs and sending it back into the herd where it was forced to stop running and move with the rest, the arrow still dangling from its wound.

The thieves hit the tuktu, yelling and cursing at the Tuktu herders, who were keeping animals between themselves and the thieves as much as possible.

"Here they come," Attu said. He ran down the hill toward the lake.

Suka, Tingiyok, Rovek, and Bashoo hid behind the skin boats in the dead tuft grass on the west side of the frozen lake. "Remember. Stay hidden until you see me attack," Attu said, then turned with the other hunters to take up their positions behind some trees on the east side.

Soantek wiped his hands and grasped his heavy whale spear, carefully checking his rope. Attu held his spear at his side and took in a deep breath to steady himself.

Then the world exploded in hooves and screaming men as the tuktu ran onto the lake, forcing the thieves with them. The ice shattered a few spear lengths from shore, and the thieves and animals sank into the water.

The lake turned into a brown mass of broken ice as the thieves found themselves thigh deep in water and muck.

The now panicking tuktu turned toward shore and thrashed out of the lake, taking small high steps with their thin legs and making sucking sounds with their spreading hooves. But the thieves had sunk into the ankle grabbing mud at the bottom of the newly frozen lake and struggled to move at all.

The Tuktu dogs and men waited on dry land with the rest of the herd. The dogs held the tuktu less than a spear throw away from the water's edge while the thieves fought to free themselves of the muck. Some had lost their bows, and several were already injured from tuktu antlers and hooves. A few panicked and thrashed about wildly, their legs pushing more firmly into the mud with every twist. Attu saw the thief farthest out into the lake struggling in the deeper water. He tried to pull himself up on the edge of the still unbroken ice there, managing to get his upper body onto it before the ice cracked and he went under. He didn't come up again.

One man had given up fighting to free himself and was grabbing at his arrow pouch to shoot from where he was trapped. Several others in the deeper water saw him and did the same. But one man just stood there, holding his weapons above the water, no longer struggling. The ones who had turned their bows toward the Tuktu on the bank yelled at him, calling him a coward and a traitor. Then the thief who had first stopped struggling aimed his weapon at the man just standing there.

Beside him, Attu felt Rusik flinch. "Do you see that? Will he shoot his own man if he doesn't fight?"

The other thief must have thought so because he grabbed for his weapons and turned to shoot with the others. The man who had threatened him began yelling again, this time toward the bank, where the Tuktu remained behind the animals.

"Toonuk, show yourself!" the man yelled. "Or are you still the coward you were when you forced me out of your Clan, hiding behind your tuktu like a woman?" He pointed his arrow at the herd, searching.

"They know these thieves?" Mantouk asked.

Attu said nothing, but his mind raced. *Why didn't Toonuk tell me the truth?*

"You were evil when we cast you out of our Clan, and look what you've done now," Toonuk walked out into the open, keeping a wary eye on the men before him. "Any of you who don't want to follow Korack anymore, come out of the lake, weapons above your heads. We won't kill you. But if you fight, you die."

Korack spat into the freezing water in the direction of Toonuk. "My men know better than to disobey me, Toonuk. We take what we want from anyone we decide to attack. And today that's you." Korack raised his bow in the air, and then, turning it parallel to the water, he pulled back and shot an arrow at Toonuk. Toonuk threw himself sideways, and the shot barely missed him.

Korack's men hooted and shouted their approval of their leader, pulling themselves through the mud toward the shore.

"You saw him," Mantouk said, moving to crouch closer to Attu. "Whether Toonuk knows him or not, Korack is a killer."

Attu nodded. He tightened his grip on his spear.

Korack, who was closest to the bank, took another step forward and suddenly grinned. He said something over his shoulder to the men behind him, then, at his signal, they struggled forward with renewed energy.

The mud is frozen near the shore. Attu opened his mouth to warn Toonuk, but Korack had already reached the frozen mud and slung his bow on his back, exchanging it for his spear in one smooth motion. He plunged up the bank and toward Toonuk. The other thieves followed.

"Now!" Attu drew back his weapon and leaped from behind the trees to the water's edge. He threw his spear at the nearest thief. It struck with a spurt of blood. The man's voice cut off in mid scream as Attu knelt by the edge and snapped his rope sharply to the side. The spear released, and Attu used his rope to pull it back, curling the rope as he did, ready for his next strike.

One of the thieves still in deeper water turned toward Attu, his eyes widening in shock at seeing more enemies. He paused a moment before pulling back on his bow. Attu threw his spear again and ducked. An arrow whizzed by Attu's ear. The thief collapsed, speared through the throat.

"Korack!" One of the thieves shouted, pointing toward Attu's men, but Korack was fighting hand-to-hand with the Tuktu and paid no attention to the man.

Mantouk yelled and fell to the ground, an arrow through his forearm. Attu ran to him. Mantouk sat up and, gritting his teeth, pulled the arrow the rest of the way through his flesh. He dropped it beside him.

"I'll be fine," Mantouk growled. He ripped off his knife belt and began wrapping it around the bleeding wound. "Ubantu's in trouble." He jutted his chin toward the lake. Attu turned.

Ubantu was struggling with a thief who'd managed to get to shore. The thief raised a knife, ready to strike at Ubantu, who was trying to fend the enemy off with only a broken spear shaft.

I can't reach him in time, Attu thought as he plunged through the dried tuft grass toward the pair. Then the thief went limp and slumped to the ground. Behind him stood Spartik, staff butt resting on the dead enemy's back.

Ubantu looked his thanks at Spartik, and the two turned away to continue fighting.

Look out! Attu mind shouted to Tingiyok across the lake as he saw a thief pull himself out of the water and run toward the Elder. Tingiyok dropped the spear rope he was drawing in and pulled his knife, ready to fight.

But the thief, instead of running at Tingiyok, veered away from him toward the hill they'd run down a short while ago. *What is he doing? None of our men are chasing him...* Then

Attu's mind froze as the thief screamed and fell face first in the long grass, an arrow jutting from his back.

Chapter 8

Attu stood at the edge of the lake. Bodies of dead thieves littered the surface of the water, many with their legs still caught fast in the mud. Several had managed to get out, like Korack, and died during the fight. The thieves had been trapped, with Tuktu in front of them and the lake and Attu's men behind them. Three more Tuktu men had been shot before the thieves had run out of arrows and Attu and Toonuk's men had been able to kill them. When the last of the thieves had fallen, a strange quiet overtook the grisly scene as the hunters and herders gathered by the water's edge.

"What do we do now?" Suka asked.

Attu turned to Toonuk. The other hunters gathered around them.

"Some of the thieves must have stayed behind with the dogs. They'll be close to our camp. Our women and children are still in danger," Toonuk said. "And once they realize we killed the others, they'll surely be after us, seeking revenge."

"If they find out you helped us, they'll be after you, too," Spartik said. "You should have stayed where you would be safe. You can't begin to understand what we're up against."

"Is that what this is all about?" Attu asked. He glared at Toonuk and Spartik. "I know you didn't ask for our help, but you didn't tell us the whole truth, either. Did we just get pulled into the middle of a Clan war? Isn't this more than just a few thieves who need to be stopped? There were at least thirty men in that group."

Toonuk looked at Attu in disbelief. "No. What I told you is true. They were renegade hunters, men who'd gone off on their own-"

"Or been shunned by your Clan," Attu added. "It looks to me like you've created this situation yourselves, or at least made it worse than it needed to be."

"How dare you?" Spartik hissed. "We didn't ask for your help. How did you even know we were being attacked?"

Attu ignored his question. "And now some of the thieves might figure out there is a Clan not traveling with a herd, but just sitting on the edge of this bay, waiting to be attacked, because you can't reconcile your differences with your own men and get them back into a Clan where they belong."

"We will never take thieves back," Toonuk spat, turning away from Attu. He picked a few men to return with the herd and more to return quickly, armed and ready to defend their women and children in case the other thieves attacked.

"We'll need to find the rest," Spartik said.

"There will only be a few left behind, maybe two or three." Toonuk turned to one of his men. "Take eight others and find those thieves and kill them." The man rushed away, calling to others to join him.

"Some of my men-" Attu began.

"None of your men should go," Toonuk said. "If any of the thieves see you, they'll know we've made contact with another Clan. You look different. Your clothes, the way you move. And you speak oddly." Toonuk called out more orders, and his men moved swiftly.

"He's right," Attu said aside to his hunters. "But we need to know that the thieves have been dealt with before the Tuktu head south again."

Suka, Ubantu, and the others nodded their agreement.

Toonuk turned back to Attu's group. He'd obviously overheard what Attu had said. "Send a man or two to our camp tomorrow. We'll let them know as soon as we're done with these thieves. Then we'll be moving south again." Toonuk glanced back toward the bodies. "You think our ways are wrong. I think you are an odd people, fresh off the ice and rather naïve. But more of us would have died today if not for your men. Thank you for your help." Toonuk strode away before Attu could reply.

"The most severely injured of our herders is still alive, but our healer said the spirits of infection are already in the man's chest wound and there isn't much hope for him." Toonuk stood to the side of the pile of weapons that they'd gathered, later that afternoon. "The others will recover."

Tuktu thief corpses had been gathered to be burned on the plain, well away from the dead grass of the lake and the trees.

"What do we do with the bodies still stuck in the lake?" one of Attu's hunters asked.

"I thought of burning them right where they are, but that would only burn the part out of the water..." Soantek said, letting his words drift away at the look of horror the others gave him.

"Why don't we use the skin boats and rope to grab the bodies? Then we can stand on shore and pull them out," Bashoo suggested. "This whole side of the lake is open water now."

"Maybe you can haul them out, but we can't." One of the Tuktu herders looked up at Bashoo, half angry at Bashoo's suggestion and half in awe of the man's great size.

"We'll use the tuktu I kept back," Spartik said. The men moved reluctantly, Attu's to the skin boats and Toonuk's to get the tuktu and pulling harnesses. No one wanted to do the grisly work of fastening ropes around the dead thieves and pulling their bodies out, but without a proper ritual and burning or burying of the bodies, the Tuktu thieves' spirits would roam in the Here and Now forever.

Attu wrapped a rope around one of the dead thieves. He concentrated on removing what weapons he could find from the man he was working on. He unfastened the heavy arrow pouch the thief was wearing so his spear rope could be passed over the man's shoulders and under his arms.

When the last body had been piled in a heap on the plain and surrounded with wood, Yural spoke the proper words of burial and of protection for her people, and Spartik did the same. Toonuk touched the wood with a torch, and flames mounted into the evening sky. Yural continued praying, and Attu knew she was praying for the spirits of the thieves, that they might go Between and wouldn't be left to roam Nuvikuanna forever, looking for a body to enter. Attu shuddered.

He looked down at his rope and his mind flashed back to dragging corpses to the muddy bank. Disgusted by all that the rope now seemed to represent, he grabbed it and threw its coils on the flames. Precious or not, Attu never wanted to touch that rope again.

Attu looked around at the others. Everyone looked as exhausted as he felt. It seemed to Attu that much time had passed since the beginning of the fight. But it had just been one day, he realized, as he looked west, where the clouds above the hills glowed red to match the fire.

Toonuk, Spartik, and the last of the herders had headed south again, and the camp was unusually quiet. Attu had sent Ubantu with them, and he returned two days later as the sun was just clearing the morning horizon.

"The rest of the thieves are dead," Ubantu reported. Then he motioned for Attu to come with him as he walked into a cleared area away from camp.

"These will have to be purified before we touch them." Ubantu rolled out the hide enclosing the weapons the Tuktu had given Attu's Clan onto the dry grass. Father and son stood a long time, listening to the wind blowing through the trees to the north. Finally, Ubantu pulled his hood up more firmly around his ears and turned to Attu.

"I was reluctant to take them, Son, but we couldn't say no to the Tuktu's gift, payment for our help. And we need the bows and arrows."

"And now it looks like we have six. That was generous of the Tuktu, since many of the weapons we recovered were broken and some were lost in the lake."

"Spartik kept asking me how we knew they'd been attacked. He didn't believe me when I told him that we heard the rumbling of the herd as it raced north. He knows we got to the lake too soon to have simply heard them coming."

"But you told him nothing else? Nothing of our Gifts?"

"No. We should tell these Tuktu nothing we don't have to tell them. They are not to be trusted." Ubantu turned back to the weapons.

Attu used a hide to protect his hand as he picked up one of the bows the Tuktu given them. "Mother will make sure these weapons carry no evil spirits." He set the bow back on the large hide and carefully rewrapped the weapons. "Will you take them to her?"

Ubantu nodded, but he made no move to pick up the bundle. Instead he sat, motioning for Attu to join him. They sat in silence for a while. "They had to kill them all," Ubantu finally said. "Toonuk said there are at least three other bands left, and the men sometimes move among the bands. Any who escaped would tell the others that Toonuk's Clan was responsible for killing Korack and his men. And they would tell the others about us. If they think nothing of killing their own men…"

Ubantu paused and looked out over the now frozen ocean, with its dusting of snow moving in swirls across the surface.

"We cannot draw close to this enemy," he continued. "We cannot talk to them, tell them we will not harm them if they will leave us alone. We cannot try to share what we have or make peace of any kind. They are outcasts of their own people, like rogue nuknuk males banded together, killing and taking what they want, angry at their own people for driving them away, and preferring to prey on the Clans that cast them out instead of trying to make new lives for themselves without them. I have no doubt they would kill us and take what we have, including our women, if given the chance."

"It's hard to believe anyone would go against the spirits so violently, killing innocent people to steal what they have, then moving on to kill more." Attu wiped loose hair from his face. He realized his hand was trembling. "Even the Ravens followed their Raven Spirit, as evil as it was."

"Do you think these Tuktu thieves are the men in your vision?" Ubantu asked.

"I don't know."

"At least now we have a few bows and arrows." Ubantu tried to smile, but Attu could feel his father's fear under his words.

"Not nearly enough." Attu turned back toward camp as a poolik started crying. Another joined in, and the camp grew loud with infant cries. Attu thought about how far such noise would carry across the frozen bay.

Ubantu picked up the bundle. "Yural will get the weapons back to us as soon as she's sure they are purified."

"We'll be prepared, but we will also hope and pray," Yural said. The Clan had been discussing the Tuktu thieves, and everyone was worried. But at Yural's words, the others seemed to calm and eventually began talking of other things.

Attu motioned with his head and rose to walk back to his shelter. He needed some time alone to think. His people had been through a lot in the last few days, meeting the Tuktu and fighting the thieves. They wanted to stop thinking about it all for a while. *But I can't. I need to consider what else we should be doing.*

"Can I speak with you?" Kossu asked as Attu moved away from the fire.

Attu stopped and turned toward the young man. "Ai."

"I've been thinking," Kossu said. "We have the bows and arrows we took from the thieves, but at least one or two are damaged. And the others got wet in the fight. Who knows how long they'll last? We need to be able to make these weapons for ourselves. And soon."

"We all need to be testing every type of sapling that grows around here until we find the right kind," Attu agreed.

"I want to try to make them," Kossu said. "I'll search for the right wood, too. I was wondering if there might be the kind of wood I need growing down by the lake..." His voice trailed off as he realized what he was saying. None of the men wanted to talk about the lake. The women had stopped using the fluff and were now digging up moss to line the wetness coverings.

"You search anywhere you think you might be successful," Attu said. "Yural is going to speak with the Clan tomorrow about the lake. She's purified the area, and there's no reason for us not to go there and use whatever we need from that place."

"Good. I was wondering after my mother was telling Trika that-" Kossu stopped suddenly, embarrassed. He glanced at Attu, then away.

Attu touched Kossu's shoulder. "I know you've explored this area better than any of us. It's difficult to be grown and ready, but not a hunter yet. It wasn't that long ago that I was where you are now. But I think of you as a hunter in all but the ceremony. And that will come soon."

Kossu smiled his thanks, and the two walked back toward the shelters.

"If anyone can make them, Kossu will," Tingiyok said the next evening as several of the hunters sat around the fire outside Attu's shelter. Rusik looked pleased with the compliment to his son. "We've all brought saplings back from wherever we've walked for the last few days. We need to begin carving them. We've got to have more weapons equal to what others may have. And we need to learn to use the bows we have."

"Meanwhile, Tingiyok says the ice is thick enough on the bay now to try hunting tomorrow," Rovek said.

The Elder gave his near toothless grin. "We may not see nuknuk, but surely a seal or two might choose to grace our cooking skins."

"We want to go," Bashoo said, as Rusik nodded.

"We're eager to learn this new type of hunting," Rusik said.

The group grew quiet for a moment as men's thoughts returned to the fight and using their spears to kill the thieves. They'd killed many Ravens to escape them, and they'd used their spears then, but this had been different. The Tuktu thieves had been attacking their own people. Attu wasn't the only hunter who felt that perhaps Toonuk and the other Tuktu were at least partly to blame for having so many rogue men from their Clans. The Tuktu had certainly been arrogant and demeaning of Attu's people. Perhaps life with the Tuktu became intolerable for some men and leaving was the only way they could resolve the arguments within the Clans. But fighting their own people?

The whole situation felt wrong to Attu, and killing those thieves had seemed like siding with evil against a greater evil. He felt the whole group's anticipation of the hunt being snuffed out like a nuknuk lamp as the other men's minds, like Attu's, returned to their misgivings about the fight. Attu looked to his father.

"We are hunters," Ubantu said, his voice loud in the silence. "I will let no enemy rob me of the joy of being a Nuvik hunter. I will hunt. And I will love the hunt!" He slapped his thigh and popped his lips.

All around Attu, the men popped their lips and slapped their thighs. Attu grinned and joined in. His father was right.

When the men had quieted again, Attu spoke. "Suka, stay behind with Soantek and Mantouk. Keanu has seen nothing in her daily flights, and we are keeping watch on any caves in our area. Tingiyok has seen no sign that anyone has used them. But some hunters should remain in camp at all times, just in case. Set up a hide at the edge of camp and practice shooting the arrows at it. Take turns shooting while others carve the wood we've gathered to see if any of it's right for bows."

Suka and the other men agreed.

"Then tomorrow we hunt," Attu said. "Soon we will be back out on the ice, my brothers. Soon."

The others laughed at his old joke.

A poolik in a nearby shelter let out a lusty cry.

"And that would be my daughter," Suka grinned. "Lean of body and large of voice." He stood and walked away toward the sound.

"Like her father," Tingiyok called. Suka paused, laughing, the rest joining in. "May you all find good sleep in the Between this night," Tingiyok said as he stood and left also.

The rest of the men headed for their own shelters. As Attu stepped into warmth filled with the smell of wetness coverings, a fierce love and need to protect those he loved overwhelmed him, and his thoughts turned again to the Tuktu thieves, his vision, and all that might still bring evil to his Clan. He opened his spirit to Attuanin. *We will fight whoever tries to harm us. No one will be allowed to hurt my people, my Rika, my children. No one. Protect and help us, name spirit of mine, greatest of all the spirits of the deep. Guide me, Attuanin.*

Chapter 9

"Rusik. Step back from the edge of the hole," Ubantu said. Rusik looked up, and anger flashed across the man's face. But he stepped back.

The man is struggling. It's hard for a seasoned hunter like Rusik to take direction from another. But he did what was asked of him.

Attu walked to the man. Rusik was muttering something, but Attu didn't catch what he said. He ignored whatever the comment was, knowing it was just Rusik's way of letting out some of his frustration. "If you stand too near the hole, your shadow can alert the nuknuk you are there. Also, the ice near the hole is the most dangerous. It may look solid enough, but there might be cracks underneath, made when we dug out the hole."

Rusik nodded his understanding, but said nothing. Satisfied, Attu turned to the other group of men, waiting near the second hole they'd made a few spear throws to the north of the first one. It was odd to have so many hunters surrounding each hole, but the holes were hard to make and this was a teaching hunt.

Bashoo had proved invaluable during the ice digging. The huge man was incredibly strong. Yet, as Attu and the others explained the process and the inherent dangers in chipping a hole in the ice in the middle of the bay, Bashoo listened. He was as gentle with the ice digging tools, when needed, as he was with little Brovik.

With the holes dug, the men waited. Bashoo looked like a large boulder resting beside the hole. Ubantu flicked his eyes, first at Bashoo, then at Attu. Attu gave the brief hunter's nod. Bashoo would make a great nuknuk hunter, if the hunt so far were any indication. He sat almost as quietly as Ubantu. And Ubantu could sit so still, breathe so quietly, his very spirit seemed to blend with the surroundings. A surfacing nuknuk would have no clue a hunter lurked above the ice.

Rusik was trying, but the man had difficulty holding still. Attu became convinced Rusik's furs must itch him constantly. He was always twitching, and twice Attu caught him moving a hand to scratch himself. Attu remembered trying to wear the Seers' woven grass clothing and feeling like his skin was raw from the constant scraping of the sharp bits. He wondered if Rusik felt the same about the furs.

Ubantu's spear leaped from his arm and pierced the hide of a nuknuk before it even got its nose whiskers out of the water. Bashoo's spear hit the animal from the other side, and the two men dragged the nuknuk up and out of the water, moving away from the hole.

Rusik leaped up and ran toward the struggling nuknuk.

"Watch out!" Attu threw out his hand to stop Rusik before he got too close to the still thrashing animal. "Stay out of the way of those tusks." Attu moved to the side, well out of reach of the nuknuk, and he and Rusik followed Bashoo and Ubantu at a safe distance as the men continued to drag the resisting animal, moving away from the hole and onto solid ice.

Earlier, Ubantu had explained to both Bashoo and Rusik how to properly honor and kill a nuknuk. As the animal struggled, its lifeblood flowing out onto the ice in a red pool, Bashoo repeated the words Ubantu had taught them. Careful to stay behind the animal and away from its tusks, Bashoo raised his killing stick and hit the nuknuk on the back of the head. The animal died instantly.

"You did well, Brother," Ubantu said, pounding Bashoo on the back.

"You struck first," Bashoo said.

"But if I had not, your spear would have taken him," Ubantu said.

"I have had much practice throwing it," Bashoo replied. "But the prey was much larger and easier to hit. This is more of a challenge." He grinned and the other hunters grinned back at him.

The nuknuk was prepared for dragging off the ice before the men settled back around the two holes to wait for another nuknuk.

Attu's mind was drifting, his eyes on the hole in front of him, his thoughts on the thieves.

Attu! It was Rika.

Tell Rovek Meavu labors. His child is about to be born.

It's not her time yet.

Perhaps, like her mother, Meavu delivers early.

Attu caught the worry in Rika's voice and told the others they needed to leave.

The men had barely made it off the ice when Suka came running down the beach. Rovek dropped his hunting gear and ran to meet him.

Ubantu threw down the rope he and Bashoo were using to pull the nuknuk and hurried to join Rovek and Suka.

Rusik took Attu's tools from his hands. "Go. Find out about your sister." Attu nodded his thanks and followed his father.

"It's all right," Suka reassured Attu as he neared Suka and Rovek. "The poolik has come. Both Meavu and the child are fine."

"Already?" Attu asked.

"Rika said it was the fastest delivery she's ever seen."

"And?" Ubantu asked.

"A boy."

"A son. I have a son." Rovek looked as if he were about to faint. The other men laughed as he sat down hard in the sand.

"You would think by his shocked face Rovek didn't even know his woman was growing a child within." Suka laughed. He was clearly delighted to have been the one to tell Rovek.

Attu well understood Rovek's bewilderment. He must have looked like that when Suka had told him of the twins. *And I just sat in wonder like Rovek is doing. This moment doesn't seem real to you now, Brother. But it is one you will never forget.*

"Go, hunter. See your woman. See your strong son," Attu said. He reached down for Rovek. A grin widened across Rovek's face and he leaped up, ignoring Attu's outstretched hand, and ran for his shelter.

Attu held his tiny nephew in his arms. "Isn't he small?" Attu whispered his question to Rika, not wanting to disturb his sleeping sister.

"No, he's a good size. And appears to be very healthy." Rika touched the newborn's fuzzy cheek. "He looks like Rovek, don't you think?"

Attu couldn't tell. He studied the little face. His nephew's eyes were scrunched shut, and he looked like he'd just eaten something sour. To Attu, he didn't look like anyone in particular except for his own little wrinkled self. The women were always saying things like, "Doesn't Yural's poolik have eyes like his father?" and "Rika, your daughter has your nose." Sometimes Nuka would look at a child and announce the babe looked just like some long gone Between relative.

Attu could see some resemblance to Rika in their pooliks now, but he hadn't been able to when they were first born. Still, he nodded at Rika now as if he could see a resemblance to Rovek and handed the squirming baby back to his woman.

She gave him a sideways look then grinned knowingly at him. "You don't see any resemblance. You never do."

"What?" He felt his face turning red. "Of course I do," he lied.

"Meavu will need to feed him soon." Rika changed the subject as the poolik squirmed even harder and mewled. "Nuka has our children, and I'm fine here with Meavu. There is plenty of wood and water, food and wetness coverings. Rovek and Meavu were prepared early."

Attu wondered if Meavu had known she would deliver before her expected time but hadn't said anything to them.

"Go join the men at the fire, celebrating with Rovek." Rika turned away from the door flap as Attu opened it, pulling a fur over the baby's face to keep him from the cold draft.

Attu stepped outside, pausing as he realized it had begun to snow.

"After those first few bows we made proved to be too flexible, Kossu and I found some harder wood to try. Here's what we made." Suka and Kossu stood with Attu, Ubantu, and some others near the edge of camp. "These two didn't break, like what happened to Toonuk, but you can see they're too hard," Suka pointed to several cracks along the length of both bows. "They will break with a few more pulls."

"Mine broke," Kossu said holding out a bow that looked like it had been snapped in two over Bashoo's knees. "I was careful to hold it away from my face the first few times I pulled it."

Attu looked at the young hunter's bandaged hands.

"Next time I'll wear miks," Kossu said. "I had my heaviest parka on, or I would have gotten shards through my arms and chest, as well."

"So, what next?" Ubantu asked.

"We're going to look for wood that's harder than the first ones we tried, but less hard than these. These are the saplings that grow along the beach between the water and the pines. Kossu's is from the ones that grow near the river. We need to check the ones that grow in the swampy area near the ocean."

"And I'll look among the pines growing north," Ubantu said. "Rusik, can you come with me?"

Rusik nodded.

"Some of the other hunters are going to check by the lake," Tingiyok said. "Kossu and I will look beyond the first set of hills, more toward the grassland. There are a few stands of trees near the edge of the next set of hills."

"The wood is out there," Suka said, seeing the look of frustration on Attu's face. "We'll find it."

The men moved to begin another search for bow wood.

Two cries pierced the air. "What is it?" Rika asked, scooping up her son as Attu grabbed for his daughter.

"What is wrong, little one?" Attu focused on his daughter's mind. Something was wrong. He felt it. Panic. Desperation. Then nothing.

"What was that?" Rika asked as a shout, then another, alerted the camp.

It's Keanu and Soantek, Tingiyok mind spoke to them. *They've been attacked, but it's over. Come quickly. Rika, bring your healer's bag.*

Attacked? Thieves? How many? Who's hurt?

There seems to have been only one. Soantek is injured. Hurry!

Farnook, come get our children, Attu heard Rika mind shout to Farnook as he grabbed his spear, Rika threw her healer's bag over her shoulder, and they ran for Keanu and Soantek's shelter. Tingiyok was standing near the entrance, and Rika ran in before Attu could stop her.

"We've only seen this one," Tingiyok said, pointing to a body on the ground as the men gathered around. "It's just Keanu, Soantek, and Rovek in the shelter. Rika's not in danger."

Attu looked at the body. "Hand me your torch," he said to Mantouk.

Attu passed the flame over the body. He was wearing the same clothing the Tuktu and the thieves wore, but torn in several places, blood oozing from multiple wounds. A gash ran from the man's neck up across his face, almost to his hairline, and his face was so bloody it was hard to see what he looked like.

Rovek came out of the shelter. "Rika said Soantek and Keanu will be all right. But Keanu is still badly frightened. Rika said I needed to leave."

Others were running toward them. "Hunters, surround the camp," Attu ordered. "Be ready for an attack. Stay low and hide behind the rocks and trees. I'll be with you as soon as I can."

The men turned away, led by Ubantu. Rovek went with them.

"Mantouk, wait a moment. You can't fight with one arm."

Mantouk scowled, but stayed back with Attu. "Stay by that body. Watch him, just in case." Attu handed the torch back to Mantouk. The hunter stood by the body, the torch he'd been carrying lighting up the area for the rest of them.

Yural ran up. "Should I ready the women and children to flee to the caves?"

"Yes. Hurry."

Yural nodded and trotted away, calling to the other women.

Attu turned to Tingiyok. "Do you know which direction the man came from?"

"No."

Someone in the shelter moaned, then Attu heard crying.

"Don't come in," Rika called out to Attu as he reached for the door flap. "Keanu's upset and needs to calm down before you question her."

The two waited for a short while. The sounds of crying stopped. Then Rika came out of the shelter. "Soantek will be all right." Rika moved to the body.

"Hand me that torch," she said to Mantouk, and he gave Rika the light. She held it over the body, trying to see the man's face and hands without getting any closer to him than she had to.

"Soantek said the man was crying out something when he came into the shelter. Something about being left behind, about being sick and starving. He demanded food. Then Soantek said he got a wild look in his eyes and attacked."

"What was wrong with him?" Mantouk asked. He leaned over to look closer.

"Don't touch him," Rika said. "Look." She pointed to his hands. "He has sores on his skin."

"Keep guard over him," Attu instructed Mantouk.

Mantouk nodded. "I won't let anyone near him."

"Good," Rika said and turned back into the shelter. Attu tried to follow her, but she stopped him. "I don't want anyone else in here besides me."

Meavu ran up "Farnook and Nuka are getting the pooliks ready to move to the caves. I don't think there are other thieves nearby. I can't be sure, but it feels like this man was alone."

"Soantek said the man spoke of being abandoned by the others. He could have been desperate for food," Tingiyok said. "He might have wandered a long time before he saw our fires and headed toward us."

Keanu began talking to Rika, her voice loud enough for them all to hear, and full of despair. "Why didn't I see him when I flew? I covered a large area yesterday. I saw nothing. What good is my searching if I can't see a thief before he attacks?"

Ubantu joined them again. "Suka has run the entire perimeter of the camp and up the nearest hill. He sees no one else. I don't think we need to move the women and children into the caves just yet. This man's attack seems all wrong."

"We think he might have gotten sick and been left behind by other thieves," Attu said. "As soon as it's light out, we've got to try to find his trail. Are you sure we shouldn't move the women and children, just to be safe?"

"It's too late to go to the caves if there are others and they're watching us," Ubantu said. "Then our women and children would just be trapped in the caves, not hidden. I'll go tell Yural to stop the move."

Attu went to check on the perimeter guard. Tingiyok and Mantouk stayed behind to guard the body and that edge of the camp.

"I awoke to put another log on the fire," Keanu explained from the shelter's entrance. Attu had come back to check on them, but again, Rika wouldn't let him in. She made them all stand back several spear lengths as first Keanu and then Soantek recounted what had happened. "It felt as if someone were trying to mind speak to me but couldn't. It felt like a warning. I woke Soantek, and he just had time to grab his spear before the thief came in through the door flap. He began shouting at us, demanding food, yelling about how he'd been cast out of his group and was starving. When I didn't move to get him some food, he must have somehow gotten past Soantek and hit me. I remember nothing after that."

"He leaped past me." Soantek shook his head. "I couldn't stop him before he hit Keanu." Soantek turned toward Keanu, his eyes filled with guilt.

"You killed him," Keanu said. "And I'm fine."

Soantek touched the bandage on his arm. "I fought him off with my spear, got him out of the shelter, then Rovek came."

Soantek reached for the shelter pole with his good arm, swaying on his feet.

"You need to lie down," Rika said. But Soantek ignored her.

"Rovek and I fought him. He kept screaming at us that he was going to kill us all. I finally struck him across the neck and must have hit the large vein there. He fell and did not get up again. I went back into the shelter to see how badly Keanu was hurt, and then Tingiyok came. It all happened so fast." Soantek leaned heavily on the shelter pole. He looked about to fall.

"That's enough," Rika said. "You can ask Rovek the rest." She moved to help Soantek back to his sleeping furs. Keanu stepped away from the entrance. As the door flap closed behind them, Keanu clutched her head where the thief had struck her.

"He has a bad cut on his arm, but he'll be fine."

Rovek had come back to check on Soantek and Keanu. Attu was standing outside the shelter, guarding that side of camp with Tingiyok.

"Why were you and Tingiyok here so quickly? Did you hear something?" Attu asked Rovek.

"Meavu Saw the attack. She woke me. She'd been feeding our son when she Saw Soantek and Keanu being attacked by a Tuktu thief. She said there was no time to spare. I had to go now. So I grabbed my spear and ran toward their shelter, shouting all the way for help."

Rika stepped out of the shelter. "I'll stay with Soantek and Keanu tonight," she said. "Rovek, you have to stay here. Do not go back to your shelter."

Rovek eyes widened as realization dawned on him.

"I can't be sure until it's light and I can examine the dead thief more closely, but we can't take any chances. You fought the thief and you were in Keanu and Soantek's shelter." Rika looked with compassion on her younger brother.

"But I only touched the man with my spear. And I didn't touch either Soantek or Keanu. I didn't even sit down when I was in their shelter…" Rovek's objections faded as he realized he couldn't put anyone, especially Meavu and their newborn son, at risk.

The light snow had stopped before the attack, leaving the ground with a thin covering of white. Bashoo was the first to find the tracks.

"We follow them. Prepared to fight," Attu said. He grabbed his weapons.

"But we stay hidden until we see how many might be in their camp," Ubantu added.

The men set out, keeping low to the ground in the open areas and staying behind ridges and trees where possible. The ground was fairly flat, and the thief's tracks were clearly visible in the new snow. Attu thanked the spirits there'd been no wind.

Rounding the corner of one of the hills to the east, Suka pulled up and dropped to the ground. The others dropped also.

119

Suka gave the signal for 'wait,' and the others remained motionless. He shielded his eyes and studied the horizon. Then he pushed himself up and crawled to where Attu lay.

"There is a sled up ahead. I see no people, but there's a dog tied to the sled. We are downwind of it, so it hasn't smelled us yet."

Attu motioned for his hunters to make a wide circle, coming at the sled from all directions, in case thieves were hiding in wait. But as they moved closer, Attu saw no one else nearby. Just the dog, which spotted them and began barking wildly, straining on its rope.

"No one?" Attu asked.

The others shook their heads.

As Attu got closer, the dog leaped at him, teeth bared. "I won't hurt you," Attu said, and pushed his mind toward the dog, sending images of a warm fire and food. The dog stopped straining at the rope, but growled low in his throat.

"Careful," Rusik said.

"Won't he attack us if we get closer?" Suka asked.

"No. I think I can control him," Attu said, pushing his mind back into the dog's for a moment.

"The thief was alone, I think," Attu said. "But the dog wants to return to where he came from." He paused, his heart sinking at the mental images he saw in the dog's mind. He felt Tingiyok's mind as well, probing.

"So there are others," Tingiyok said. "Many others. But they were at least two days' journey to the east, at the foot of the mountains, when the man and the dog left."

"Yes. The man said he'd been cast out," Attu said. "But maybe he was forced to leave because he was sick? Who knows where the rest of them are now. We've got to get back. And we've got to burn this sled. Don't touch it."

Ubantu looked to the blue sky. "It should be a clear, still day. If you let the dog go now, you can fly and follow its trail as soon as we get back to camp."

The others agreed. Attu hurried to slash the rope with his knife where the dog had been biting at it. The rope broke, and the animal took off at a dead run to the east, disappearing over the next rise.

"Look!" Mantouk had walked up to the sled while Attu was cutting the dog's rope. He pulled out a bow and arrows. "It's huge and well made."

"Don't touch those!" Attu pushed Mantouk away from the sled. The bow and arrows scattered into the snow.

"Why did you do that? We have to burn everything." Attu glared at Mantouk. "I told you not to touch anything."

Mantouk scowled at Attu. "They were sitting on top, and I just wanted to…" his words trailed off when he saw the fear in Attu's eyes. Mantouk's face paled as he realized what he'd just done.

We found the thief's sled. Mantouk touched it. Attu mind spoke to Rika. When she answered him, his heart sank even lower. "Mantouk, you need to step away from the rest of us." Attu tried to keep his voice even.

Mantouk looked down at his hands. He'd spent the night guarding the thief, looking at his sore-infested body. Now he pulled the sleeves of his parka up as if he would already find sores there. "What do I do?" Mantouk asked. Attu had never seen a man more terrified.

"Head back to Keanu and Soantek's shelter," Attu said. "Don't let anyone else near you. I'll tell Rika you're coming. She'll know what to do."

Mantouk turned back toward camp. "I'll go with him," Ubantu said. "At a distance."

Attu turned toward the others. "Tingiyok, can you oversee burning the sled? The bow and arrows, too. Touch them with a hide covering your hand and burn the hide as well. I've got to track that dog." He turned and ran back toward camp.

Chapter 10

Attu settled himself in his shelter. The fire had long burned out, and it was cold, but Attu had no time to build one up. He grabbed an extra fur from the sleeping area and wrapped it around himself.

"We have to know where they are. They could be heading toward us right now," Attu whispered to himself as he reached out with his mind to the sky. He found one of the common brown birds winging its way back to the shelter of the rocks near the caves. Attu entered the bird's mind gently, explaining his need to protect his children by finding the predators stalking them. She was willing to fly across the plain toward the mountains in the direction the thief's dog had run.

No more snow had fallen, and there had been little wind, as Ubantu had predicted. Attu saw his men near the smoldering heap of the sled and picked up the tracks of the dog heading east. He flew and flew, the bird needing to stop and rest twice before Attu found himself flying in the bird over the thief's camp. It was well hidden under a cluster of pines, almost to the mountains, and if he hadn't had tracks to follow, Attu knew he would have missed it.

Perhaps this is why Keanu didn't see anyone. And it is on the edge of where she could fly in a day.

Attu circled lower to get a better view.

No! He felt his mind reflexively trying to return to his body, which he couldn't do safely from this distance. Attu forced himself to calm down and remain with the bird. *And I have to see it all. I have to be sure.*

As Attu flew back to his own camp again, he barely remembered to thank the bird, sending it a quick blessing of a warm spring and many eggs in a safe nest before he opened his eyes and found himself back in his shelter.

The physical reaction to what he'd seen hit him then, and Attu gagged, choking on the gorge rising to his throat. He struggled to settle his mind against the possibility of the horrors he had seen happening here, to his Rika, to his children…

Farnook, are my children with you? Are they safe?

Of course. Elder Nuka and I have them. Many of the womean are here with us. Why? What's wrong?

In his relief, Attu let his mind briefly relax. He felt Farnook's mental shudder and quickly pulled his thoughts back to himself.

I'm sorry. Don't tell anyone else what you saw just yet. Thank you for keeping my pooliks away from… This time it was Attu who shuddered. *Thank you.*

Attu stepped out of his shelter and stood motionless, his hand resting on the entrance pole for support as Suka walked up. "Do you need me to-" he looked at Attu and grabbed his shoulders. "What in the name of all the trysta spirits did you see?"

Attu said nothing, but turned and ran toward Soantek and Keanu's shelter, where he knew he'd find Rika.

"I was careful not to touch him. I saw enough with the open sores on his face, neck and hands," Rika said as Attu stood at a distance and fired questions at her about what she had touched, what she had done. "Why? What did you see?"

"We are safe for now," Attu said, keeping a tight mental barrier up. "But no one else must even come close to Keanu and Soantek's shelter. Where's the thief's body?" Attu knew his voice was beginning to sound frantic, but he couldn't stop himself.

"The men who'd stayed to guard the camp moved the body using long tree branches, keeping as far from it as possible. They pushed the body away from the camp, downwind." Rika pointed to where the smoke from the thief's burning body was rising. "Yural said the words and prayed, but she also stayed at a safe distance."

"And you?" Attu's heart raced as he thought of Rika, covered in sores and perhaps dying from this horrible sickness.

"Look at my skin," Rika said. It was red and raw from being scrubbed. Attu knew his woman had used the harsh paste the women made of ashes and fat to scrub herself. "The furs I was wearing are burning with the thief. These are some of Meavu's. Mantouk has gone to wash and burn his clothes as well. We'll keep him isolated and wait. Trika knows, and she understands she can't go near her man until the threat of sickness has passed."

"What about Keanu and Soantek?" Attu said.

"I gave some of the paste to Keanu. She scrubbed herself and helped Soantek wash also. He is awake and has no fever from his wound, so I think I got it cleaned and bandaged before the fever spirits could enter. Keanu has a bad headache, typical after such a blow."

Rovek walked up from the edge of the clearing, stopping a distance from both Attu and Rika. "I've washed as well, and will have to stay away from everyone until we make sure the evil spirits have not entered my body. Mantouk and I will set up shelters on the edge of camp. Rika says we must not come near each other, either." Rovek looked grim, but determined.

"Have you flown?" Ubantu walked up to Attu, his face grave.

"Yes. There is no immediate danger." Attu avoided his father's gaze. He tried to look calm, but he knew his voice carried an edge. "I will tell everyone as soon as we can gather. Right now, this is more important. Rika, what about you?" Attu asked.

Rika shrugged. "I'll have to stay away also." She turned away from them.

"But what about-"

Nuka, helped by Farnook and Veshria, hobbled up beside them and interrupted Attu. "Farnook..." she paused and glanced at Farnook. Farnook shook her head. "I can't be sure, but I believe I might know what evil spirits of sickness took hold of the thief." She pulled back her sleeve, showing scars that looked like small, healed burns.

"When I was a child, a lone hunter stumbled into our camp," Nuka said. "He said he was hungry. He was weak, but we thought it was from starvation. We welcomed him, fed him, and he spent the night in my parents' shelter because my father was the leader of our Clan."

Nuka looked off into the distance, toward the smoke still rising from the dead thief's body. Her face grew pinched. "The next morning he was dead. My parents were terrified when they examined his body and found he had sores on his chest and back. The rest of our Clan moved their shelters to the other side of the rocks we were camped on. My parents burned their shelter and furs with the body. But it was too late. My family had been in contact with the man."

"What happened?" Rika asked as Attu felt a low moan trying to escape his lips. He clamped them shut. *I know.*

"The evil spirits entered us. All of us caught the sickness. My brother died. He was just a toddler at the time."

Several others had gathered while they talked. A few of the women gasped. They looked to each other, and Attu could feel the fear growing among them.

"And your parents?" Rika asked.

"Once my brother passed Between, my mother stopped fighting to live. She died two days after my brother. The three hunters and their women who had also shared the meal with the stranger got sick and died. One of our Elders died. Everyone who'd come in contact with the stranger isolated themselves as soon as they realized he had carried evil spirits of sickness into our camp. But it was too late. Hunters who'd been gone until two days after the stranger died stayed away from the rest of us. They didn't get sick. Those who hadn't come near any of us before we'd isolated ourselves didn't get sick, either. But of those who did, only my father and I survived."

Ubantu turned to Attu. "Did you touch the rope you cut?"

"No. Only my knife touched it."

"Give it to me," Rovek said. Rovek held out his hand, and Attu undid the waist strap holding his knife in its pouch. He tossed the strap and knife to Rovek.

No one spoke. All eyes were on Attu, but he couldn't speak. If he did, he'd give his fear away. And the last thing they needed was to have their Clan in panic.

"What do we do now?" Rika turned to Nuka. "What else do we need to do to prevent these evil spirits of sickness from coming for us and our children?"

Nuka's brows narrowed in concentration. "Rovek, you're sure the only thing you touched the thief with was your spear?"

"Yes." Rovek looked hopeful.

"But you went back into Keanu and Soantek's shelter after the attack."

Rovek nodded. He looked grim.

"It must be burned. I believe I will not get this sickness again, because my spirit has fought it off once and I carry the scars, which will protect me from it if it tries to return. I will help Keanu burn their shelter, including a fire where the man's body lay."

"What about Soantek? He still needs a healer," Rika asked. "I've already been exposed-"

"No. I don't want you to go near them again," Nuka said, her voice emphatic. "I'll continue to dress Soantek's wound and take care of them both. Just give me what I need."

"But-"

"Do as I say, child," Nuka said. "The evil spirits of sickness may not have entered you yet. We can hope and pray they haven't. And I want to do this."

Rika met the Elder's eyes, and then nodded as tears filled her own. "Thank you."

"I'll gather the wood with the others," Ubantu volunteered.

"I'll get new clothing for Keanu and Soantek," Farnook said. She turned toward Veshria and the woman nodded. They moved to ask Nuka a question, and then the three women hurried away, Veshria steadying Nuka.

"Burn these?" Rovek asked. He held his spear in one hand and Attu's knife pouch in his other like they were poison.

"Yes. Where you burned your clothing," Rika said. "You can retrieve the points once they've cooled. They will be safe then. I'll have Attu bring you more of the strong washing paste. Wash again in the ocean like you did this morning so if there are any evil spirits on you from the weapons, Attuanin can catch them in the deep. Then wash again in the river near the ocean so no evil spirits get caught in the rocks to contaminate any others of the Clan. They do not like the cold, but we can't count on the cold weather and snow to protect us."

Meavu rounded the corner of a shelter and stopped several spear lengths from Rovek.

"Rovek will remain outside camp," Rika said to Meavu. "He can't hunt for you, either. You must not touch game he's touched."

"Our new son…" Rovek's voice trailed away as he began to take in what this separation   would mean for his family.

"We'll be fine," Meavu said. "The Clan will take care of us until the threat of this sickness is past."

Attu's heart sickened in him. *It has to pass. It has to…*

"We will be fine," Meavu repeated, softly. Rovek and Meavu's eyes met.

Rika walked away from the couple, Attu following her, but when he drew too near, she motioned for him to stay back. Despair darkened her eyes. "You know I can't come back into camp," Rika said. "I touched Keanu and Soantek and other things in their shelter. I cleaned the wound the thief's knife made." She turned away, but not before Attu saw her eyes filling with tears. "Thank the spirits I didn't return to our shelter or touch our children."

"Meavu and Farnook took the babies after we ran to Keanu and Soantek's shelter. I haven't touched our children since."

"I know," Rika looked resigned. "Several women have volunteered to feed our son and daughter. They must eat."

Attu couldn't speak as realization of what this meant for Rika hit him.

"They'll have to feed them for me for the next half moon at least. I must be certain I won't become ill before I come near any of you again. I was exposed more than Rovek. I will need to build my own shelter and stay away from him, too."

Attu nodded. "I was back in our shelter, with the knife."

"Wash yourself and burn your clothes. Then you must burn our shelter too, Attu. Set a torch to it. Burn it and everything in it. Many in Nuka's Clan died." Rika brushed away the tears flowing down her face. She straightened her back, turning to look at him with the fierceness of a mother and true healer. "I will not let what happened to their Clan happen to mine."

Attu burned their shelter. When all Rika and he possessed was engulfed in flames, Attu asked his father to gather the others.

"Rika and Nuka are doing everything they can to stop the thief's sickness from spreading," Attu began as his people gathered near a fire in the center of camp. It seemed odd to be together like this in the middle of the day. Attu could feel his people's fear. It mirrored his own.

But heads nodded as the others agreed. Shelters had been burned and any possible carriers of the evils spirits had been isolated. Attu took a moment to thank Attuanin silently and ask again for his help before continuing. "First, I want you to know I don't think we are in danger of being attacked by any other thieves from the attacker's group." Attu was careful to guard his thoughts now, pushing away the images that kept trying to take over his mind.

"How do you know that?" Ubantu asked.

Attu hesitated, knowing his information was going to terrify his people. But they had to know. He took in a deep breath and continued. "As I flew over the thieves' camp, they lay everywhere, dead. Most had been dead for several days, perhaps even a half moon, well before the other thieves attacked the Tuktu. I believe the thief who attacked Soantek and Keanu was probably fleeing the sickness. But he'd already been infected."

"No one buried the dead?" one of the women asked.

"No. It looked like they'd all gotten sick around the same time. Some might have been able to bury the first who died, but I saw no sign of it. They were a large camp, probably as many as the other thieves had. There were at least ten sleds and many dogs. Some of the animals had apparently died of thirst, dead at the end of the ropes they had been tied with. Some looked like they had died fighting other dogs. They were lying torn on the ground, ropes still around their necks. But some of the dogs had either been loose or chewed through their ropes. And as I flew over the camp, there were a few dogs still alive." Attu paused, swallowing reflexively with the memory. "Maybe five or six. And they were eating the dead."

Details flashed into Attu's mind, overwhelming him as they had the first time he'd seen them. *Two dogs fighting over a human arm, pulling it between them like a stick. One dog gobbling the inner parts of another dog, blood smearing its muzzle as it gorged on what could have been its littermate. One of the smaller dogs pulling at a half-eaten corpse, trying to drag it into some nearby bushes where it could eat it and not be attacked by the larger dogs.*

All around him, Attu could see the horrified faces of his people. He knew they were terrified that this same fate might happen to them. Would they all get sick and die so soon that they wouldn't even receive a proper burial? It was unthinkable that they had been exposed to this sickness and might even now be spreading the evil spirit of this sickness among themselves. To think their bodies might then be eaten by animals after their spirits were gone Between? It was too much.

A few of the women began moaning. The men looked sick. Many began whispering and a few moved to get up, as if they must put distance between themselves and any other person, to be safe from the sickness.

Veshria stood. "We must get rid of the dogs," she said. "What if they're the cause of the sickness?"

Several others murmured in agreement. A few stood up, as if to take out their anger and fear on the closest target, the dogs.

"No!" Ganik was on his feet, shouting at his mother. "I won't let you kill him." He grabbed the large pup at his side by the collar and turned and faced the rest of the Clan, his eyes wild.

Attu stood. "That is nonsense. The Tuktu have dogs, and they've told us every other Clan they know of has dogs except for ours. How could dogs spread evil sickness spirits to people?"

"It's not possible," Yural stood. "This will not happen to us." She looked at the others who had stood and they sat again, looking embarrassed. "Nuka survived the sickness and has told Rika all that must be done. We are doing everything necessary to keep this sickness from our Clan." She looked around, her face challenging, as if she dared anyone to disagree with her spiritual authority. The whispering stopped.

"I'm so sorry you had to see this," Yural said. She moved to her son, wrapping her arm around Attu's shoulders. He felt like a child again, safe. He leaned into her, accepting her comfort. After a moment Yural

turned toward everyone else again, the center of the Clan clearly in the space she now occupied.

"We must pray for the spirits of those thieves," Yural said.

Even Attu was surprised at his mother's words. Lips popped all around him and one man started to speak, but an upraised hand from Yural stopped him. "We must pray to all the spirits that these men's spirits travel swiftly to the Between. We burned the bodies of the thieves who attacked the Tuktu. We prayed for them. But I believe it's too dangerous to go near these who died of the evil spirit sickness. We must do this for them from here."

"Yes," Ubantu stood beside Yural, supporting her as spiritual leader now, as she had always done for him when he'd led the Clan.

"We must pray to keep ourselves safe," Yural continued. "We must pray to keep the evil sickness spirits now released from these bodies, as well as the spirits of the thieves, away from our camp. And we must understand something else." She turned toward the cluster of women. "The dogs were doing what any animal will do if its normal source of food is no longer available. The thieves fed these dogs. Eventually, the dogs will begin hunting on their own. But first they will eat the food supply around them. Even among the Nuvik, when one is starving, it is done."

Most of the women and even some of the men cringed at Yural's last words. It was never spoken of, but among the Nuvik on the always frozen Expanse, if the game grew scarce enough, long enough, and someone had died within the last few moons, there was a ceremony that could be performed to allow the Nuvik to eat the deceased one to save themselves from starvation. It was considered the greatest sacrifice, both from the deceased, who would be rewarded in the Between, and those who partook of the flesh, who would then be forever in debt to the deceased's name spirit. Attu had never experienced such a time of hunger, but he knew it had happened once when his father was young. He glanced over to see a guarded look pass between Ubantu and one of the older hunters.

Yural waved a hand across her face, her spirit necklace gripped between her fingers. Several others did the same. "The thieves' camp was close enough that some of their dogs might wander this way looking for food. We must keep our three close to camp and kill any strange dogs if we can't scare them away."

"Do you think any other thieves left the camp?" Suka asked.

"No other tracks led away from the site." Attu clutched his own spirit necklace. "But some could have left before the snow."

Suka gripped his spear and looked out into the growing darkness.

Chapter 11

Soantek became ill with the running sore sickness six days later. Keanu refused to leave his side. Within days, she was sick as well. Mantouk became ill the same day Keanu did, and he moved to the shelter set up for Keanu and Soantek. Rovek burned the one they'd set up for Mantouk.

Nuka nursed all three of them, not allowing anyone else near the shelter. No one questioned her decision. Nuka had encouraged Keanu to place their temporary shelter as far away from the others as possible, and downwind, but still on the beach for safety. Attu was glad the Elder had been so careful.

Trika and Chonik came daily with fresh water and wood, drawing as near to the shelter as they safely could, staying until Nuka could take a moment to step out and give them an update.

"It's not good," Rika told Attu. "The evil spirits are attacking Mantouk from the inside. He has hardly any sores, but

Nuka said he is in great pain and has started coughing up blood."

Rika stood at the edge of camp, a safe distance from Attu, but where he could still hear her and they were out of earshot of the others. *Why had Mantouk rushed forward to touch the bows and arrows?* But Attu knew Mantouk had seen the bow and he'd reached out of impulse.

"And no matter how much white tree bark powder Nuka gives Soantek, she can't get his fever down," Rika continued. Rika and Nuka were almost as worried about him as they were Mantouk. "But Keanu is recovering. She had fewer sores, Nuka said, and has no cough at all. Nuka says the fever spirits left Keanu's body and she hasn't needed the powder now for two days. I believe she will live."

"And Mantouk and Soantek?"

"It's too soon to say." Rika turned to go. "Nuka says I must gather more white bark to grind and dry. It's the only thing I can do right now. I feel so helpless. Nuka's tried the other potions from my healer's bag that I thought might help, but none have done any good. There's nothing else I know of to help Nuka treat them."

Attu yearned to hold his woman, but he dug his spear butt into the ground instead. "I am building a snow house for our children. Our first as a family," he said, trying to cheer Rika. He knew how much she had missed living in one. "Soon you will join us in it."

Rika said nothing. She stood still, her back toward Attu.

"Rika?" Attu took a step toward her.

"I'm fine," Rika said. She turned enough so Attu could see she was holding herself, her arms wrapped tightly across her chest. "I miss my babies. It's an ache like no other I've ever experienced."

"I'm so sorry." Attu looked at his woman. She was so small, so vulnerable. He ground his teeth in frustration. "Is there anything I can do? Do you have enough meat? Enough skins?"

"Yes. The only good part about this waiting has been the sewing I've gotten done. Once we know the clothing is safe, you'll see I have made more than enough for all of us, as well as cured new sleeping furs. Rovek has been hunting constantly. He has a cache of frozen meat in a small cave to the east that I think could feed the whole Clan for a moon." Rika smiled at him, and Attu felt as if his heart would break. "In his spare time he's trying to make a bow."

"And?"

"Nothing he's tried has worked."

Attu tried to hide his disappointment.

"If you are building a snow house, I won't need any more nuknuk hides." Rika faced him now, and Attu could see how hard she was trying to be strong. "I'm still fine, and for that we may thank the spirits. Go now. Hold our children. Tell them their mother will return."

"Soon," Attu reassured her as he reassured himself. "You will be back with us soon."

Attu woke the next morning in their new snow house. As he opened his eyes, it was as if he'd stepped back in time to when they'd lived on the Expanse. The crisp clean air of the interior was so much better than the smoky air of their hide shelters. A nuknuk lamp the length of his forearm sat on a flat rock in the center of the house. It was all that was needed for warmth, and the lamp gave off little smoke, just the scent of burning fat, a heady aroma that filled the house and made it seem like Rika was there, cooking him something delicious.

But Attu was alone. The weight of all his worries fell on him as he remembered, and the moment of joy was gone. He prayed, as he had been doing constantly, for the safe return of his woman, well and whole, and for the healing of Keanu, Soantek, and Mantouk. He asked Attuanin to guard Rovek, to keep him from the sickness, and he prayed the same for all of his people. And, as his mother had instructed, Attu prayed for the spirits of the thieves, that they would be able to go Between and wouldn't be forced to roam the Here and Now searching for a body to enter.

Attuanin, keep us safe from wandering spirits of sickness. Pluck them from the air and drown them in your deep waters. Thank you. Two of the four bands of thieves are now dead. I pray the others are far away from here and they stay away. But I must keep watch.

Attu reached to the mind of a nearby hawk and searched the area for thieves. There were none.

Satisfied, Attu swung his feet off the sleeping platform. The blocks of ice that made their beds were set around the edge of about half the snow house's exterior wall, curving with the circular design of the house and at a good height for sitting during the day and crawling up onto to sleep at night. The cold air fell to the floor, making the raised sleeping area warmer. Attu shivered now as his bare feet touched the freezing ground of the shelter's floor. It had been scraped clean of snow, but Attu had no extra hides to cover it. And the nuknuk lamp had gone out while he'd flown with the bird. The snow house was chilling fast.

"Rika would never let that happen," he said aloud. "That is why she is keeper of the fire and not me."

He glanced around the new snow house. The other half held the cooking and storage areas. They were almost bare. Attu knew Rika would fill them with the new clothes she'd made. Yural had given Attu her old nuknuk lamp after Attu found theirs cracked from the fire. The storage niches now held the rock utensils and bowls salvaged from the ashes. The knives needed new handles. Attu's ice bear teeth had also come through the fire, darkened but not damaged. *I can make new tools from them as well.*

Attu checked the interior walls. The snow was hard-packed, no chinks, and the shape was holding well. All was ready for his family. *Soon,* he worked to reassure himself as he had reassured Rika the day before. *Soon.* He moved to the storage area and picked up his ice bear tooth spear point. It was undamaged. Attu put it back. *I thought I had the best weapon in all of Nuvikuan-na. Until the Nukeena came with their iron ones. And now the thieves' bows and arrows make even the iron weapons insufficient...*

Attu crawled out the tunnel door. Suka was nearby, wrapping rope into coils, fastening it with small pieces that could be released with a single pull.

"Is it time to hunt again, Cousin?" Suka asked. "I'm ready for some fresh nuknuk."

"We are low on meat," Attu agreed, "since we can't eat the mountain of game Rovek has stored yet. First, let me check on my family. Then we'll discuss the hunt."

Attu walked to Meavu's shelter, where Farnook was helping her with the twins. They were the third pair taking on the task, and although it felt to Attu like his children were being passed around like little hide balls, they seemed to be thriving with all the attention.

"Your daughter rolled," Farnook announced upon Attu's arrival. "She fussed and fussed and then she pushed herself with her arm and over she went." She grinned at Attu. "Her brother was lying beside her, and I swear he saw her do it and would not be left out. He began fussing as soon as she rolled, and he squirmed and twisted like a small fish caught in a net until he managed to roll, also." Meavu handed Attu his still-wriggling daughter. "You will have your hands full when these two get older and begin competing with each other to see who is best at whatever they're doing."

Attu sat beside Meavu's fire. "Perhaps your son and mine will be like Suka and I were."

"You still are, Brother." Meavu grinned at him.

"How is your son?" Attu said. It felt good to be teased again. Almost like old times, when he didn't have so many worries.

"He's fine. Sleeping. Which he does most of the time, unlike your two." Meavu tightened the flap on her door. Attu felt the draft coming under the skins.

"Move into my snow house for the next few days until Rovek can come back. Or let us build you one."

Meavu shook her head. "I'm fine. I'll stay the short while until Rovek returns. Then he'll build us a strong snow house, and we'll move into it together." Meavu's voice had grown wistful. Attu understood. She turned away from him, placing another log on the fire. The shelter warmed. Attu decided not to press the point, even though he knew Rovek would prefer his woman stay with her brother.

Attu reached for his son, holding his children feet to feet as he had done the day of their birth. His daughter wiggled her toes under their shared fur, accidently tickling her brother. He squealed with delight, and Attu could barely hang on to his children as he laughed with them.

"See?" his sister teased again. "They are already too much for you to handle."

His daughter wiggled her toes again, and they all laughed with Attu's delighted son.

"Look what Ganik made." Chonik ran to Attu, grinning. He held up a small bow.

"It works," Ganik said, running up behind Chonik. He was holding a small bunch of sticks with sharpened points. "I killed a rabbit with it."

"Yes, because the rabbit sat still long enough for you to shoot three times," Chonik said.

"But I killed it." Ganik scowled at Chonik.

Chonik grinned back at his friend. "Don't be so proud of yourself. You know what Tingiyok said."

Attu took the bow. He could see where the wood was already holding the bend more than it should. "How many times have you shot it?"

"Just a few. They don't last long. But they're easy to make, so when one starts to bend too much, I just cut another."

Attu could see the bow was no more than a cut branch with notches carved in the ends for the bowstring. "Good work. Keep trying different wood, and if you find any that doesn't keep the bend, let me know."

Attu turned away from the boys.

"I think some of those wild dogs have been coming close to our camp," Ganik said.

The hair on Attu's neck rose as he turned back to them. "What?"

"We saw a rabbit torn up beside its shelter hole," Chonik said. "It was in the grassland between the hills. Ganik thinks a thief's dog did it."

"And what do you think?" Attu asked. A look passed between the boys.

"I think it must have been one of our dogs," Chonik said. "The tracks were small, like Tingiyok's dog."

"I'll ask Tingiyok," Attu said. "Let me know if you see anything else, and don't go out again into that grassland without Tingiyok or another hunter with you. It's too far from camp."

Attu turned away as Ganik whispered fiercely to Chonik, "Now see what you did? Why did you have to tell him we'd gone that far?"

Attu would have laughed at the pair, but what Chonik had said disturbed him. There could be dogs from the thieves' camp nearby. He would have to warn the others again to keep watch for them.

Attu crawled into Yural and Ubantu's snow house, stopping at the entrance to the large circular room. "I bring no evil," he said.

"Come in," his mother called.

Attu was surprised to see Veshria in his parents' snow house, busily working on piecing together some nuknuk hides.

"Then you place them on the floor, hair side up, but you must lift them daily to check for moisture underneath," Yural said. "If they get wet and stay damp too long they'll rot, even against the cold of the frozen ground. If you can keep them good through the winter, you can use the same hides for your summer shelter. By the end of the winter, most of the fur will be rubbed off from walking on them, and it will be a simple task to remove the rest."

"Thank you. That is good to know." Veshria used her woman's knife to cut the sinew she was using to sew the tough nuknuk hides together. She began gathering them, but Yural stopped her.

"Just leave them here where they'll stay dry. Ubantu and Rusik will be finished with your snow house by the end of the day tomorrow. Then I'll help you arrange things," she paused, "if you want me to?"

"Yes," Veshria said. "And I'll need your help again with the nuknuk lamp. I can't trim it to keep it burning efficiently without smoking."

Yural chuckled. "Most women take seasons to learn the nuknuk lamp. You're doing well, Veshria, having only lit your new lamp a few times, but I do have a few more tricks I can show you."

Attu thought of his own nuknuk lamp and how it had gone out on him just that morning.

Veshria gave a quick nod of acknowledgement in Attu's direction and left the snow house.

"She's better," Attu said.

"The spirits have healed her, and most of the time Veshria is teachable," Yural agreed. "She still has her moments, but she's strong, and strong women will sometimes disagree." His mother smiled to herself as she moved to check on her sleeping son. "She has allowed Ganik to keep the pup, and she's stopped talking about them carrying sickness. She's been training it with Suanu's suggestions. They've become friends."

Yural adjusted the furs more closely around her sleeping poolik.

"How is my brother?" Attu asked as he watched her. "He seems to sleep much more than my two."

"He is a passive baby," Yural said. "At first I was worried because both you and Meavu were so active, but your father assures me he was just like our new son when he was a poolik. He said his mother used to pinch him, just to make him cry once in a while."

"Why?"

"In times past on the Expanse, women were told by their healers that a poolik must cry each day to strengthen its lungs against the cold. Ubantu's mother said he never cried on his own. So she pinched him." Yural ran her finger gently across her sleeping son's brow. His little face was darker than her own, like Ubantu's, with straight thick brows and hair, also as black as his father's. Yural looked at the handsome babe with adoration.

"And you?" Attu asked.

"What?"

"Will you pinch your son to strengthen him?"

"That is utter nonsense." Yural flicked her hand in dismissal as she moved to sit by the fire again.

She took up the sewing she'd left. "I say a Nuvik woman should know better than to disturb a sleeping poolik. No mother should inflict pain upon her child for no reason."

"I remember the time I fell and the bone handle of my knife broke." Attu shuddered at the memory. The shards of bone had penetrated through the fleshy part of his palm and out the other side. He traced the small pattern of scars on his right hand with his left.

"Yes. You howled good and long while I pulled out the fragments and cleansed the wound. But you lived. And you healed." Yural looked at him, and Attu felt the love in his mother's eyes. He realized, as he gazed back at her, he now understood that love in a way he'd never been able to before he'd become a father himself. She smiled, and Attu knew Yural knew what he was thinking. His mother had no need of mind speech where her son was concerned.

"Did you need something?" Yural asked.

"I-"

Farnook called from the snow house entrance. "Yural, come quickly. Mantouk has gone Between."

Yural's face filled with grief as she picked up her sleeping son and slipped him into her parka hood. She crawled out of the snow house, Attu right behind her.

Chapter 12

Trika wept as Yural tried to explain to her that she must not touch her man. "I cannot paint the Between of death symbols on him? I cannot hold his head while all the Clan women wash and wrap him?" Trika looked devastated. "Oh, Yural, I must touch him again. I must kiss him and-"

Veshria stepped up. "No, you must not," she said. " Yural is right. Think of Chonik. You must not allow the spirits of sickness to enter your body. Promise me, Trika." Veshria took Trika by the shoulders and looked into her eyes. Trika's hands clenched and unclenched her women's garment. Finally, she nodded then stiffened as new agony crossed her face.

"What will happen to his spirit?"

Attu turned away as Veshria and Yural continued to work to calm the grieving woman. He motioned for other men to follow him. They would have to burn Mantouk's body as far away from the camp as they could safely drag him.

"More death," Suka said, catching up to walk beside Attu into the trees to gather wood. "I feel so helpless. What else can we do? Two other groups of thieves are wandering out there. Who knows when they might find us? Evil spirits of sickness have come into our midst and there's no place to go. We couldn't travel right now anyway, with the snow and the pooliks, but I feel like jumping into my skin boat and paddling far away from this place with my woman and child, somewhere I feel is safer."

"And we can't even do that." Attu looked out over the frozen bay. "There's nothing else we can do." He turned and resolutely began gathering wood.

A few days later, Attu joined his mother at the evening fire in the group snow house.

"What is it?" Yural asked as Attu wrapped a hide around himself and sighed. She reached up and touched his cheek. "You look tired."

"No more than anyone else. How much longer do you think we should keep Rovek and Rika away from camp?"

"Ah… you think you can't make this decision. Nor Rika. Your hearts are too involved to hear the spirits plainly."

"Yes."

"And mine is not? It's not my decision to make. It is our healer's."

"Rika's thinking about Mantouk's death. We know that if she and Rovek haven't gotten sick by now, the chances must be slim that any evil spirit sickness is in them. But Rika is afraid to put anyone else at risk."

"Then I will pray about it, my son. When I have an answer, I'll tell you. I, too, want our family to be reunited. And I worry about Keanu and Soantek, still weak and on the fringes of camp. They are so vulnerable…" she let her words trail off as she turned to meet his eyes.

Attu saw his own fear reflected in them.

The next nuknuk hunt was postponed for two days, so Kossu could have his hunter's ceremony and join the men. While Attu waited for the day, he spent his time finishing his new ice bear tooth nuknuk spear and checking on the pups.

Attu sat beside Suanu in the huge snow house Bashoo had built for them. At first, Attu was confused at the size of the structure, a full arm's length taller than the others in the camp. Then he'd laughed at his own confusion. *This is how high Bashoo can reach. He's made his snow house just like the others, but to fit him.*

"How is your pup's training coming along?" Attu asked. He watched the dog playing with a piece of hide near the sleeping platforms. She had grown considerably since being rescued, but still had the gangly look of a young animal. Her fur was much like her mother's, black on her back, with strong brown patches on her face and upper legs, white on her lower legs and belly. The contrasts in color had increased as the pup grew, and Attu was fascinated with how one color stopped and another began with little or no blending.

"She is remarkable looking, isn't she?" Suanu had apparently noticed Attu's interest in the pup's coloring. "Watch," Suanu added. "Come, Dog."

The pup came to her side. Suanu motioned with her hand and the dog lay near her. She motioned again, the hunter's signal for "wait," and the dog sighed and rested her head on her paws. "She will stay there until I tell her to get up," Suanu said.

Attu was impressed. He pushed his mind toward the dog, to hear her thoughts as he did for mind speak. He felt her contentment at being beside this other female, but also as he listened, he sensed an edge of hunger, which was mounting. The meat in the cooking skins smelled so good. But she must not touch it. The female beside her was lead dog. She decided when the pack ate.

Attu relayed the information he'd gleaned to Suanu. She didn't seem surprised. "She'd better think of me as lead dog. I do control the meat."

They laughed.

Bashoo came in through the entrance tunnel, smiling when he saw Attu. The pup began to rise, but a look from Suanu was all it took to make her lie flat again. Her tail wagged back and forth furiously, and she whined. Suanu smiled and gave a quick flicking signal as if to say, "Enough, Dog. Go play."

The pup launched herself at Bashoo and licked Bashoo's face while the big man held her off the ground. He sat down, still holding the pup, and she wriggled in his lap until he pulled out a piece of dried meat from his pocket. The pup stilled, looking at him expectantly. "Watch this," he said, sounding much like Suanu.

Bashoo held out the piece of meat. The pup sat, her whole body vibrating with excitement, but she held in place. Bashoo set the piece of meat on the pup's snout.

Attu popped his lips as the pup held steady and did not eat the meat. Attu could feel her tension as he reached out to the pup's mind again. But he also felt a sense of satisfaction. She knew what was coming next, and knowing gave her the confidence to hold still while the aroma of the meat in her nostrils made her salivate.

"All right," Bashoo said, and the treat disappeared into the pup's mouth. She jumped up, wagging her tail in delight. Then she sat, eyeing Bashoo expectantly, ready for him to set more meat on her snout.

Bashoo ruffled her neck fur and laughed. Brovik awoke and scrambled from the furs where he'd been napping, leaping much like the pup had onto Bashoo's lap. The three of them wrestled.

"This is how my man spends his time, playing like a pup with our son," Suanu tried to sound as if she were annoyed, but Attu heard the pride in her voice and saw the adoration in her eyes for this bear of a man who had rescued her baby from the river and had filled their lives to overflowing with his love.

Veshria had trained their pup much as Suanu had, and Ganik took the dog wherever he went. The pup wanted nothing more than to bring back sticks the boy threw or wrestle with him in the snow. This pup was large, twice the size of the others, and there was a wildness in his mind that was absent from the two females. When Attu walked over to Veshria's shelter, Ganik was playing with a small sled. He held a rope in his hands, the other tied over the dog's shoulders. At his command, the large grey pup pulled and the sled moved across the ground, Ganik balancing precariously on it. As Attu watched, the sled picked up speed.

Then a movement in the snow beside them caught the pup's attention and he veered to the right. Ganik flew sideways off the sled and landed face first on a jumble of snow and rocks.

"Are you all right?" Attu rushed over to the boy. But Ganik was already pulling himself up, laughing. "That was fun!" He ran after the pup, who was dragging the sled around in circles, biting at the rope.

Still reckless. But Attu couldn't help smiling. *Now we know at least one pup will pull.*

Tingiyok was working on a new spear. The small dark female pup was curled on some furs on the sleeping platform. She raised her head when Attu entered, calling out the familiar greeting, but a look from Tingiyok was all it took for her to relax again. She stretched out on her side and fell back asleep.

Attu compared Tingiyok's pup to Suanu's. She was the smallest of the three, black, lighter only on her underside, which was grey. Unlike the other female, this pup had a thick ruff of fur around her neck, and he knew her tail was also thicker, lighter at the end, but still much darker than her sister. As if the pup had heard his thoughts, she moved from her side into a tight ball, curling her furry tail around her front paws and face. Now the pup's tail resembled the fur around the Nuvik's hoods.

Tingiyok set his weapon aside. "You are here about the pup. Suanu told me you'd finally gotten around to checking on them." He raised his hand before Attu could speak. "Her words, not mine."

"How is your pup?" Attu knew Tingiyok understood why he'd had no time for the pups until now. Attu settled on some furs near the nuknuk lamp, which, like his own without a woman to tend to it, was only burning with half its regular flame.

"Warm Fur is doing well."

"You have named her?"

"Yes. Did you know the pups' first teeth are falling out?" Tingiyok held up a sharp-pointed tooth. It was so small Attu had to look closely at it before he recognized it as being a tooth and not a sliver of bone. "Much larger teeth are coming in behind them. It seemed an important enough development, from pup teeth to true hunter teeth, to warrant a naming. And she is a warm fur in this old man's bed at night." Tingiyok grinned. "When I touched her mind, she agreed to the name. She likes her fur to be warm. Some mornings I have to pull her from the sleeping platform."

As if in response, the pup rolled to her side again, pushing her body deeper into the furs beside Tingiyok.

"Then Warm Fur she is," Attu agreed. "And your mind speech with her?"

"Is more like impressions of senses and some thoughts. She does know a few words, ones I've used enough for her to understand, but she thinks in images, remembrances of what she's seen and experienced."

"Much like the impressions I get when I mind blend with animals."

"I think so, from what you've told me. I can send her an image of what I want her to do, and she'll do it." The Elder grinned his nearly toothless smile. "Most of the time."

The old man sat back. "It's curious, though. She sees things differently than we do. The white snow shows up brightly in her mind, as well as the white of the rabbit furs this time of the seasons. But the red of blood she sees looks brown in my mind, and the blue of the unfrozen water in the river looks brighter, like the white."

"Do you think she sees as well as we do?"

"Better, when it's dark. She sees movement before I do. And she can find animals by their smell. I've already speared two rabbits just because I followed her as she followed their scent trail. It's hard to hold her back, but she will approach quietly with the promise of her share of the meat, and she seems to have been born knowing to come from downwind toward prey." Tingiyok sat back.

"I know you have done much with Warm Fur," Attu said, hoping his tone conveyed his thanks as he made his decision. "Would you consider taking on the job of continuing to train all the pups – with the others' help, of course – eventually teaching them all to pull sleds and hunt with us? Guard us?"

"And do what we ask with mind speech. Yes." Tingiyok pulled his shoulders back, pleasure lighting his face. "I will gladly accept this responsibility." Attu rose with Tingiyok and pounded the man's back in a quick hunter's embrace.

Attu stood with his Clan, the men in an inner circle, the circle of women behind them as the words were spoken over Kossu. The fresh tattoo of the People of the Waters stood out on Kossu's bicep, and the rest of his body shone with nuknuk fat. His hair was now braided in the single braid of a man, the end cut off and ready for the fire. The shadows made Kossu appear taller and older as he stood, proud and lean, in his place beside the blaze.

All members of the Clan were present to witness the hunter's ceremony. Attu saw Trika nearby, her son Chonik at her side. She looked sad, but also determined. Attu knew she wanted her son to see this ceremony he would one day have to look forward to, but Attu also knew Trika's grief must cut like a knife, knowing her son no longer had a father to walk with him from childhood to manhood.

Even Soantek had insisted on coming, knowing how important this was to the Clan. He sat, wrapped in furs, at a small fire Keanu had built far enough away from the gathering not to endanger anyone, but so they could still see. She sat beside him. Both looked wan, but they were recovering. Attu thanked Attuanin again for sparing their lives.

Yural spoke the words, and Veshria, Ganik, and Tishria each placed a hand on Kossu's chest, fresh with the blood of his last kill, as Kossu pledged to hunt for them all until he took a woman of his own. Rusik threw Kossu's hair into the fire, and lips popped as it erupted in a quick flame of many colors.

"A good omen," Ubantu announced, and the others agreed. Then everyone was surrounding Kossu, clapping him on the back and congratulating him.

If Rusik were any prouder, I think he would burst, Attu mind spoke to Rika. She stood at the edge of camp, longing to be right in the middle of things. He was showing her what he could.

Kossu is a son to be proud of, she replied. *May our son be like Kossu when he is grown.*

"I thought I had it," Tingiyok said.

Attu and the other hunters were gathered around Tingiyok, Suka, and Kossu, looking at Tingiyok's latest attempt at bow making.

"What's wrong this time?" Suka asked.

"The wood has enough spring in it, but that's the problem." Tingiyok showed them three bows he had made. "This one is new. Looks good, right?" He pulled on the bowstring and the bow bent well. He let it go, and the string twanged viciously.

Lips popped.

"But look," Tingiyok said. "This one has been pulled a few times." He showed them the second bow, which was more bent than the first one. "And this one. I've shot it about twenty times." He held up a bow so bent that even strung, the bowstring was limp.

"This is so frustrating," Suka said, examining the third bow. "Either the wood is too hard and it breaks, or it's too

156

flexible and won't hold its shape." He handed Tingiyok back the ruined bow.

"I'm not sure there's any wood left to try," one of the other hunters said. The men turned away, discouraged.

"I'll keep trying," Kossu said, his eyes fierce with determination as he spoke to Attu. "I won't give up. There has to be wood somewhere that will work. The thieves' bows didn't come from the Between."

Attu couldn't help but admire the young hunter's determination. "I'm counting on someone finding it." Attu grasped Kossu's shoulder in encouragement before turning back toward his shelter. "I'm not sure what we'll do if we don't," he murmured to himself, feeling his own discouragement at Tingiyok's latest failure.

"I believe the spirits of sickness will be gone from Soantek once his sores have scabbed over and he hasn't run a fever for at least half a moon." Yural stood near Attu, speaking with Rika from a safe distance. "But it has been long enough for you and Rovek. I believe you can both return."

"Now?" Rika sounded unsure.

"I know of no evil spirit of sickness that can exist in the air alone for longer than half a moon. Soantek has been recovering for many days now. In a few days, it will be a half moon since he had a fever. Then we can be sure the evil spirits of sickness have left him. For you and Rovek, it's been a full moon. You must be safe."

My children. My man. My home. Rika's mind overflowed into Attu's. And then she ran into his arms.

"I'll tell Rovek." Yural grinned and turned away.

Chapter 13

Attu shared a nuknuk hole with Rusik. He'd been pleased to see the man had learned from his first few hunts and now stood back from the hole at a reasonable distance. Attu had thought Rusik would want to hunt with his son, but Rusik said Kossu was nervous and preferred hunting with Suka and Tingiyok his first time out with the other men.

Attu understood. "I wanted to prove myself to my father so badly that I botched my first few nuknuk hunts, throwing my spear too soon and scaring away any game that came close."

Rusik laughed. "I may do that as well. This is so different from hunting game on land like we Seers always did. My son may well bring a nuknuk home to his mother before I do."

Attu heard the pride in Rusik's voice. So far, Rusik hadn't been able to spear his own nuknuk. *But he desires his son's success in the hunt over his own. He is a good father and a true hunter.*

Rusik still had trouble crouching and remaining motionless, but Attu knew such ability required much practice for most hunters. They sat opposite the hole now, and Attu's mind drifted while his eyes and ears remained alert.

Finally, a bubble broke the surface. Attu's spear shot out and was first to hit the nuknuk. Rusik's spear followed. The two men grabbed their ropes and pulled, each at an angle away from the other, but both in the same direction away from the hole.

"We have only angered it," Attu hollered as the two pulled on the thrashing nuknuk. "We hit no vital organs. Be careful of its tusks."

Rusik had a huge grin on his face as he pulled, and Attu remembered the thrill of the first few times he'd speared one of these large animals. Even now, Attu still felt a surge of excitement at the kill.

Attu stopped pulling when he thought they were far enough onto solid ice. He approached the animal cautiously. It had stopped thrashing, but was breathing heavily, and there was little blood. Attu pulled at the rope connected to his spear. He knew he needed to spear it again before getting any closer.

"No!" Attu shouted, as Rusik rushed past him toward the now-still nuknuk. "He's not-"

Rusik screamed as the animal thrashed its powerful head and caught his lower leg with its tusks. Attu heard a sickening ripping sound as the tusks tore through Rusik's hide pants and into his muscles. Rusik fell, and the animal rose up on its front flippers, arching its head back and striking Rusik's chest and abdomen with its twin points of sharpened bone. Rusik screamed again, then fell silent.

Attu pulled his spear loose and hauled it in by its rope. He threw it again, catching the animal in the side and forcing it to turn away from Rusik. He pulled out his killing club. Attu knew he could be impaled as easily as Rusik had been, but he had to remove the threat. The animal might strike Rusik again in its anger. Rusik groaned and rolled to his side.

"Don't move!" Attu shouted. Attu waved his arms, making loud noises to attract the nuknuk's attention. It worked. The huge animal turned toward Attu, glaring at him as Attu approached, raising its head to Attu's height and daring him to come any closer. Attu darted to the animal's side and struck it on the back of the head as hard as he could, then speared it again.

The nuknuk swung its head around, barely missing Attu's legs with its tusks. The blow was hard, however, and the nuknuk dropped its head after it turned. Attu took the chance and pulled out his spear, causing the animal to thrash again. But Attu could see the nuknuk was weakening. Attu dodged its tusks a second time and plunged his spear through the animal's ribs from the back into its heart. The nuknuk dropped like a stone. Attu clubbed it again, in the killing spot this time, just to be sure. Then he stood for a few breaths, his sides heaving from the exertion, before he turned back to where Rusik lay in a pool of blood on the snow.

"Rusik?" Attu asked, kneeling beside the man, cupping the hunter's face in his hands.

Movement to the side caught Attu's attention. Kossu, Suka, and Tingiyok were racing toward them across the ice, careful even in this emergency to follow the tracks Attu and Rusik had left.

"Your son is coming. Hang on," Attu said.

Rusik tried to roll onto his back again, and Attu helped him. Rusik took in a deep shuddering breath, and Attu thought he was about to speak, but then Rusik's body relaxed and he stared sightless toward the grey skies above the frozen bay. As Rusik's eyes glazed over in the Between of death, Attu gently closed them.

Kossu fell at his father's side, clutching his body, tears blinding him as he called out to his father again and again until he collapsed on Rusik's bloody chest and began to moan, a deep haunting sound of grief that tore at Attu more painfully than any nuknuk tusk ever could.

Attu had alerted Rika, who reported that Veshria had fainted at hearing the news of her man's death. But when the men brought Rusik's body into camp, Veshria was there, silent, motioning to the others where she wanted the body placed in her snow house, sitting with the other women as they began to wrap Rusik for burial, holding his head on her lap and stroking his hair much as Elder Nuanu had done with Elder Tovut's body. She said nothing as Suanu began painting the Clan symbols on Rusik's cheeks, just under his closed eyes. Even Trika had joined the women, and as she cried with the others, Attu felt his mind screaming with the pain of their grief. And his own. He left the snow house.

"Attu."

Attu turned to see Rika. She had followed him. She said nothing, but wrapped her arms around him for a moment before pulling away. "You need some of my calming tea. Your whole body is shaking." She looked up, studying his face.

"I'll be all right," Attu said, meeting her eyes. "It's just that I couldn't do enough to save Rusik. It all happened so fast." Attu struggled to stop trembling, turning away from his woman and pounding his fist into his other palm. "First the thief's attack, then the sickness and Mantouk dying. And now this." He looked around. Several of the others were watching them. "I can't talk about this. Not here." He strode away.

Rika let him go.

Attu and Rika sat in his parents' snow house. Yural had insisted they join them for the evening meal. For once, all the pooliks were sleeping. Attu didn't want to talk about any of the events of the past day, but he knew he had to, as the Clan's leader. He had to know how everyone was dealing with another death on the heels of Mantouk's.

"Is Veshria in shock?" he asked.

"I can't tell. When Veshria came back from the Between of unconsciousness, she was calm, moving about to get her man's things ready for burial. But as far as I know, she hasn't spoken a word since we told her."

"I've never seen a reaction like this from a woman who has lost her man. I'm very worried about her." Yural rose to adjust the nuknuk lamp.

"It's like part of Veshria died with her man. Rusik's death has shocked us all. But it has also helped Trika grieve her own man, preparing Rusik's body as she couldn't do for Mantouk. You saw how Mantouk's death cut Trika's heart with grief, but she's still with us, still talking. Veshria's reaction…" Yural clutched her spirit necklace.

"We had gone for so many moons without anyone dying. All the women gave birth and survived. All of the pooliks were doing well. And in spite of my vision, Broken Rock Bay still seemed the best place for us. And then the Tuktu came with their talk of thieves. The thieves came and we fought them. The lone thief came, and then the sickness, and now this…" Attu felt something inside his spirit break, and the words rushed out of him before he could stop them. "What am I doing wrong as our leader? How could I bring my people to this place? What was I thinking?"

Attu felt ashamed to break down in front of Rika and his parents, but he couldn't hold in his feelings any longer. "My vision hasn't even come to pass yet, and still two of our own have died in just a few days."

"Attu-" Ubantu began, but Attu couldn't stop.

"Toonuk was right. I am naïve. I can't even begin to understand why the Tuktu have thrown out so many of their own or made life so difficult that many of their men prefer to leave the Tuktu Clan and roam as bands of thieves. We know there are two of those bands left. We've seen no other enemies, and the Tuktu spoke of none, so I think we can assume the men in my vision are probably one of those bands. We know if they discover we're here, they won't hesitate to kill us to get what they want. We think we can see ahead, see danger and stay safe, but… " Attu covered his face with his trembling hands.

"Meavu Saw the thieves attacking the Tuktu." Rika touched his arm. "She Saw the attack on Keanu and Soantek."

"But she barely Saw them in time. And no one Saw that Rusik would be attacked by the nuknuk."

"This is not about being naive, Attu," Ubantu said. "It's not even about Gifts. This is about leadership in the difficult times. You are facing what every leader must face: the consequences of decisions made in the interest of everyone, the responsibility and the grief of seeing people you love dying and the resulting grief of us all, and the uncertainty of life and death in the Here and Now. Did you think to protect us all from everything that could hurt us? From all the spirits and the animals and the other people in Nuvikuan-na who mean us harm?"

Attu dropped his hands and looked to his father. Ubantu's eyes were filled with tears of compassion for his son.

"You are Attu, a Nuvik hunter," Yural spoke up. "You are honorable and you serve your people well, using what we all are learning about this place. You do what you can do. That is all. And that is enough."

"People die," Rika's voice was almost a whisper. "I know what it feels like to think you should have been able to do more, to look back and question yourself after someone has died, and to come to the conclusion you are somehow inadequate to the task, be it healer or leader. Yural and Ubantu are right. Life is hard and death comes to us all. It is the way of the spirits, Attu. It is not your fault. None of it."

The nuknuk lamp sputtered as they sat in silence for a long time. Finally, Attu took in a deep breath, and as he let it out, he felt his body stop shaking. He looked to his parents and

Rika. "I know in my spirit that what you are all saying is true. But it is so hard seeing others die. I guess it was easier for me to think I could have done something else, something different, to avoid what has happened to our people in the last few moons," he looked down at his now steady hands, "because then I would still feel like I had control over everything."

Rika sighed and opened her arms to Attu.

They buried Rusik's body at the top of one of the six hills, farthest from camp. The area was rocky and the ground blown free of snow. Suka found a natural depression and they used that, piling up the rocks and creating a mound to keep Rusik's body safe from predators.

Attu shivered as he remembered the dogs in the thieves' camp and added another rock to the pile. "We will guard his body for the full time granted a Nuvik hunter, for he has proven himself worthy of our Clan," Attu said.

The next few days passed. Veshria spoke to no one, but she resumed her woman's work and spent much time with Keanu and Soantek, preparing meals for them, helping the still weak Keanu with her woman's chores, and sending Ganik and Tishria on various errands to keep them busy.

The two children came to Rika and Attu's shelter a few days later, bringing the pup with them. At first, Rika didn't want the large young dog in her shelter with the pooliks, but Attu assured her he could control him if necessary. Attu was surprised when it was Tishria, and not Ganik, who spoke after motioning for the grey male to lie down. The pup obeyed, placing his snout on his paws.

"Healer Rika, Mother needs some of the white bark powder," Tishria said, pulling Attu out of his thoughts. "She said you would have some."

"She told you?" Rika asked, leaning toward the girl in her eagerness to hear Veshria was finally speaking again.

"No, but I know what she wants." Tishria looked away from Rika, as if embarrassed.

"I don't under-"

"Tishria knows what we all want before we say it," Ganik said. He seemed at once both contemptuous of Tishria and awed. "She even knows what Grey Wolf wants."

"Grey Wolf?"

"The dog's name."

"He doesn't like being called a dog. He is Grey Wolf, like his father," Tishria scolded Ganik. "You must remember that or he won't respect you."

Attu crouched in front of Tishria, eye to eye. "So, you hear the dog's – I mean, Grey Wolf's – thoughts?" Attu tried to ask as nonchalantly as he'd seen Tingiyok do with Meavu when she'd shared an emerging Gift with them.

"And he hears mine," Tishria said, her voice a whisper.

"And when your mother needs something?"

"She thinks to herself, but I hear her as if she said it out loud," Tishria said. "I'm not lying. I do." The little girl stuck her chin out, as if she'd been told before that she was making things up.

I believe you, Attu mind spoke to her.

"Your voice is so clear in my-"

Don't speak your answer. Think it.

I hear you. Tishria looked with wonder at Attu. *Not like Mother. Mother's thoughts are all jumbled. It's hard to know what she's thinking since Father...* Tishria stopped communicating as her eyes filled with tears. She tried to brush them away. "Mother doesn't..." she switched to mind speak, *like it when I cry.*

Poor child. Rika held out her arms to Tishria, and the girl fled into them.

"So amid all our heartache and grief over the deaths of Mantouk and Rusik, there is a great joy as well, to discover strong Gifts are among us in at least one of our children." Yural sat near the nuknuk lamp in the group snow house, talking with Farnook, Suka, and Attu.

"Our daughter has a Gift," Suka said.

"What?" Farnook looked at her man, perplexed.

"The Gift of the loudest cry in the camp. It gets her what she wants, as well."

Yural and Attu popped their lips as Farnook punched Suka in the arm.

"Ow!" he cried.

Yural turned back to the nuknuk lamp, touching the wick here and there with a small bone tool. The light flared even brighter than before.

How does she do that? Attu thought as he stretched in the renewed heat of the lamp and told himself he needed to get up and go back to his own shelter, where Rika lay sleeping with their pooliks. *Just a while longer,* he decided. The night was cold, and they'd had no more snow to build tunnels from the group snow house to their family ones. Attu had guarded the camp last night and was tired.

How long do we have before the Tuktu thieves find our camp? It was a haunting thought Attu could not dispel, which came to him whenever he grew quiet. The hunters had all learned to use the bows they'd gotten from the Tuktu. One had broken the first time it was drawn back, probably damaged in the fight, so there were only five. They'd stocked plenty of arrows and made pouches for them. Bashoo and Ubantu had gotten to be quite good with the bows, so if a fight came, they would use the best two. The others were stored with Attu, Tingiyok, and Suka.

But if they were attacked by as large a group as Attu had seen in his vision, those few weapons would never be enough. The thought was so disturbing, Attu no longer felt comfortable in the heat of the nuknuk lamp. He excused himself and returned to his own shelter, where he could be with Rika and his children, where he could see them, hold them, and protect them.

Chapter 14

Kossu held up his latest failed attempt at bow making. Attu examined the bow, its form bent too much from just twenty pulls.

"Were the first few shots good with it?" Attu asked.

"Almost as good as the thieves' bows. Then it began weakening."

"Can you show the other hunters the wood you used to make this one?"

"Why?" Kossu looked down at the bow in disgust.

"Because this is the best one anyone's been able to make so far, and if we need to fight, our hunters could use a few of these bows each to get off a few shots at an enemy before they bent too far. It's better than just having the five bows we have now."

"And it might make those thieves think we all have decent bows. At least at first." Kossu looked down at the bow in his hands with more interest. "But I'm not going to stop searching for the same wood the thieves used to make their bows."

The weather grew still colder, and Attu relished the crisp air, so much like the Expanse. Everything around him looked richer in the light of the slanting sun during the short amount of daylight each day. The women brought their pooliks to the group snow house and spent much time there through the dark hours. Although the air within was damp with the smell of wetness coverings, the happiness of the women and the squeals of the delighted babies at play filled Attu's heart with joy.

Attu sat near one of the nuknuk lamps with Ubantu and the other men not guarding the camp. There was no need of the heat when so many were in the large snow house, so the women kept the flame low, but it was a gathering place of long habit, and the light was welcome to them all.

"I'm concerned about Kossu," Ubantu said. "He is long absent from camp."

"I spoke with him before he left this time," Attu said. "He is determined to find the right wood to make more bows. He's tried every type of tree the others found, and now he's ranging farther and farther away to find others to try."

"It is not wise that he goes alone." Tingiyok's concern reflected in the others' eyes. "Being the man of his family now, he should be here when not hunting, to protect his mother and siblings. And what if he is attacked by another lone thief or one of the dogs they left behind?"

"I have shared this with him," Attu said. "He showed us the wood to make the temporary bows, but in his grief that's not enough. Kossu has thrown his energy into this quest to find the bow wood, even though no one has been able to find it. I've been reluctant to stop him. I'm not sure what he would do if he didn't have this idea to keep his thoughts from the death of his father. And the wood must exist. It may just be too far away from here."

"Rusik was a fine hunter. May his star light the night for all of us," one of the hunters said.

The others nodded, and no one spoke for a time.

"I pray the spirits reward his efforts and Kossu finds the bow wood," Tingiyok said.

"Imagine all of us with bows and arrows as good as the few we have now," Soantek added.

"Attu glanced at Soantek's face in the light of the lamp. The man now carried scars, angry red pits in his skin. But Soantek had lived, and he was strong again. Attu pushed away his thoughts of Mantouk after saying a quick prayer for his spirit, and for Trika and Chonik.

A dog started barking, and the other two joined in.

Attu looked up as other hunters grabbed their weapons.

"What is it?" one of the hunters asked.

"Attu!" Suanu called from the edge of camp.

Attu and the others ran to where Suanu crouched behind her shelter, holding the rope attached to Dog, who was leaping and barking wildly as Suanu struggled to control her. As the men reached Suanu, Dog stopped leaping and stood frozen, glaring past the shelter into the dark where long grass grew beside the camp. A deep growl rose in her throat.

"Something is out there. I couldn't see it, but Dog did. I grabbed her rope before she could go after it."

Attu gave the silent signal, and his hunters spread out and moved forward cautiously. Attu saw that Tingiyok had thought to grab one of the bows and had it nocked and ready.

"No!" Ganik cried as a blur of grey fur raced past the men and into the long grass. Grey Wolf barked once, then the grass erupted with the sound of animals fighting.

Suka ran into the grass, toward the fight. "Dogs!" he shouted as he drew closer. "At least six of them."

Attu pushed his mind into Grey Wolf's. *Run from them*, he mind spoke as he created a picture in his mind of Grey Wolf running from the other dogs out into the open area where the hunters could spear them.

Grey Wolf pushed back. Attu sensed the dog's revulsion at the idea of running instead of fighting.

Attu pushed the idea at Grey Wolf again. *Too many for you. Pack fight with you.* He sensed the dog's agreement.

"Get ready," Attu said. "They're coming out this side."

Grey Wolf shot out into the open area, a pack of screaming dogs at his heels. He turned and grabbed the throat of the first dog behind him and the pair rolled away from the others, white sand flying as they churned it up with their feet, Grey Wolf trying to maintain his grip and the other dog trying to get away.

Before the rest of the pack could realize the danger they were in, Attu's men speared them, dragging each dog like a nuknuk and striking killing blows when they could.

One dog tried to run away, but Tingiyok caught the animal in the back with an arrow. The dog howled in pain as it fell to the ground. Tingiyok ran to it and killed it with a blow to the head.

Attu felt his gorge rise as the last dog fell to Ubantu's spear.

Grey Wolf stood over the dog he'd attacked. He was bleeding from a cut on his ear, but otherwise looked all right.

Ganik ran toward him, but when he drew close, Grey Wolf growled at the boy. Ganik stopped, drawing back in sudden fear.

"The other dog isn't dead yet," Bashoo said. He walked over to Ganik and picked him up like a toddler, stepping away from the still growling dog.

"Let me kill it," Attu said aloud, walking toward the dog with his killing club. He opened up his mind to show Grey Wolf what he was going to do. But when he touched the dog's consciousness, the wild fierceness that swept over him made Attu stumble. He stopped his approach.

"Your kill," Attu said aloud as he sent the message to Grey Wolf.

Suka had taken a step forward, but he held back with the others at Attu's words.

"You defended your pack well this day," Attu continued. "Do you kill this one, or do I?" He sent a picture of himself, using the killing club.

Grey Wolf stopped growling. He looked around, as if realizing that there were no more enemy dogs to fight. He stepped back, away from the dog that lay before him, still alive, but bleeding out fast.

"I will allow this animal to die with honor," Attu said. He spoke the words over the animal and then struck it with the killing club.

Grey Wolf watched Attu and then walked away, toward Ganik.

Attu winced, but didn't move to stop Grey Wolf.

Tingiyok mind spoke his own hopes to Attu. *We need to know he can do this, can kill to protect, then turn off that violence and become the gentle friend of the boy again.*

Ganik looked at his bloody dog, and for a moment Attu thought he would run from the animal. But Ganik took in a deep breath and held his hand out for Grey Wolf. The great dog licked it, as if asking forgiveness for growling at Ganik earlier. Ganik petted the top of Grey Wolf's head, and Grey Wolf leaned into the boy, his eyes sliding shut in pleasure at Ganik's touch.

"I think that might have been all the wild dogs." Attu agreed with the other hunters later as they discussed the night's events. "But we need to keep our own dogs close to camp, both to protect them and to alert if other dogs are coming."

"Grey Wolf couldn't have fought all six of the other dogs on his own and lived," Ubantu said.

"But I bet he would have taken more than one of the thieves' dogs with him into the Between where dog spirits go," Suka said.

Lips popped. Tonight the other hunters had seen what Grey Wolf could do. Attu realized that although he and Tingiyok had told the others about how the pup's parents had gone after the moose, they hadn't elaborated on the animals' ability to fight because they'd wanted the others to let the pups into the Clan.

Now that the other hunters knew, Attu had expected at least some of them would be concerned about the young dogs. But by attacking the thieves' dogs, Grey Wolf had become a hunter like them, a true defender of the Clan.

Attu realized that's what Toonuk had meant about their dogs being "almost people." Surely the Tuktu thought of their dogs the same way Attu's hunters were thinking of Grey Wolf now, as defenders of their herds and their families, companions as well as fellow herders.

"If there are any others, we don't know how bold they might get, especially with it being winter and the game scarce," Tingiyok was saying as Attu turned his attention back to the conversation. "When I'm out with the boys, we'll watch for tracks. But I want to take Warm Fur with me when we go out, for protection. I know the dogs are still pups, and Warm Fur is much smaller than Grey Wolf, but she'll let us know if other dogs are in the area so I can keep the boys safe."

Another moon passed. Guards were still posted day and night, but no more of the thieves' dogs came near camp and

Keanu saw no sign of any thief bands on her daily flight. The days were beginning to get longer, but like it had on the Expanse, the weather became colder. Not the deep cold of Attu's childhood, but colder than the Clan had experienced since coming off the Expanse.

Attu walked through camp on one of those cold days. His foot miks squeaked on the snow as he heard Ganik and Chonik arguing near the ocean edge of camp. As he approached them, their voices raised even louder.

"I did so beat you," Ganik shouted. "My spit went farther than yours by at least an arm length."

"No it didn't," Chonik said, his voice full of stubborn resolution. He glared at Ganik. "I won't play this game with you if you keep cheating."

Attu thought about playing spitting games with Suka when they were boys. Each would stand on one side of a line they had drawn in the snow. Then they would spit. The winner was the one who spit the farthest. When they'd played that game, it had been to have an excuse to spit, to see their saliva freeze in the air and shatter as crystals of ice when it hit the ground. And just like for these two boys, it had been a game to be played at the edge of camp, away from the disapproving eyes of their mothers.

Ganik shouted even louder. He pushed Chonik, who fell backward in the snow. Before Attu could stop them, Chonik was back on his feet and the two were fighting, throwing wild punches with their mik-clad fists, doing little damage to each other, but escalating both boys' anger.

"Enough!" Attu moved to push between them, but before he could, a grey blur shot past him, bowling Chonik over onto his back again. The boy stopped moving, his eyes wide as Grey Wolf planted his front feet on Chonik's chest and growled, baring his teeth.

"No!" Ganik shouted, grabbing Grey Wolf by the scruff of his neck and pulling him off Chonik.

Attu thrust out his mind to the half-wolf as he shouted, "Lay down!"

Grey Wolf dropped to the ground. His eyes squinted and his ears flattened. Still in Grey Wolf's mind, Attu saw the scene as the animal understood it – the two boys fighting, his boy shouting – and Attu knew Grey Wolf had thought Ganik was about to be hurt by the other boy, even though Ganik had started the fight.

No. Attu showed Grey Wolf how he had seen the argument, and then, inspired to try something else, Attu thought, *Pups wrestling. One gets ear bit. Then fight. Adult wolf stops fight when pups get too rough with each other.* He conveyed his ideas visually, a combination of mind speak and mind blending.

Grey Wolf's confusion vanished. To Attu, it felt like something slipped into place in the animal's mind. He knew the wolf understood him. At the same time, Attu had a realization. When he thought of the other two pups, he thought of them as their mother was, as dogs. But he couldn't think of Grey Wolf that way.

Wolf, Grey Wolf's thought intruded on his own and Attu drew back, startled. He hadn't meant for the pup to hear his last thoughts. But then, out of curiosity, he moved into Grey Wolf's mind again, wondering if the wildness he'd sensed there during the fight with the thieves' dogs would still be as strong.

Attu saw two grey wolves standing beside each other, one larger than the other. As the image became clear, he realized this was how Grey Wolf saw himself. Tishria had been right. The pup saw himself as wolf, as his father, not as a dog like his mother. Grey Wolf picked up on Attu's thoughts of his mother.

Gone. Attu felt the immense void left where the pup's parents should have been.

We are your pack now. Attu projected images of Grey Wolf and the other two pups, running with the children, then grown, hunting with the adults, pulling sleds, guarding the camp and fighting the wild dogs. Before he could stop himself, Attu also saw Grey Wolf, now a fully-grown male, attacking a Tuktu thief. He pulled back from that thought, but felt a question from Grey Wolf as the pup's eyes continued to gaze into his own.

Someday, Attu tried to communicate. *All people are not pack. For now, hurt no human.*

Grey Wolf stood, walked to where Chonik had pulled himself to his feet, and sat in front of the boy.

"He wants you to know he's sorry," Ganik said. "Pet him."

Chonik reached out a tentative hand. Grey Wolf wagged his tail twice and licked Chonik's mik.

The bark of the bushes near the lake turned a brighter shade of red. Attu's people grew restless as the weather warmed above freezing several days in a row. It was still cold, but the long days of winter had given way to the growing daylight of early spring. The pooliks were growing too, and Yural's son, the first to be born, was also   the first to sit up.

"Soon it will be time for his naming," Attu's mother crooned at her sturdy son, out on this milder day and riding in Yural's hood.

"Will you have my brother's naming soon, or wait for the others?" Attu asked as they walked through camp toward his shelter. Yural wanted to visit with Rika, but since the weather was warmer, she had ventured outside, rather than use the snow tunnels linking their shelters with the group snow house.

Many of the Clan were out today. Men worked on hunting equipment or helped their women clean the sleeping furs. Attu watched as Rovek piled snow onto one of the furs, grinding the snow into the fur with his miks. Meavu was working on another smaller fur, which had apparently lain in the snow long enough. She picked it up and shook it, sending snow everywhere to the delight of her son. He squealed as the snow fell on Meavu's hood and some landed on him. He reached out his mik-covered hand, trying to catch some of the sparkling whiteness.

The love of snow, Attu thought. *We are born with it.*

"I did it!" Attu turned as Kossu came running through the camp toward him. "I did it! Look!" The young hunter held out a bow. "It works!"

The Clan gathered at the edge of camp to see Kossu's bow in action. Kossu was right. The bow pulled hard but didn't break, and the arrow flew much farther than anyone had expected. After the shot, Kossu held up the bow, so all could see it had retained its original shape.

"How many arrows have you shot with it?" Ubantu asked, reaching for the bow. Kossu handed it to him.

"At least forty," Kossu said. "This one is different. I'm certain it will keep its shape."

Tingiyok took the bow from Kossu. He unstrung the sinew bowstring, examining how the bow straightened to what must have been its original shape, with only the bit of curve Kossu had carved into it.

Soantek took the bow then and tried to restring it. He couldn't bend the bow far enough to hook the string onto the notch at the opposite end.

"Here," Kossu said. "Brace the bow against your foot mik, like this." He braced the butt of the bow against his instep and then slowly bent it until Attu thought it must surely break. But the bow held, and the sinew string slipped on.

"Even if the bow only held for a few shots like the others we made, still it is a weapon worth making," Soantek said. "This bow bends harder than the ones the Tuktu gave us, so our arrows will shoot farther."

Lips popped, and several hunters pounded Kossu on the back. The young hunter beamed.

"Where did you find this wood?" Attu asked.

"Down by the lake. It was hidden in the middle of a thick stand of tall bushes surrounded by larger pine trees. The bow wood trees are small and all have a tight slick bark that peels off easily. Underneath, the wood seems too wet, as if it would bend and break. But I slipped the bark off and then let the wood sit near the fire for a few days to dry. I bent one too soon, and it cracked like a green twig."

Lips popped again, now in dismay at the loss of one of the weapons.

Kossu nodded his agreement. "So I left the others for a few more days, about half a moon in total. Then I began to carve the curve and the notches. I didn't say anything to anyone this time, because I wasn't sure that drying the wood would make a difference. I didn't want to get our hopes up for nothing. This is my first finished one. I took it out this morning to try, and I've shot it over and over again. I think it's going to hold up. Look at how it snaps back, right to its original form."

"How many can you make?" Ubantu asked.

"Enough for everyone. I will need to cut more, let them dry-" Kossu began.

"Do not cut them all," Yural spoke up. "Be careful to leave the smaller ones, and do not step on the smallest if there are any."

"There are, and I have been careful," Kossu assured her, looking to all of them. "My spirit drew me to this place, and my name spirit warned me to be careful," he added. "I believe my father also guided me from the Between."

"Then we thank the spirits and Rusik," Yural said. Everyone dropped their heads, paying respect to the dead.

Veshria stood beside Keanu and Farnook. Tears streamed down her face, and a look of both pride at her son and fresh anguish at the loss of her man mingled there. Attu looked away, his own eyes filling at the sight.

"You must show these trees to the rest of us, so no one accidently cuts any for the fire," Attu said.

"I'll show everyone, but it's very hard to get to them. I had to cut through the thorn bushes and avoid the swampy areas. I don't think anyone would try that hard just for kindling."

Several men, including Attu, went with Kossu toward his snow house to examine the other trees to be made into bows.

"Bows that powerful will need better arrows than the ones we've been making." Ubantu grinned.

"We can harden them and straighten them even more using fire, like we Nukeena did to shape pieces of our canoes." Soantek ducked into the snow house with the others. "I still have one of the tools."

"Feathers will need to be added," Tingiyok said, stepping inside just ahead of Attu. "We can use the same pine glue we use for the skin boats to seal the seams. Just a touch should keep the feathers on the end of the arrows."

Including the five bows they already had, soon all the men had bows and arrows of their own. Even Ganik and Chonik had small ones. Kossu took the bow that had split, cut off the broken middle, and used the two pieces on either end to carve two small bows, lighter and thinner than the men's, yet true weapons.

"This is much better than the ones I could make." Ganik grinned when Kossu gave him the small bow. "Come on!" he called to Chonik, and the two ran down the beach to try out their new bows.

"Not too far," Kossu called after them.

Attu laughed as Ganik shot at a water bird walking on the beach. He missed, and the bird flew away, its cry shrill.

"Nothing will be safe from those two now," Kossu said.

"Tingiyok will instruct them in the proper use of the bow. He'll make sure they respect the animals, or Ganik will find himself without his new weapon." Attu walked toward the other men. He needed to practice shooting as well or Suka was going to make another contest out of it when he saw how much better he could shoot than Attu.

"Veshria still isn't speaking, but yesterday I saw her smile as Ganik stood at the target with the men, practicing shooting his little bow," Rika said. She stood stirring the cooking skins over the nuknuk lamp. She brushed a drip of melting snow from her face, glancing up at the roof of their snow house. "Should we start building our hide shelter soon? The weather is warming, but it still seems too early."

Their son and daughter were rolling around in the furs on the sleeping platform. Attu was watching them, careful not to let either child fall, but letting them move and crawl as much as they could. "Like our children, who seem too young to be crawling about, the winter seems too short here. When it was so cold, it felt like we were living on the Expanse again. But that time has passed. The seasons will change here; the ice is beginning to break, and I must admit I'm looking forward to getting back into my skin boat again."

His daughter had made it to the edge of the platform and began sliding down the side, her small hands clutching the fur she was on, as if she were riding down a snow hill on a hide sled.

"Oh, no you don't," Attu said, and moved her back to the safety of the middle.

"Yural says at the next full moon we'll have the naming ceremony." Rika scooped some fish stew into their bowls, handed Attu one, then moved to sit on the opposite end of the sleeping platform where she could keep an eye on her son.

"I believe it's a good thing to name all the pooliks at once. Meavu's is almost six moons, having been born early. My brother is eight moons, but Mother wanted to wait and name him with the others. Have you women gotten together to make sure none are named the same name?" Attu asked.

Rika laughed. "Do you know how tricky that is to do? Without giving away the actual name ahead of time?" She snatched her son from the edge of the platform, playfully rolling him back toward his sister. The boy wrestled with the fur he was holding before shoving it into his mouth.

"I'd better eat quickly," Rika observed. "Our son is getting hungry.

"The rest of my meat cache is gone," Rovek told Attu the next day. "I know I had at least two more seals and part of a nuknuk stored there."

"Do you think more of the thieves' dogs got into it?" Attu asked.

"I couldn't tell," Rovek said. "I'd brought Ganik and Chonik with me. I told them their mothers could have the meat if they helped me drag it back to them. Grey Wolf was with them, and he smelled the cache first and sniffed around it so much before I reached it and found it open and empty that I couldn't tell if all the tracks were his."

Rovek shrugged. "I don't need the meat. But I thought you should know."

That night, as Attu slept, he dreamed of the vision. He awoke with a muffled cry, working to calm himself and not awaken Rika or the babies.

Remember, he told himself, *in the vision it is winter. And it is now spring. The snow is almost gone. My people are building their hide shelters again. It may snow again, but the ground is so muddy now, sleds won't travel well. As soon as they stopped, they'd be mired in the mud on the plains. Thieves may come, but not by sled, at least until next winter. And right now, with all this mud, no one can travel far.* Then Attu thought of the missing meat. *Still, the wild dogs may be lurking nearby. We will stay prepared.*

The next morning, Attu went to Keanu's shelter. Soantek welcomed him in with a finger to his lips. "She flies," he said, motioning to where Keanu sat, her eyes wide but unseeing. "But stay. She'll be back soon."

Even with the mud surrounding them, Keanu was entering a bird's mind every day and, with the bird's permission, flying over a large expanse. She watched for tracks in the dead grass and mud, rather than for people, since they knew the thieves could hide themselves well during the day. She had been flying for most of the winter, ever since she had recovered from the sickness and was strong enough to do so.

"You have other responsibilities," Keanu had told Attu when he objected to her patrolling every day without his help. "Let me do what I'm good at." Attu had realized the wisdom of her words and made no more objections.

A few days ago, a Clan of swift gulls had taken up residence in the rocky hills to the north. Keanu had promised them no one from the Clan would take eggs from their nests if one of them would be willing to fly with her whenever she asked them to.

"They are simple birds and their eyesight is not as keen as the hawk's I flew in over the winter, but they aren't distracted by every rock rabbit or mouse animal they see." Keanu rolled her eyes as she stretched, coming back into the Here and Now of the shelter and her visitor.

"The gulls are worried that Ganik's getting too close to their nests with his stone throwing and bow and arrows," Keanu said. "You must warn him again. He can bring home all the rock birds he can kill in the rocks near the caves, but the hill where the gulls are is off limits. I must keep my promise to the gull Clan."

Attu nodded. "And no sign of the Tuktu?"

"I don't think they can travel north yet in all the mud. Not until the ground thaws more and dries out."

"I hope they come north close to us again," Attu said. "We need to know if other Tuktu Clans have fought the thieves."

Attu and Keanu exchanged looks, and Keanu rubbed her arms, shivering as a chill overtook her.

Chapter 15

"And that was the last full night of sleep I've had in six moons," Attu said as he and Suka laughed about the day Attu's twins had been born. They were preparing their skin boats for their first hunt since the ocean ice had broken. A few large chunks still floated in the bay, but it was safe to paddle once again.

Attu worked his fingers along his rope, checking for splits. The breeze off the bay was warm today. Attu was eager to go seal hunting again. The seals were swimming north along the coastline, and many swam into the bay to rest before braving the currents again.

"And what are your pooliks to be named?" Suka teased as he readied his boat, checking the seams near the front one more time.

"I'm glad that's not up to me. But it's been interesting, listening to the women giving hints to one another and trying to figure out what to name each child without using the same name twice."

Suka looked out over the bay, his eyes drinking in the beauty of the blue water, calm today under a clear sky. "Oh, it will be good to be back on the water again."

Attu, help! Tishria's high mental voice cut through Attu's thoughts.

What is it? A wild dog?

Ganik, Chonik, me. North. Along the shore. A nuknuk.

Attu grabbed his spear, shouted to Suka and the others, and ran up the beach. A nuknuk roared, its voice echoing against the rocks.

"Oh no," Attu said, and he ran faster.

Around the first jumble of rocks, Attu saw Ganik, Chonik, and Tishria. Ganik was high up, wedged into a crevice in the rocky hill where he had been forbidden to gather the gull eggs. Chonik and Tishria were at the base of a narrow opening between the rocks, blocking the only path to the water for the male nuknuk that stood up on its hind flippers just a few spear lengths from them. It bellowed again, then dropped to all fours and began weaving back and forth.

Attu searched for a clear path around the jumble of boulders, so they could flank the animal, but there was none.

"What do we do?" Suka asked.

"We-"

Grey Wolf ran at the nuknuk, barking fiercely, the hair on his back standing up, his ears flat to his head.

No! Attu heard Tishria's voice. *Don't get too close, Grey Wolf. Listen to me.*

Grey Wolf stopped a spear length in front of the nuknuk, between it and the children. The huge animal reared up and roared at him.

Attu pushed at Grey Wolf's mind, but Tishria's thoughts stopped him. *I can do this. Too many voices in his head will confuse him.*

The nuknuk lunged at Grey Wolf. The dog danced away from the huge beast, and Attu felt Tishria encouraging Grey Wolf to draw the nuknuk away from them, farther north on the path. One spear length more, then another.

"Run!" Attu hollered at Tishria and Chonik.

Tishria ran to Attu, then turned to face Grey Wolf and the nuknuk again. But Chonik didn't move. He looked at them, his eyes wide, his face blank. The terrified boy had never seen a full-grown live male nuknuk this close. Chonik knew what had happened to Ganik's father and was obviously too scared to move, for fear the animal would turn from the dog and attack him as it had Rusik.

Grey Wolf snapped at the nuknuk's sides as the animal moved away from Chonik another spear length.

Not so close! Tishria mind shouted. Grey Wolf backed away again and the nuknuk lunged, barely missing the dog's flank, and drawing closer to Chonik again. But Attu could see that Grey Wolf's instincts had kicked in. He was learning about this prey, and he moved quickly in and out, drawing the animal farther away from the boy again.

"Stay back," Attu ordered Tishria and she nodded, but kept her eyes on Grey Wolf and the nuknuk.

"I can get him," Suka said.

Attu nodded and Suka ran toward Chonik. He grabbed Chonik up like a seal and turned, sprinting back up the beach where the others stood.

"Stop!" Attu shouted at Grey Wolf and mind spoke to him as well. He and the other hunters backed away from the nuknuk, opening up a space for it to get to the water.

Let it go. We're safe now, Attu heard Tishria coaxing Grey Wolf to give up the fight.

Attu watched as Grey Wolf backed away from the nuknuk, closer to where the hunters stood ready in case the nuknuk charged them. The nuknuk followed, keeping its tusks facing the dog. The water near shore was deep, and when the nuknuk reached it, he gave one last roar toward them all and then disappeared under some broken ice near the shore.

Attu looked up. Ganik was gone. He'd apparently been able to climb the rest of the way up the hill to safety. *For now,* Attu thought, *until Keanu finds out you broke her promise to the gulls...*

Tishria slapped her leg and Grey Wolf ran up to her. He licked her outstretched palm and whined.

"You are a good wolf. A good protector of your Clan," Tishria said aloud. Attu could feel her mental push in pictures toward the animal's mind. Grey Wolf stopped his whining and stood tall before Tishria. Their eyes met and Attu felt a deep communication between them, deeper than any he had ever felt between a person and an animal. Then they turned and began walking up the beach where the rest of the Clan had gathered.

"Mother will be worried about us. And Ganik is in big trouble," Tishria said as Attu walked beside her. "I told Ganik not to go. But he said he wanted fresh eggs to eat and no one would stop him. So I found Chonik because you said we weren't to go this far alone, and we came to bring him back."

"And Grey Wolf?"

"I made Ganik leave him behind. I called for you, then I called for Grey Wolf, too." They walked a few more steps before Tishria reached for Attu's hand, pulling him aside.

"The nuknuk wouldn't listen to me." Her eyes looked to Attu's with concern.

"You tried to mind speak to the nuknuk?"

"I did mind speak with him. Before I called to you. I thought if I could convince him we would just go, he'd leave us alone. But then Chonik wouldn't budge and…" Tishria shuddered and Attu caught a fleeting image of an angry nuknuk eyeing the children. "He told me he was defending his part of the beach. He would have attacked us if you hadn't come."

"Tishria mind spoke to Grey Wolf and was able to keep communicating with you at the same time?" Rika asked Attu as they sat talking about the morning's near tragedy.

"After she couldn't convince the nuknuk not to attack them." Attu took a bite of his stew. "Tishria is incredibly brave. And Grey Wolf may have saved a hunter's life today. Who knows what would have happened if one of us had been forced to confront that animal?" Attu shuddered at the memory of Rusik, gored by the nuknuk.

"And the nuknuk was going to attack them for being on the beach he'd claimed?"

"Yes. I caught a glimpse of his thoughts through Tishria. The children must not play along the shore until all the ice has melted and the nuknuks have moved north again."

"And Ganik?"

"Tingiyok asked to take care of his punishment. Ganik will be hauling wood to every shelter for the next moon. And I know Tingiyok already took his bow and arrows."

"I hope he learns from this. His actions almost got his sister and his best friend killed."

"Do you know how many fish Soantek's going to have to give the gulls because our promise has been broken?" Keanu stirred her cooking skin so hard, Attu thought it might spring a leak. "I can't risk what the evil spirits might do to our Clan after I told the birds they would be safe and then Ganik took their eggs anyway."

"Are the gulls refusing to let you fly in them?" The gulls were the fastest flyers, and Keanu had been relying on them because there were so many and they'd been willing to take turns flying with her for almost half a day so she could look as far as possible from camp.

"They will continue to fly, but I've lost their trust, at least for this spring, so I might need to find more willing birds, anyway," Keanu said. She moved from the cooking skin, her stirring stick still in her hand. She waved it for emphasis. "Birds have short memories, and I'm sure the gulls will have forgotten about it by next spring. But the spirits never forget. I prayed about it, and my name spirit gave me the idea of making amends with fish."

"Tingiyok will make Ganik fish, too. And I will ask Yural if there's anything else you need to do. She may need to perform a ceremony to make sure we're doing everything we can."

"And as angry as I am at Ganik, I don't want him to invite evil spirits to harm him by being the one to break our Clan's promise. He just doesn't seem to understand how serious this all is."

Attu left with the promise to speak with both Yural and Tingiyok. Punishment was one thing, but Ganik needed to see the danger he was putting himself in by breaking such a serious promise to the gull Clan. If the spirits chose to, Ganik could grow up to be the unlucky hunter, never getting game and always wondering why, when the reason was that he'd been disrespectful of the animals of Nuvikuan-na as a child and was now paying the price. *Perhaps that nuknuk was part of some immediate retribution from the spirits…*

The Clan gathered the next evening at sunset. The full moon would rise soon, but they'd begun when the fire spirit met the water spirit, to honor the Nukeena Clan. Each mother stepped forward, her man beside her, and all the Clan formed a protective circle around them, the sign of the Clan's strength and unity in the raising of the young. Soantek spoke a few words over each poolik, sprinkling each with both water from a nearby spring and ash from the sacred fire he had built at sunrise and prayed over until it had burned completely.

As the full moon rose over the mountains to the east, the mothers moved closer to the water. One by one, each man and woman knelt on Yural's ceremonial robe, laid out on the ground in the sand. When it was Yural's turn, Soantek would perform the ritual, but right now he stood aside, watching and learning as Yural performed the naming for each new family.

Meavu chose the name Tovut for her son, and all agreed the Elder's name should live on in the Clan. Attu knew Meavu secretly hoped her boy would have some of the Gifts Elder Tovut had possessed, even though the Clan hadn't recognized them as more than the ramblings of an old storyteller until it was almost too late.

Attu laughed with the rest as Farnook named her daughter Nipka. She grinned at the Clan's approval. As if to seal the appropriateness of being named "she with the spirit to speak loudly, is strong, is heard among the Clan," Nipka began crying, her tiny body squirming in frustration at being bound with her parents' hands in the ceremonial rope. Once again, Attu was amazed at the loudness of the squalling red-faced poolik.

Yural took her turn before Attu and Rika. The honor of being last would go to the Clan's leader and healer. As Yural and Ubantu knelt on the robe, Soantek spoke the words over them and their son. "I name him Kavut," Yural said, and all was quiet before heads began to nod. Kavut meant "of strong brows," and Yural and Ubantu's son had his father's strong features. But the Clan knew it also meant possessing the Nuvik spirit of inner strength, a calmness and wisdom greater than the person's age. Attu hardily agreed with his mother's choice of name for her quiet, alert boy.

When it was Attu's and Rika's turn, Rika handed Yural the rope, and Attu remembered the two of them, not so long ago, holding out their hands to Elder Nuanu as she bound them together under the light of the full moon as they floated on the ice chunk. That night they had sworn to share their lives forever, even though they might never escape the ice chunk to have any time together.

Attu looked to Rika and saw she was remembering, too. She placed her hand upon his, and Rovek, holding his nephew's tiny hand, placed it upon Rika's. Meavu, standing on their other side, held out her niece's hand. Yural wrapped them together. For once, their pooliks didn't squirm.

Attu's daughter looked at him, her eyes wide in the moonlight. Attu's heart melted yet again at the sight of her. His son was studying his grandmother, watching her hands as they moved over the bound ones, speaking the words of binding yet again. "And you will be one family. Your children will be protected with your lives. No one and nothing will take them from you until the Between of death separates you. You will guide your daughter, Rika, and you will guide your son, Attu, in the ways of the women and men. Rika, you will love the child of your heart, your son, and teach him to respect all women and treat them as precious. And you will guide your daughter, Attu, in the ways of the true honorable man, so she may trust the man of her own heart one day, and have no fear of him, but be assured he will hunt for her and protect her always."

Rika flinched. Attu knew she was thinking of her own father, who had also sworn this oath in front of his whole Clan, then dishonored it.

Our daughter will never fear me. He looked into Rika's eyes, baring his spirit to her to the deepest part of himself.

I know. Thank you. She smiled and looked up to Yural.

"What do you name these children?" Yural asked.

All around them the Clan leaned in to catch Rika's words.

"Our son shall be named Gantuk," Rika said, "'he who smiles and makes others smile,' for he was born second, bringing a smile of surprise to all of us."

Lips popped in agreement with her as Attu chuckled, remembering what a shock he'd had when Suka had first told him his woman had given birth to twins.

"I could tell you that I have set my spirit to the search, and it has returned time and again with the name our daughter will have," Rika continued. "But I cannot. This child was named before she was born, by her namesake. On the night I was bonded, before the ceremony had even been performed, Elder Nuanu told me my first child would be a girl. I was to name her Nuanu, 'For she will be my eyes and ears in the generation after you. She will be as I was, for the Clan.' Therefore, because the spirit of Shuantuan within Elder Nuanu bid it, I name our daughter Nuanu."

Some of the women gasped in astonishment. Others shook their heads. It was one thing to name a child after a beloved Elder, such as Elder Tovut. But to name a child after the woman all believed had become the personification of Shuantuan, the most powerful of all trysta spirits? And to say Elder Nuanu had told her to do so before Rika was even bonded?

Rika opened her mind then, and Attu, Farnook, Tingiyok, Keanu, and Soantek all saw her memory. Tears flowed down Farnook's face, and Attu realized Farnook was remembering how she'd seen Elder Nuanu in visions, guiding her along with Vanreda and Farnook's own mother from the Between.

"It is true," Elder Tingiyok said. "It must be so. Elder Nuanu told Rika to name her child Nuanu."

Rika drew in a deep breath. As she let it out, the Clan had also drawn a collective breath and was relaxing into the celebration once again. Their daughter would be raised until her woman's ceremony with the name of Nuanu. Attu was convinced she would remain with the name, as Meavu had and he had, but that her name was Nuanu was enough for now.

Fires were lit on the beach, and the sound of the waves accompanied the drumming and singing and dancing that followed. The Clan feasted on some of the new greens the women had collected, smothered in the fat from fresh moose meat. The moose were heading north again. Attu wondered, as he took a juicy bite, if the Tuktu would come back soon, driving their tuktu herd before them through the fast-growing grass of the small plain to the east.

"Come! Dance with the men," Suka held out his arm for Attu to join him. Attu took his last bite of meat before letting Suka haul him up. The men were dancing the dance of the seal hunt. Soon Attu was sweating with the rest of them as they circled the fire. Feet pounded and arms flung imaginary spears. Wind swirled the smoke among them and rustled the pine trees until all of Nuvikuan-na seemed to be joining in the celebration of the naming.

Chapter 16

"They are about two days travel to the south, I think," Keanu said to the group gathered outside Attu's shelter. She had been flying in the gull and had returned to tell the Clan that she'd seen the Tuktu coming over a rise in the hills. "But their numbers are few. Less than half the people they had in the fall. Perhaps it's another group. I couldn't recognize any of them, but I was far away. The gull was afraid of them and wouldn't fly too closely."

The Tuktu arrived late the next day. The men guarding the camp to the south alerted the others, and Attu went out with most of the men to greet them.

"We bring no evil," the Tuktu leader said as he approached with his men, "but we bring news of evil."

"Before you draw closer, brothers, are any among you sick with body sores?" Attu asked.

Some of the Tuktu herders murmured among themselves, but said nothing loud enough for Attu to hear. Several said nothing at all and looked away, instead, eyes to the ground.

Finally, Toonuk spoke up. "No. We know what you're describing. Our Clan escaped that sickness. But we have suffered in other ways this winter. I have much to tell you." The Tuktu leader's face was drawn, and he looked older than Attu had remembered him. He also seemed to have lost much of his arrogance.

"Come then. You are welcome to set up your camp and take care of your herds. Tonight we'll feed you all as you rest yourselves by our fires. You can tell us everything then."

"Thank you," Toonuk said, smiling briefly in genuine thanks before turning away. As the Tuktu leader walked back with his men, he seemed to sink into himself, appearing smaller. Toonuk's shoulders drooped, as if he'd been holding himself straight while speaking to Attu, but didn't have the energy to remain that way.

Attu watched with his men as the Tuktu herders began gathering in their animals. Instead of the arrogant stares most of the Tuktu herders had given Attu and his men during their first visit, several smiled wearily as they moved past Attu's men, working to get the animals settled in within the area where the hills and some rocks along three sides made a natural enclosure. With fewer men, they were struggling.

"Let us help you," Attu called out to the men.

One shook his head, but several others nodded and motioned for Attu and his hunters to spread out on the east side of the herd, blocking them from escape and helping the Tuktu funnel the animals into the more enclosed area.

Once the animals were secure, the Tuktu called out their thanks and Attu and his men started back to camp. "I'm not sure I want to know what happened to them," Rovek said, "to lose so many of their numbers."

"They seemed almost relieved to be back here again, don't you think?" Ubantu asked.

"Yes. These are not the same people who stalked out of here last fall after killing the thieves and declaring themselves as the ones with all the knowledge of right and wrong, while claiming we knew nothing." Attu looked back at the herders, now working with their women to set up shelters. "Something very bad happened to them."

"Whatever it was, half of them are now gone, and Toonuk said it wasn't because of sickness," Suka said. "Do you think they were attacked? Do you think that many herders left the Clan? Maybe there's another group of thieves out there now."

Attu shuddered at the thought.

"No," Soantek said. "They were missing women and children, as well. They may have had a division in the Clan, but I don't think so."

"I think they were attacked and lost that many people, and now they're grieving," Ubantu said.

They walked the rest of the way back to camp in silence.

The Nuviks and Tuktu gathered around several large outdoor fires in the warmth of the spring evening. They feasted on fresh seal meat, fish, and greens from the surrounding woods. Then all gathered to hear the Tuktu's leader.

"Thieves attacked our camp this winter," Toonuk said. "A large group, like the ones we killed last fall with your help."

Lips popped at Toonuk's words, though none were surprised.

"We fought hard and many of us were killed," Toonuk said. "The thieves set fire to our shelters. We lost women and children, as well. But we also killed all of the thieves who attacked us."

Lips popped again. "How were you able to defeat them?" Attu asked.

"It was my son, Martu," Toonuk said. He glanced to where Martu sat near Kossu and several of the other younger hunters and young Tuktu women.

Martu looked up at the mention of his name. Pride gleamed in his eyes as his father spoke.

"Martu was the first to spot the enemy coming. He alerted the rest of us. When he realized the thieves would reach our camp before the women and children could get away, Martu used the dogs and the tuktu herd to create a wedge between as many of the thieves as he could and our shelters, driving the attackers away and forcing them up against some cliffs nearby. Then he and the other boys scared the tuktu into stampeding right to the edge of the cliffs. A few of the tuktu were lost, but the thieves he'd been able to corral also fell to their deaths, their bodies broken on the rocks of the shoreline below."

"The rest were too close to the shelters and had set fire to several before we could fight back. We fought to protect the women and children," Spartik said. The Elder's face was drawn, his brows furrowed as he remembered the fight. "The thieves became confused when their band was divided, and many of their men got caught in the tuktu herd. And when we began shooting arrows at them, I think they were shocked. They ran. My men chased them down. More of our herders died in the close fighting. But the whole band of thieves was killed.

"When we spoke with the other Clans at the winter gathering, we learned that another Tuktu Clan was attacked by thieves around the same time as we were. They were too far from us for it to be the same thieves. Many Tuktu died in that fight. And the thieves got away." Spartik spat off to the side.

"We are sorry for the loss of so many of your people," Yural said. She rose and placed her hand on first Toonuk's then Spartik's shoulder. "We will pray for their spirits and for yours as well, in this time of your grief." She spoke a prayer aloud then, and the group hushed to hear her. Attu felt his spirit joining in the prayer as the smoke rose from the fires into the night sky, carrying Yural's words to the trysta spirits and beyond.

When she finished, all was quiet for a moment. "Thank you," Spartik said. "We thank you." He moved his arms out, drawing all his people into his words of appreciation. Heads nodded and many of the Tuktu men and women smiled at Attu's people.

"And now you will want to know of the sickness," Toonuk said. Attu heard the reluctance in the man's voice, but also his determination to share this, too, with Attu's people.

"You said you escaped the sickness. But others did not?" Attu asked.

"We usually winter near other Tuktu Clans; the one we are closest to makes camp to the east of the fire mountains near the river, we on the west near the ocean. I think you know the place. You spoke of it when you told of escaping the Ravens."

Attu's people agreed. "We hunted just south of there for the wild tuktu," Rovek said.

"Yes. The grass grows near the mountains and the warm springs, even in the winter. It is a beautiful place. We make our camps and visit back and forth, trading and telling stories during the long nights. Many of our people are related through exchanges of women and men among us. Before this winter, it's always been a time of joy to reunite with that Clan again." Toonuk stopped as his voice broke. He tried to continue, but couldn't.

Toonuk's woman, Nealria, spoke up from her seat beside him. "As our Clan's healer, what happened is almost too hard for me to tell. But you need to know. Two thieves stumbled into another Tuktu Clan's camp as they headed south. The other Clan was just a few days behind us.

"One of the thieves grabbed a Tuktu woman and tried to take food from her shelter. The other Tuktu hunters killed the thieves, but by the time the Tuktu realized these thieves were not just suffering from starvation but also suffering from the open sore sickness, it was too late. Many had touched the bodies and the amazing bows and arrows."

"Being ahead of them saved our lives and cost them theirs," Spartik said. "Within days of the attack, nearly everyone in that Clan was ill. Within a moon, they were dead."

"How do you know? Did any survive?" Rika asked. Her fingers closed tightly around Attu's as she spoke.

"Two of their older children caught the sickness but lived. A few of the men had gone ahead, looking for grazing, and the others kept them away from camp when they returned. One of them is with us now. The others died in the fight against the thieves who attacked us."

"Two children out of fifteen families," Nealria said. "When they didn't come to the winter gathering place, some of our men went looking for them. The last ones set a guard to watch for us, knowing we would come. They flew the red hide, so we'd know something was wrong."

"The red hide?" Tingiyok asked.

"Normally it means sickness in the herd, so others don't come near our tuktu with their own animals. We take one of the sledge poles and erect it in the middle of the camp with a hide stained red from the red flower plants that grow near the fire mountains. The color stands out against both the green of grass and the white of snow."

"Clever," Attu said. "But I'm so sorry it had to used by your fellow Tuktu."

"My grandfather was the last to die." A young hunter Attu didn't recognize stood. He looked to Toonuk, who seemed grateful not to have to tell the rest and sat, letting the young hunter continue the story. "I am the only hunter from my Clan who survived both the attack on our Clan and the attack on Toonuk's. I was with the other hunters of my Clan, looking for grazing, when they were attacked by the sick thieves. Grandfather would not let us near the others when we returned. My grandfather did not become ill. He was a strong and robust hunter, even though he was old. He buried all who died, giving them the proper rituals for the full time we Tuktu guard the graves of men, a full moon.

"Then he set fire to every shelter, burned every possession of his people, and culled the herd. He believed the tuktu would not carry the illness, but he did this just to be safe."

"So all their weapons, their bodies, their clothing was burned?" Rika asked.

"Yes." The young hunter paused. "My grandfather waited with the two remaining children most of the winter, until they were completely healed of the sores and fever free for two moons. Then he came to us."

"We took the children," Nealria said. "It was the right thing to do."

"Our Elder Nuka had the sickness and lived," Rika said. "When others among us got the illness, she was able to care for them and not become ill again herself."

"Some of you got the sickness?" Toonuk stood up, several of the others with them. "Why didn't you tell us?" He glared at Attu, fear and anger making him look like the Toonuk Attu remembered.

"All is well. There is no danger," Yural said. "We would never take such a chance. No one among us is sick."

She looked to Nealria, who reached up, touching her man's leg. "Sit, Toonuk. Listen to them."

Toonuk sat. Attu felt the other Tuktu sliding away from his people, as if on reflex. But no one got up to leave.

Attu told the Tuktu about the thief who attacked Keanu and Soantek, about what they'd found and the precautions they'd taken. He told them about Keanu and Soantek's illness and Mantouk's death.

"Probably those two who attacked the Tuktu Clan left the thieves' band when the others got sick, like the one who attacked us did," Attu said.

"That was about the same time," Spartik agreed.

"Where is your grandfather now?" Tingiyok asked. "I'd like to-"

"Just before Grandfather gave us the children, he explained what he felt had to happen," the young hunter said. "He was not seriously ill yet, he said. But he might become ill. He'd touched the children, as well as the others, been in contact with clothing, tools, the very ground he'd been walking on for moons. And he'd developed a cough he could not shake. He was afraid he was somehow carrying the spirits of the sickness, and that it might erupt in him at any time. He said he could not risk ever coming into our camp, not knowing how long it might be before he could become ill enough to infect us all. He had the children wash in the pool by the mountain, one the rest of us could avoid without trouble. Then he sent the children to us, naked. He didn't risk touching them or going near them again."

"Then what did he do?" Rika asked.

"Grandfather made his peace with the spirits," the young hunter answered. "I went with him – at a distance, of course – to the top of the fire mountain. He was determined not to infect anyone else with the evil spirit of this terrible sickness. He called out to his name spirit, explaining why he had to do what he had decided to do. Then he walked to the top of a high cliff overlooking the fire from the mountain and jumped into it."

And he jumped. Attu saw it, as if from the hunter's own eyes, as he spoke those words. He saw the Elder leap into the molten redness of the fire mountain, his face filled with pride, his staff in his hand as he disappeared into the smoke and heat. Attu felt the grandson's grief, and a pride that reflected his grandfather's, and a love so intense it overwhelmed the grief.

"As our Elders did in the time of the great cold of the Expanse, walking out onto the ice so others might not starve but have their portion to eat, this grandfather gave the ultimate sacrifice for his fellow Tuktu." Toonuk hit his chest with his staff three times. The Nuvik men stood. Attu and the other hunters returned the acclamation with their spears.

In spite of the lateness and the pooliks asleep in the shelters, the women of Attu's Clan began the ululation cry, joined by Toonuk's people. They called out long and loud to the spirits of the Beyond to accept the Tuktu hunter into the Between as if he had been buried in the traditional manner, to see the bravery of his sacrifice, and to reward him in the Between of death.

Attu watched as the Tuktu women hauled down the large Tuktu shelters and rigged two of the heavy shelter poles into sledges with the hides, much like the Seers had done to haul tuskie meat. But instead of people pulling the sledges, a harness of hides was strapped to a tuktu, and the animal willingly pulled the sledge.

"It is a good life for them, most of the time," Yural said. She stood with Attu apart from the others, at the crest of the last hill. Kavut sat in his carry sling, his eyes wide to the sights around him, quiet as usual.

"This has been a hard winter for all of us," Attu said. He turned to his mother. "I know the Tuktu need to head north again to the lush grass of the plains there, but I felt safer with our combined numbers." He watched as the men moved out first with the herds, the women following. "Last time I could hardly wait for them to leave."

"This time is different," Yural agreed. "We both need all the people we can get to help us stay safe. Last fall, Toonuk was full of himself. Now, he's experienced two attacks on his people, one devastating, and the sickness wiping out their sister Clan."

Attu met his mother's compassionate gaze. "But he will be a better leader now that he knows he's not as in control as he once thought."

"Perhaps these tragedies will help all the Tuktu people in the end." Yural looked out over the hills where the Tuktu were slowly making their way north. "The spirits' ways are sometimes strange, but it is clear that these people's arrogance in leadership brought about the existence of roving bands of thieves in the first place. The sickness may well be the result of such evil in their midst for so long. They need to listen to their strong young men and give them a place. Not just try to cull them from the herd like raging bull tuktu."

They stood in silence for a while longer before turning back toward the camp, joining Suka, Kossu, Tingiyok, and the few others who'd come to see the Tuktu leave.

"Did you notice that Kossu spent all of his time with Spartik's youngest daughter while they were here?" Suka asked

Attu. "What is her name?" He turned to Kossu, a teasing grin on his face.

"Chirea," Kossu said, blushing.

"And does she like you?" Suka asked.

Kossu said nothing, but grinned at Suka before running ahead.

"Suka," Yural said, "let the young hunter have his privacy." She tried to sound reproachful, but couldn't. She looked to where Kossu was still running, her face now thoughtful. "Many of us are looking forward to the Tuktu's return in the fall. I will ask the spirits for a good reunion between Kossu and Chirea when they meet again."

Attu chuckled. "Now who's meddling?"

"He's gone!" Ganik screamed as he ran from his family's shelter. "I tell you he's gone! And I'm going after him. Grey Wolf will not go back into the wild like his father. He's my dog!"

Tishria stepped out of the shelter as Attu and Yural approached. Ganik was running over the hill.

"Should I go after him?" Attu asked.

"The dog has run off before. He'll be back."

"No, he won't," Tishria said. "Grey Wolf told me he's going to find a mate of his own."

It was growing dark. Ganik was still missing, and now Chonik was gone, too.

"How could my brother do something so stupid?" Kossu asked. He and Attu were searching where they'd first found the pups, thinking Ganik might try there first. "There are predators in these hills. And there are so many ravines Ganik could fall into. What if there are wild tuktu and he stampedes them? Or a moose?"

"Ganik and Chonik are both aware of the danger. Trika said Chonik took her fire starter and his bow and arrows, along with his hunting knife. I think Ganik told him where he was going to look first. So if Chonik can find Ganik, he should at least be able to build them a fire to keep the predators away tonight." Attu topped the next hill and searched the horizon. Nothing.

Chapter 17

Both Soantek and Keanu had flown to look for the boys. No one had seen either the boys or Grey Wolf. There had been no one at the old den and no sign they'd been there.

"We need to head back toward camp and try circling more to the south," Kossu said. "The boys and Grey Wolf often went that way, exploring."

"Good idea," Attu agreed.

The two struck out from the top of the rise and headed down into the next ravine between the hills.

"Help!" A call came from the next rise. "Help us! Someone help us!"

"Ganik!" Kossu raced up the next hill, Attu at his heels. They stopped as the moon finally made its appearance over the mountains, lighting up the top of the ravine and revealing Ganik and Chonik, huddled behind a large rock, peeking out just enough so Attu could see their faces in the shadow. Sprawled at their feet was a man.

"He's not dead," Ganik yelled, as Attu and Kossu approached. "But I think he's hurt."

As Attu and Kossu approached, they could see the man was lying with his knee bent at an impossible angle. Sweat poured from him, beading up in the moonlight and making his pale face glisten. His eyes were open and wild. A bow and arrows lay on the rocks nearby, and the man looked like the thief who'd attacked them, but even more ragged.

"What do we do with him?" Kossu asked. "He looks like he might have the sickness. We shouldn't touch him."

The man was seriously injured. They couldn't just leave him there to suffer until he died. *Should I end his life quickly with my spear and then burn his body, spear and all?*

It was the thing Attu needed to do. Even though this man was an enemy, no one deserved to die a slow painful death alone, or be attacked and eaten by a predator.

Attu raised his spear. *Do not kill him. Save him.* The voice stopped his downward thrust, and Attu's mind reeled at the power of Attuanin in his mind.

Why?

Save him.

How can this man, this enemy, this thief, possibly be so important to my people that we must risk the illness to save him?

Save him.

Attu felt himself drifting, his mind moving in circles between the Here and Now and the time with the whales.

Attuanin's voice had drawn him back, and he remembered being with the great killer whale fish, swimming with him, hunting with him, and all he had learned about listening to the spirits and following Attuanin for the greater good of his people.

"Attu?" Kossu asked. "Attu! Are you all right? What do we do?"

Attu looked around and realized he had lost track of time. The boys shivered behind the rock and Kossu was looking at him strangely. The thief's eyes were closed, and the moon had risen farther in the sky.

"Stay with him while I take Ganik and Chonik back to camp. I need to talk this over with everyone. Let's go." Attu motioned for the boys to follow him and started down the hill.

"I'm not going back," Ganik grumbled as they walked beside Attu. "I haven't found Grey Wolf yet."

Attu stopped and turned to Ganik. "If Grey Wolf wants to come back, he will," Attu said. "If not, then he's gone. There's nothing you can do about it." Attu let his anger show. "That could have been one of the Clan," Attu said, pointing back to where the thief lay. "One of us, lying on top of this hill with a broken leg because we were out looking for you." He met Ganik's eyes and waited until the boy finally hung his head and looked away.

Attu turned toward Chonik. "And I thought after you nearly got killed, you'd learn not to follow him everywhere."

"Ganik said he was going no matter what. So when I realized he'd left, I followed him and brought the things I knew he'd forget to take, to protect him." Chonik met Attu's gaze and didn't look away. "I wanted to prove to the Clan I wasn't scared. Not this time. What else could I have done?"

"You could have come and told me, and I would have spoken with Ganik and helped him see that chasing after Grey Wolf was a foolish idea."

"He would have gone anyway, as soon as no one was looking," Chonik said. He looked down, kicking at a stone much like Attu did when he was frustrated.

"Come now, and we'll talk about it later," Attu said. "This injured man must be dealt with."

Ganik reluctantly followed Attu toward camp, Chonik bringing up the rear as if he expected Ganik to make a run for it back into the night.

"Kill him," Suka said. "We know they are our enemies. I think we should kill him and be done with it."

"He may be contagious," Rika said. "We can't bring him into camp."

"We can't, but Soantek and Keanu could take him to the edge of camp, like we did with them, until we can find out if he carries the evil sickness spirits." Attu looked to the pair. Both had been summoned back from their flying search.

"Why do you wish to save this thief's life?" Ubantu asked.

"What are you thinking, my son?" Yural asked.

"When I was up on that hill, I-" Attu began.

"He is thinking what I know to be true, that this man's life must be saved," Meavu interrupted. She stepped out from the group behind Attu and looked at her brother, and Attu knew

Meavu had Seen something. "His life is linked to saving ours. I know it. When the last band of thieves finds us," Meavu hesitated as someone's lips popped and many shook their heads. "They will come," Meavu said, and her voice held a certainty that made the hair on the back of Attu's neck rise. "This thief has not been found by chance. The spirits directed Ganik and Chonik out on this night to find him."

"Then we must try to save him," Rika said. Others nodded. Many looked at Meavu with wonder. They had known Attu's sister had Gifts, but none had seen her so strong, so sure. It convinced many.

More discussion followed, but Attu knew in his spirit it had been decided. Soantek and Keanu moved to the edge of camp, near where their shelter had been in the fall when they'd been ill. People came forward with older hides, a small lamp with a chip in it, some old cooking skins, and soon they had a shelter ready.

Meanwhile, Attu and the other hunters had been building a sledge to drag the thief back on. Rika had prepared healing herbs and bandages for the man's leg, and Soantek had assured her that if the thief's leg was broken, he knew how to put it back in place with Keanu's help. "I will be near if you need me," Rika said.

It took the rest of the night, but by dawn the thief was in Keanu and Soantek's temporary shelter. He was delirious with fever, but there were no sores on him. His leg did not appear to be broken, but his knee had been knocked out of joint. Soantek and Keanu put it back with the help of Elder Nuka, who dosed the man with her own painkiller. Still, Attu and the others heard the screams when Soantek jerked and twisted the thief's dislocated lower leg back into place. After that, Nuka said, he passed into the Between of unconsciousness.

Attu walked to Veshria's shelter midday. Ganik was awake, groggy, but sitting up eating some cold fish when Attu arrived. "I bring no evil," he said as he stood at the door.

"Come in," Tishria said. Veshria nodded as Attu entered and moved to get him a hot drink.

"I know I must not try to get Grey Wolf back," Ganik said. He looked like he'd been crying. "Kossu said holding an animal against its will is wrong. It's not the Nuvik way. I wouldn't be a true hunter if I did."

"He's right," Attu said, glancing at Kossu. Kossu met Attu's eyes with thanks before looking to Tishria. "Our sister helped to convince Ganik, also."

Tishria sat calmly beside her mother like any other small girl. *But she is not. She's remarkable.*

Thank you. Tishria nodded her head.

You should not read my thoughts without my permission, Attu scolded, then added, *but it's true. And my thoughts still leak more than they should.* He smiled at Tishria.

"She's talking to you right now, isn't she?" Ganik asked. His voice held wonder and more than a hint of jealousy. "I wish I could mind speak."

"Well, you can't. So there's no sense in wishing for it," Kossu said. It sounded to Attu like an exchange they'd had before.

"Do you think the thief will be able to help us against the others, once he's better?" Tishria asked. Veshria looked up from her sewing, her eyes locking with Attu's at the girl's question.

"Meavu thinks so. I didn't have a specific vision, but I believe I heard Attuanin speak. The thief must stay with us. The spirits often lead me like they may have led you last night, Ganik, to find the thief when you thought you were only searching for Grey Wolf."

"Chonik wanted to head around the hill, and I couldn't do it. I had to climb to the top. Something did seem to pull me there." He looked eager to believe that perhaps he did have some kind of Gift, after all.

"And you and Kossu were within hearing when the boys found the thief," Tishria added.

Veshria studied them.

"You, too?" Attu asked. "You think there is something special about this thief?"

Veshria nodded. Attu caught a glimpse of fear in her eyes, but Veshria didn't waver from his gaze. She nodded her head again.

Attu stood away from the shelter's entrance later that day. Soantek had sent for Attu when the thief awoke.

"He's very weak," Soantek said. "But he's been talking since he woke up."

"What has he told you?"

"He says he's called Senga. And he says that he means us no harm."

"Then what was he doing so close to our camp? Was he sent by the other thieves to spy on us before they attacked?"

"He says he left the band of thieves he was with just before the first big snow last winter. He says they weren't sick when he left, and when I asked him, he said he knew of Toonuk, but had never seen him. He may have been with the group that attacked the other Tuktu Clan. But I can't tell if he's telling the truth or lying."

Soantek turned back toward where the man lay on furs in the shelter. He exchanged words with the thief and then turned back.

"He says he's not lying. He wasn't part of the group who attacked Toonuk's Clan."

"And Toonuk said his men killed all the ones who attacked them."

"He's lived on his own since then. That's a long time," Soantek said.

Attu thought that was hard to believe, but it was possible, he supposed, if the man were a good hunter, and very lucky. *Except the thief fell and dislocated his knee. That certainly wasn't lucky.*

"Let me know if he tells you anything else, anything that can help us," Attu said.

Soantek agreed and turned back to the thief.

That evening, Attu again stood as near as he dared to the entrance of the shelter where the thief lay.

"And you say you've been by yourself all winter? How did you survive?"

"I found meat. In a cave near here. I was near starving when I found it. The meat saved me." Senga's voice was raspy but strong enough now for Attu to hear him. "I will hunt and pay back for the food. It was yours?"

"Rovek's cache," Soantek said. "He must have found it."

"Why did you leave your band?" Attu asked.

"I never wanted to be a part of them in the first place," Senga said. "But my Clan leader didn't approve of me. He forced me out. I had nowhere else to go."

"What did you do to made him do that?"

"Fought over a woman." Senga said. "She was mine. She had promised to bond with me. But Poltow, our leader, wanted her for his brother. After he made me leave, I found out Poltow made her bond with his brother."

Attu heard the anger in Senga's voice. Then it changed to grief. "When I got the chance, I tried to get her back. The band I'd joined up with came upon my Clan again many moons after I'd been forced out. I snuck in among them to find her. But her mother told me she had already died in childbirth."

"What did you do then?"

"I wanted to fight with the other thieves. I wanted to kill Poltow." Senga's words were strangled with emotion. "But the rest of the Clan were my family, my friends."

"So did you? Kill Poltow? Fight with the others?"

"No." Senga's voice grew quiet. Attu strained to hear him. "What good would that do? Another of them would have taken his place. Probably his brother. I convinced a few of the others not to fight either, but the rest were angry at the way we'd all been treated. And in the end, the ones I'd convinced said they had to fight so as not to be called cowards and forced to leave the thieves, too."

"Is that when you left?"

"Yes." Senga coughed, then spoke again. "They called me a coward, but I could not fight my own people just because of Poltow. Thank you for not killing me up on that hill. I don't know why you didn't, but thank you."

"The spirits told me not to. That is the only reason you are still alive." Attu kept his voice firm. "And if you do anything to make any of us think you are dangerous, we will still kill you. Do you understand?"

"Yes. I won't hurt anyone. I will do whatever you say."

"And when your leg is healed?"

"I don't know. I have no place to go. No Clan. I guess I will go off on my own again."

Attu heard the edge of despair in the man's voice.

The Clan was gathered near the evening fire. A moon had passed, and Senga showed no signs of breaking out in sores. He was walking again, stiff-legged, with the help of two sticks, one lashed on each side of his knee. Attu had ordered him to stay near the shelter at the edge of camp and not to interact with anyone but himself, Keanu, and Soantek. Senga had agreed and had done exactly as the three of them instructed.

Attu sat, wondering what to do with Senga now, as he watched Warm Fur snuggling into Tingiyok's side. The two remaining pups looked like adults to Attu. Warm Fur was Tingiyok's constant companion, and Dog was nestled between Brovik and Suanu.

Rika reached out a tentative hand to stroke Warm Fur. The dog stretched at her touch, lying on her side and offering her belly to be rubbed. Rika laughed and gave the dog her wish. Turning back to the fire, she caught Attu watching her.

"What?" she asked.

"Nothing," Attu said, and turned to the others.

"Rika says it's safe for Senga to come into camp now. But what do we do with him?" Tingiyok asked.

"I've been thinking about that." Attu looked to the others.

"We can't just let him walk around freely. He is our enemy," Suka said.

Many nodded their heads in agreement with Suka's words.

Others voiced concerns, and a heated discussion followed.

"I don't know what to do with him, either," Attu said when Ubantu asked his opinion. "I just know we're supposed to keep Senga here."

"I will take him." Lips popped as Veshria moved to the front of the fire, turning toward the others. Her voice sounded like sand scratching at the side of a hide shelter, and she cleared her throat before speaking again. "It is the will of the spirits that I help this man regain his strength and heal."

"What do you mean?" Yural asked.

"I cannot explain it, but ever since Rusik passed to the Between of death, I have been halfway there with him." Veshria looked toward the fire. Her eyes threatened to fill once again with the far away look that had been there since she'd heard her man had been gored by the nuknuk. "But last night I dreamed. I saw myself standing with Senga, only he wasn't a thief anymore. He was one of us."

"No!" one of the hunters shouted. "That can never be."

"It is true," Veshria said. "And now, since I woke from that dream, I can speak again. Isn't that proof enough?" She glared at the hunter who'd spoken.

"You did not speak, Woman, because you didn't have reason to speak." Suka looked to Veshria, taking up the other man's argument.

"My mother speaks the truth," Ganik said. He stood up among the people, his voice clear, even though Attu could see the boy was trembling. "She has wanted to yell at me many times these last moons, but she couldn't. I could see it in her eyes."

A few of the people chuckled, but Veshria's face remained serious and the laughter faded.

"I am to take Senga into my shelter. We are to be bonded."

Another gasp, and all eyes turned to Attu.

"Senga has agreed," Soantek told Attu the next day. "I don't know if he's agreeing because he knows he can't survive on his own yet, or if he truly wants to become one of us. He's met with Veshria. She has made her wishes known to him, and he is saying yes."

Nuka moved to Veshria's shelter with Senga, so Veshria would not be alone with him until they were bonded. Five days later, at the full moon, Veshria stood beside Senga. The words were spoken, their wrists bound together, and without another word after the ceremony, Veshria disappeared into the shelter with the thief.

Kossu had looked disgusted throughout the ceremony. He'd moved out of his mother's shelter when Nuka and Senga had moved in, and although he'd vowed to continue to hunt for his family until he took a woman of his own, he had told Attu he would do nothing more.

"Why is she doing this?" he asked Attu again as they walked away from the dying fires. "It makes no sense? Does she like having trouble surround her?"

Attu had been wondering the same thing. But his spirit felt right about Veshria's choice. Before her husband's death, Veshria had shown she could be unstable, but since his death, except for not talking, Veshria had given no one any trouble. She'd changed. And Attu was convinced this stranger among them, one of their proven enemies, was vital to them. It was more than Meavu's announcement or Veshria's dream. He'd felt it the moment he'd laid eyes on the thief. Hadn't he heard those words, deep in his spirit? *Save him.*

"Kossu, fall is coming in a few moons," Attu said, deciding it best to change the subject to something he'd been wanting to talk about with Kossu. "If the Tuktu return, is there one among them you might consider? To start your own journey as hunter and protector of your own family?"

Kossu turned an eager grin on Attu. "Oh, they will return. Chirea has promised me they will..." Kossu turned red in the firelight, and his eyes shifted away. But the grin remained.

Chapter 18

"Senga is telling the truth," Tishria said, "about what happened to him." She looked at Attu, then away. She bit at her lower lip as her cheeks turned red.

"Tishria, have you been looking into Senga's mind?"

The little girl hung her head.

"You know that's wrong, don't you?" Attu knew that Keanu had begun working with Tishria, but apparently it wasn't enough yet, or Tishria hadn't understood or been willing to follow Keanu's instructions.

"I know. It's the first thing everyone told me. I don't do it on purpose. I'll just be in the shelter with him and suddenly I will be in his thoughts, especially if his knee is hurting. It still hurts him, you know. I can't block his thoughts then; they're too strong."

"I need you to walk out of the shelter if you sense Senga's thoughts and you can't block them. Distance should help. You must never look into another person's thoughts without their permission."

"All right. I'll try that." Tishria looked pleadingly at Attu. "But I've seen enough of his memories to know he is telling the truth. His leader, Poltow, did force him out of his Clan just because of the woman he loved. And he did try to get her back. And Senga did leave the thieves because of their fighting his own Clan. That memory is very strong. He thinks about it when his knee hurts, how no matter what, he couldn't have fought his own people. Do you want me to show you? I give you permission to look into my mind."

"I believe you. There's no need for that. But promise me you will try very hard not to look into Senga's mind any more." Attu looked at Tishria, his eyes steady.

"I promise." Tishria's bottom lip trembled, and Attu was struck with how young she was and how hard it must be for her to have such a great Gift and not be able to control it. He reached out to brush away a loose hair from Tishria's braid, but she leaned into him and Attu hugged her instead.

"Didn't you know you couldn't survive on your own?" Attu asked Senga as they pulled skin boats back to shore a few days later. Tight hide wrappings had replaced the sticks, but Senga still moved slowly. He'd taken to paddling and fishing to provide for Veshria. He couldn't swim well, but he was good in the boat.

227

"All Tuktu boys fish when we're near the rivers or the ocean. I had never hunted big game, but I thought I could fish and survive." He looked out over the water. "I wanted to fish and to learn to hunt the tuktu again, like our ancestors, maybe even start a herd of my own."

"But the bay had frozen once you got to the ocean again."

"I was starving. Then I found the meat. When the meat was gone, I wandered again. I was near starving when I thought to return here, to look around farther east, to see who lived here and had stored the meat. But before I reached your camp, I fell and twisted my leg and the boys found me."

Attu popped his lips. "It's a good thing that you fell, then."

"Why?" Senga let the rope he was holding go slack. His eyes widened as he realized Attu's meaning. "You would have killed me like the sick thief who attacked you?"

"One of us would have probably shot you with an arrow before you even got close enough to explain yourself." Attu lifted his skin boat back onto its rack above the high tide mark.

"It has been a few moons since I came. Do the others still think of me as an enemy? Do you?" Senga asked. He sounded desperate again, as he had on that first day, a man with no Clan to belong to. "I am grateful to be here. I have bonded with Veshria; I have done what you asked of me. What else can I do to show you I want to be part of your Clan?"

"We don't trust you," Attu said. "Because of all that's happened with the other thieves, it's going to take a long time before everyone accepts you. Veshria has, and Tishria, too. But in our Clan, Veshria's opinion about things has often been wrong…" Attu let his words fade. He knew the truth hurt

Senga, but the man needed to know where he stood with the others.

"I have seen that Veshria is not well liked by many," Senga said, setting the skin boat he'd borrowed from Suka on the rack beside Attu's. "It hurts her deeply."

What has Veshria been telling Senga?

As if Senga could read Attu's thoughts, he added, "Veshria has told me many things. It has been a long time since she has had someone to share her heart with." The man turned away, as if he'd said too much. He lowered his eyes and studied the ground in front of him as walked away, leaving Attu standing beside the skin boats, wondering.

"Didn't any of the thieves try to take women again, make a life for themselves like before?" Suka asked Senga as they gathered their catch the next afternoon. Several of the hunters had gone fishing, and now they stood, gathering up their fishing tools and catch to head back to camp.

"The leader of our group wouldn't let us," Senga said. "We had three leaders while I was with those men. They were always fighting among themselves for leadership, just like the Tuktu Clans."

"Did you ever hear of one called Korack?" Ubantu asked as the men walked back up the beach toward their shelters.

Senga struggled through the sand, and Ubantu slowed beside him. Senga was walking now without a limp. He still wore tough hides around his leg, however, and the deep sand at the top of the beach was hard for any of them to walk through.

"I never heard of him," Senga said. "Why?"

"He was the leader of the thieves who attacked the Tuktu Clan we met. He shot one of his own men when he tried to run away from the fight. Why didn't your leader shoot you?"

The other men leaned in to hear Senga's reply. "Because I snuck away from the others just before the attack on my Clan. I got away in the commotion that followed. I knew I couldn't stop the attack, so I got close enough to the camp to set the dogs barking as the others approached. That gave my Clan a better chance when the attackers came."

"If this is the attack Toonuk told me about, many of your people died. But they did fight the thieves, and many of the attackers died as well."

Senga looked at them all, deep sadness etching lines in his face. "When will this all end? If our leaders can't stop fighting their own people, throwing men out of our Clans and causing those desperate men to seek revenge, we're going to destroy ourselves."

"I tried to tell Toonuk that his Nuvik ancestors weren't violent and controlling like the Tuktu are now, by telling him of our ways when they first arrived," Ubantu said. "He didn't believe us."

"He said we were naïve and fresh off the ice," Attu added.

"The leader of my group of thieves, as you call them, was just as bad as this Korack that Ubantu speaks of. They mimic the leaders who've pushed them out. No one seeks the peace I see you have among yourselves. Toonuk should have listened to you." Senga regarded the other men solemnly before turning to struggle through the sand again.

A brisk wind was blowing as the men neared their shelters. The scent of the Clan's cooking fires filled the air.

Trees in the distance had turned to bright reds and yellows. By the next moon, snow would fall again.

"Ganik! Climb down from there," Veshria called to her son as he scrambled among the rocks behind the camp.

Senga stepped out of the shelter into the crisp air. "Your mother calls," he said. "Come down."

"You can't tell me what to do. You are NOT my father!" Ganik shouted back and scrambled over the top of the hill.

Attu turned back to his tool sharpening and wondered if Veshria had made a mistake. Attu knew Kossu was angry with his mother, and obviously Ganik was as well. Only Tishria seemed content to have a new father.

"No, Nuanu. Hot," Rika said, and Attu heard rustling as Nuanu was scooped up and Rika walked out of the shelter. "Watch her," Rika said and plunked the poolik in Attu's lap. "I have cooking to do."

Attu snatched the arrowhead he was sharpening away from Nuanu's little fingers as she reached for the small, notched stone. "Oh, no you don't," Attu said, and gave his daughter a strip of sinew to play with. She took it, her eyes intent as she waved it back and forth, concentrating on how the dangling part moved.

"She misses nothing," Veshria said. She stood beside the fire, and Attu could see the longing in her eyes as she watched Nuanu. "May I?" Veshria reached out.

Attu gave Nuanu to her and Veshria sat beside him, cuddling the poolik and talking to her. She looked up. Tears were flowing down her cheeks. "This could have been my time to be a new mother again. I was a fool, Attu. And my man's life was taken because I disregarded the life within me."

Attu was speechless. *Does Veshria believe Rusik died as her punishment for not following her healers' directions about using the root for her toothache when she was pregnant?*

"The spirits do not-"

"I know no one else believes me, but in my spirit I know it's true." For a moment Attu saw the old Veshria, the petulant stubborn one. But her face cleared and she spoke again, this time with no malice or spite in her voice. "I believe I was punished, yes. But it is over now. I came to talk with you about Kossu. Senga does not know our customs, so he can't speak for Kossu, and Kossu is angry with me right now. I can't talk to him. But you can. I know he wants to be bonded to Chirea from the Tuktu Clan when they return. Can you help him?"

"Yes. And from what Kossu has said, Chirea was willing when the Tuktu moved farther north for the summer grazing. She promised him she would be back. It could be any day now. But he will have to have something to trade as well."

"He's been making a few more bows and arrows for the Tuktu, to go with the wood we gave them and the few we had to spare last time they were here." Veshria grabbed one end of the sinew string Nuanu was holding and tugged it gently. Nuanu tugged back. Veshria tugged again. Nuanu pulled her hand back, giggling at the game. Veshria looked up, smiling. "Will you help him?"

"Yes. And bows and arrows will be more than a fair trade. I can't believe Spartik will say no to those."

"Thank you." Veshria smiled at Nuanu through her tears as she stood and handed the poolik back to Attu and walked away. Attu sat with Nuanu playing in his lap as he wondered if Veshria had taken Senga just so she might have one more chance at having a child before she grew too old. *Perhaps she thinks that through Senga, the spirit of her stillborn baby will come to her again, now that she has paid the price of grief she insists was necessary.*

Attu knew the rebirth of a baby's spirit into another baby was possible, but the Nuvik had never believed someone else you loved had to die first. *That is Veshria's guilt at work.* Attu decided to speak to Yural about it.

The Tuktu came three days later. Attu and a few of the other hunters were upriver in their skin boats when a sound like thunder came rolling over the water. Attu looked up and in the distance saw a rising cloud of dust. The fall had been dry and as the tuktu ran, they were leaving a trail of flying dust and dirt behind them.

"Why are they running?" Kossu said. He stood in his skin boat to see better, but the slim craft veered and he fell back into his boat, nearly capsizing it.

"What if they're being chased?" Suka turned his skin boat and began paddling furiously back toward camp. The others followed.

Chapter 19

"This animal is the reason the tuktu bolted." Toonuk held a long rope. On the other end was Grey Wolf, pulling and twisting and biting at it as the leader of the Tuktu yanked him along. "One of my tuktu just had to be killed because your dog bit its back leg and cut the main tendon. You will give us something in payment for it." The Tuktu leader glared at Attu.

"So much for the friendliness of last visit," Suka whispered. "And here we stand, having run to help them, weapons ready, for nothing."

The other hunters stood with Attu, looking equally chagrined.

Grey Wolf, however, just struggled at the end of the rope. Toonuk could barely hold him.

Enough. Attu mind spoke to Grey Wolf. He stared at the dog.

Grey Wolf quit struggling. His tail dropped, and his eyes slid away from the humans and toward the camp.

"He ran away, like I said he would?" Toonuk asked. He looked surprised at the dog's sudden stillness.

"Yes. In the early spring. This is the first we've seen of him. We will repay you for the loss of your tuktu."

Toonuk made a sound in his throat. It sounded derisive.

Attu said nothing, but he couldn't help agreeing with Suka. Toonuk seemed as arrogant as he'd been on their first visit. Perhaps Yural was wrong, and Toonuk hadn't really learned anything from the experiences of last winter.

"Grey Wolf!" Ganik cried as he came around the corner of his shelter.

Grey Wolf began wagging his tail, and Toonuk let go of the rope. "He's skin and bones. I think he'll be glad to be back among you. This time, perhaps he'll stay."

"Keep him away from our herd," Toonuk added as Grey Wolf bounded over to Ganik. The dog jumped up and the boy fell backward, laughing and hugging Grey Wolf to his chest. Attu was amazed at how large the animal had grown in the few moons he'd been gone. But Toonuk was right. He was also very thin.

"Are you hungry?" Ganik asked. He took the rope off Grey Wolf and shot a glance at the Tuktu leader before the two headed back toward Ganik's shelter.

"My men will kill him if he harasses the herd again," Toonuk said. He turned angry eyes on Attu.

"I have spoken with Ganik and the others. Neither Grey Wolf nor our other two dogs will come near your herd again," Attu said as Toonuk and Spartik walked into camp later that day and moved to sit by Attu's fire.

"He was fast, I'll say that. He grabbed at one of the smaller animals, and before we could stop them the tuktu were stampeding across the small plain just north of here. They didn't stop until they came to the lake."

"I think some of the older animals recognized the place," Spartik said. "They stopped well back of the water and by the time we caught up with them, the dogs had circled the herd back and they'd settled down to eating the lush grass by the lake. It's the best grazing we've had for the tuktu in many days."

"The smell of fine grass will stop any tuktu from running," Toonuk said. The men exchanged nods. Toonuk no longer looked angry. Instead he seemed relaxed, as if his earlier sternness had been more of a show of power than true anger.

"I am glad you've come back," Attu said, feeling the tight coil in his stomach relax a bit.

"I would have been forever banned from my shelter if we had not," Spartik said, and he grinned broadly at Attu. "There is a certain young hunter a certain daughter of mine could not stop talking about all summer. We have much to discuss. It has been a peaceful and good summer for us. For you?"

"No attacks. And it has been interesting. But I will tell you about it all when we meet later. Do you wish to receive the gifts Kossu has for you now?"

"Someone said they include bows Kossu has been able to make. Are they as good as the talk I have already heard?"

"Yes." Attu smiled.

"Then they can wait. Let the young pair have some time together first. They have not seen each other for a long time. I want to make sure Chirea still wants her young hunter before I accept his gifts."

Attu nodded, but he would bet a nuknuk that Chirea's answer would still be yes.

And knowing how skittish these Tuktu are, it will be good to have the young people back together again, where all can see how well matched they are, before I tell the Tuktu about Senga.

The sun was dipping below the ocean as the Clans gathered to exchange stories and information, as well as to make the announcement that Kossu and Chirea would be bonded. The young people sat at the fire, and as Attu approached, he could hear congratulations and teasing surrounding them. Both looked uncomfortable, but Kossu kept Chirea's hand tucked firmly in his own and they kept stealing longing glances at each other. Attu couldn't help remembering his own tempestuous feelings toward Rika and how hard it had been when he'd thought he'd lost her forever. Hopefully, this young pair would never have to endure such hardship. Their time apart had been with the promise of future bonding, and it seemed to have made them both sure of their choice.

The early evening passed in celebration and good eating. The Tuktu brought fresh meat from the animal they'd had to kill and berries from the north, dried and mixed with some seeds the women harvested from the longer grass they walked through as they followed the herd. Attu's Clan provided fresh fish and the greens and roots the women gathered and cooked in seal fat on hot stones. Everything was delicious.

"Now there are some things we need to discuss," Attu began as most had finished eating. "We have one among us who is new since the last time you came through our land. It may seem strange to you, so I wanted to explain before you met him. We took in an injured Tuktu this spring."

"One of our men was injured and came to this place?" Spartik asked. "What Clan was he from?"

"Actually, he had been cast out of his Clan."

Spartik leaped to his feet, grabbing his staff and shoving it butt first into the ground. "You have an enemy in your camp? You have allowed him to live?"

"No," Attu said and stood to face Spartik, his own weapon held loosely at his side. "No, we have a man named Senga in our camp, who was banned from Poltow's Clan and traveled with a band of thieves for a while, but he left them. We took him in and helped him heal. He has taken a woman. He is part of our Clan now."

Toonuk and the other Tuktu stood. "You have let our enemy come into your camp and you welcomed him? And he took one of your women for his own?" Toonuk spit to the side in disgust. "I don't believe it. After all we have been through with these murderers? You are a weak leader. And your people are stupid for following you." He motioned for the other Tuktu to leave.

Spartik pulled Chirea away from Kossu. She began crying, fighting her father. He picked her up and put her over his shoulder, as Kossu pulled his own spear back.

"You will not take her from me," Kossu took a step forward, menacing Spartik with his spear.

"I had just begun to explain. Let me tell you," Attu said, his voice rising so all could hear above the commotion.

"Tell us what? That you are friends with thieves? After they attacked us? After they brought sickness to both our peoples? You've welcomed this murderer into your camp and you didn't think we'd mind?" Spartik looked at Attu with such hatred, Attu took a step back from the man. "Show him to me. I will kill him myself."

"Enough!" Yural appeared in the light of the fire, Senga at her side. "This is the man. We are not your enemies or your enemies' friends. We know what the thieves have done, to us and to you and to others with their attacks and their killings and their bringing of sickness. But there is a good reason this man is among us, alive and almost well." She glanced at Senga's still-wrapped knee. "Sit down. Hear my son."

Ubantu stood beside Yural. "Think with your heads and not your weapons, my brothers, for we are indeed still your brothers, your distant kin. We would not let this man among us if it were not for the best for both our Clans."

The Tuktu muttered among themselves.

"Sit. Listen to what I have to say," Attu said. He kept his voice calm although several weapons of the Tuktu were now pointed at him, while the rest still aimed at Senga. Attu admired how the man stood, his face calm, looking neither intimidated nor fierce, but strong. Attu turned to include everyone in his words. "And when I've explained, you will all understand. Then Kossu can gift Spartik with the bows and arrows he's been able to make. We can teach you all how to make them as well. Please sit."

Toonuk looked toward the other hunters. Several had lowered their weapons and were looking between Attu and Kossu now. Kossu had lowered his own spear and was nodding at them. "It is true. I have many bows and arrows to give Spartik for the privilege of taking Chirea from you to be my woman."

Spartik let Chirea slide to the ground. She turned and straightened her woman's garment. Spartik put his hand on her shoulder, but she didn't try to return to Kossu. She stared at Senga instead, as the rest of her people were now doing.

Attu sat. Yural nodded her agreement with his decision and sat also, Senga and Ubantu on either side. The rest of Attu's Clan saw what their leader had done and a few muttered their reluctance, since this put them in a vulnerable position should the Tuktu decide to attack. But they followed Attu and sat. He gave the sign of being about to speak and motioned for the Tuktu to sit also.

An incredulous glance passed between Toonuk and Spartik. Then Toonuk looked around as if he couldn't believe how quickly Attu had calmed his own men, and how they all had sat, ready to listen. Toonuk stood for a long time, looking genuinely perplexed. The longer he stood doing nothing, the tenser his men became.

"Father?" Martu began. Attu could see the young man was trembling, but he held himself straight and met Toonuk's eyes without wavering. "I want to hear what Attu has to say." And Martu sat.

A collective gasp arose among the Tuktu hunters as first the young hunter who'd lost his grandfather moved to sit beside Martu, then several more.

"Please, Father?" Martu asked.

Toonuk's brows drew together, but he nodded at Martu and the other young men then sat, motioning for the rest of his people to sit as well.

Attu took in a deep breath, and in a voice that was both calm and loud enough to be heard by everyone, he told the story of Senga. Attu explained how Senga had been forced out of his own Clan, had gotten caught up in the thief band, and then left when it meant attacking his own Clan. He told how Senga had wandered and eventually injured his leg and been found by the boys.

"Once Senga was banned from his Clan, what else could he do?" Attu said. "He didn't want to be a thief. He wanted a chance at life in a Clan, a woman of his own, a place to belong."

"But how do you know what he's told you is true?" Toonuk asked when Attu finished. "He could have lied to you to get help and to stay here where he is safe."

"That's possible. But it's not the point." Attu felt the frustration rising in him and worked to hold himself back. "Your Clans have no way to keep this from happening – over and over again – men getting pushed out of their Clans with no place to go. What else do you expect them to do besides banding together and turning against those who have thrown them out?"

Attu knew he'd taken a great risk, speaking to Toonuk like this in front of all the people. But someone had to at least start the Tuktu thinking about how to stop creating their own enemies, or more than one band of thieves would be roaming again before long.

"How dare you say our Clans are wrong to make such men leave? I-" Toonuk began.

"I did nothing wrong." Senga stood, his voice strong, although Attu saw his hands were shaking. "I loved a woman. She promised herself to me. And Poltow threw me out of my own Clan to give her to his brother." He looked around. Martu and the other young Tuktu men were nodding. Even the older herders no longer looked angry.

"I never wanted to leave my Clan. I was forced to. I never wanted to fight them. So I didn't. And because I've found these people, who will let me have a chance again at a good life, you say they are now your enemies and I should be killed? You are wrong."

Lips popped among the Tuktu. Attu watched as Toonuk puffed himself up. He looked around at his older men, and his face grew still as one by one, they refused to meet his gaze. He looked to Martu, and something passed between them.

Toonuk seemed surprised. He started to stand, when his woman put her hand on his arm, turning her face upward to whisper to him.

Toonuk scowled, but did not pull away from her. She spoke rapidly, and after a few moments, Toonuk's face calmed. He sat back down, as if he'd changed his mind. "We are not done here," Toonuk announced, meeting Martu's gaze again.

Attu was proud of the young Tuktu herder as he held his father's eyes with his own steady one. Toonuk looked away first. "But my woman has reminded me that you welcomed us as friends," Toonuk added, "and that tonight is for Chirea. Now. For the exchange of gifts."

The rest of the evening was tense. Kossu demonstrated his weapons. The Tuktu were eager to get them. Much bargaining resulted in Kossu being gifted with several tuktu hides and various other supplies as well as Spartik's willingness for his daughter to become Kossu's woman. But feelings were far from smooth. Attu gave Toonuk several nuknuk hides and much dried fish in payment for the tuktu that had been culled after its injuries. Toonuk took the payment, but said nothing.

"At least the young couple are enjoying themselves," Rika said. It was growing late. Most of the pooliks were asleep, and people were talking quietly in groups around the fire.

"Let's hope Toonuk doesn't get Spartik to change his mind about them now that they know about Senga." Attu glanced at the pair.

Chirea sat blushing beside Kossu as the last embers were dying from the fires. Soon the two young people would be parted for the night. The full moon was in two days. They would be joined then.

Spartik and Ubantu were seated directly across from Attu. He realized they were also talking about Chirea, and he began listening to their conversation.

"Chirea was a daughter born to me when most men become grandfathers," Spartik said, glancing toward Toonuk.

"My second son was born just before my first grandchildren," Ubantu said. "I think about him growing up, and I wonder if I will be there to see him find a woman someday."

Spartik nodded. "I am glad to see this day, but it will be hard to have her go. Only the spirits knew she would find a man among those we didn't even know existed until a year ago. And her man found the bow wood! A better match she could not find, to have such a clever man."

"Next day, Kossu will show you the types of trees that make the bow wood and how he's learned to dry it to make the best snap back once the arrow is released," Ubantu said. "There must be clumps of such trees near many of the lakes you stop at with your herds."

Spartik smiled his agreement.

An understanding look passed between the two older men. Spartik's eyes drifted back in Toonuk's direction. Ubantu followed his gaze and his eyebrows furrowed. Toonuk was sitting away from the fire, silent and brooding.

"Toonuk loves his son," Spartik said, his voice so quiet Attu almost missed his words. "Now that Martu has proven himself as a herder who can protect his Clan..." he paused. "Martu is strong-minded, like his father. If Toonuk can't learn another way to deal with such young men as his own son..." Spartik shrugged. "I have tried to talk to him." Spartik's words faded. He looked across the fire and met Attu's gaze, his eyes filled with quiet desperation.

"We speak. Now." Toonuk stood outside Attu's shelter. Attu answered the leader, but took his time getting up and coming out.

The sun was only a hint of lightness in the eastern sky.

"Walk with me," Attu said, moving away from the shelter and down to where the water moved restlessly along the beach. He did not look back. If Toonuk wanted to play a power game with him, then so be it. The man Attu knew would respect nothing less.

Toonuk humphed and followed.

"I will let you keep this thief, but know it is the wrong thing to do," Toonuk began.

"I say who is with my Clan and who is not," Attu said, keeping his voice and face calm. "You overstep yourself."

He felt Toonuk draw himself up as if to protest, but then his shoulders sagged and he stopped, sitting down in the sand instead, facing the ocean.

Attu sat as well, both looking out over the grey moving waves rather than each other. Attu felt the Tuktu leader working to say something. A long moment passed.

"The thieves are destroying my people," Toonuk said, finally breaking the silence. "Nealria has spoken her women's wisdom to me, long into the night." Toonuk made a scoffing sound. "Spartik also, with Martu, after we left last night. You have spoken as well…" He stopped as if unable to continue.

Attu knew this admission was hard for Toonuk. He said nothing, waiting for Toonuk's next words like a hunter over the nuknuk hole.

"By the trystas you are so patient!" Toonuk swore. Then he grew thoughtful, as if considering his own remark. "No one has left your Clan since you arrived on this land. My men have told me this. In fact, your numbers have grown. Your people are happy. You have your arguments, but they don't end in bloodshed, as your father has said. And now you've even taken in this thief. And it is working for you, at least so far. How do you do this? We are Nuvik, too. What have my people lost since they came off the ice so many generations ago?"

Toonuk turned to Attu, his eyes filled with grief over the state of his Clans. Attu saw a desperate man, not the puffed leader from the night before, making the others believe he was in control, but the man Attu's mother had hoped Toonuk would grow into, one who could admit his people were wrong.

I never believed I would get this chance, Attu prayed. *Attuanin, give me the words to teach this man the ways of the true leader. And give Toonuk the ears to hear the truth. He is just one leader among the Tuktu Clans, but he is a powerful man. It is a good beginning.*

The sun was dipping into the ocean two days later as the Nuvik and Tuktu gathered at the mouth of the river near the grassy upper edge of the beach. Chirea sat on a sledge pulled by a single tuktu. Shells along the sides of the poles jangled as the tuktu walked, guided by her father toward the edge of the river, where Kossu and Soantek stood with Yural off to the side, standing near a nuknuk hide laid out for the second part of the ceremony.

They reached the edge of the beach. Chirea walked with Spartik the short distance to the river's edge. Her tuktu hide dress was elaborately beaded, her hair swept up on her head and decorated with beads also. Her hair had been pulled back so tightly her eyes and eyebrows slanted up even more. Her skin gleamed against the light tuktu hide. Attu knew Chirea had allowed the Nuvik women to use seal fat on her skin. It made

Chirea look even darker, a rich color. She seemed to glow from within.

Farnook stood with Suka, his arm protective around his woman and Nipka, who for once was being quiet, her eyes large as she studied the tuktu now grazing where it had been left.

Keanu and Meavu stood side by side, their men behind them. Meavu was bouncing Tovut in his carry strap and Keanu rested her hands on her rounding abdomen. She would bear a child this winter. It made Attu anxious to think of Keanu in such a vulnerable condition during the time when the thieves might come.

I'm worried... Attu began mind speaking to Keanu.

Not today, Attu. Today is not the time to think about what might happen in the future. Enjoy this moment, leader of our people. See and celebrate today. Keanu motioned with her hand for Attu to look back to the ceremony.

You're right. Attu looked toward the river. Kossu and Chirea were entering the water. Chirea had taken off her elaborately beaded dress and had been wearing a light grass shift under it. Kossu wore only the man's undergarment. Soantek had his body paint on, the red for fire and the blue for water, in the swirling designs of the Nukeena's spirits. He led the way into the water until he and the young couple stood waist deep in the slow current where the river widened to flow into the ocean.

Soantek gave the blessing, pouring the water from his sacred vessel on both Kossu and Chirea. He threw powders into the air and light exploded above the couple. Even though they'd been told ahead of time about this part of the ceremony, some of the Tuktu still grabbed for their weapons, looking embarrassed when their hands came away empty, all weapons having been left behind on this day of bonding.

Kossu and Chirea disappeared under the water and stayed under far too long. Spartik took a step forward, but Nealria placed a calming hand on his forearm and he stepped back as the young pair rose again.

Lips popped and thighs were slapped as the two walked back out of the river. The first part of the ceremony was accomplished. Chirea paused, Tuktu and Nuvik women surrounding her. When she stepped away, she was back in her beaded dress, the wet grass garment in the arms of another woman. Kossu disappeared behind a mounted hide screen, emerging again with a hunter's shirt and pants on.

Next, they walked to Yural, who tied their hands together with the ceremonial rope as they knelt on the nuknuk hide and she spoke the words of bonding over them. When she said, "And you, Kossu, will be a true hunter to Chirea, bringing her the game for as long as she lives," Rika placed her hand in Attu's and squeezed. She had tears in her eyes. Attu knew she was thinking both of their own bonding and the future bonding of their children. He squeezed back.

But the ceremony wasn't complete yet. Kossu picked Chirea up in his arms, and Yural and Soantek followed, each carrying a corner of the nuknuk hide. It was placed over the tuktu hide of the sledge, and the almost-bonded pair settled on top of it. At this point, Spartik approached the sledge. He painted symbols on the side of the tuktu pulling the sledge, then symbols on the foreheads of Kossu and Chirea. The young couple lifted their feet, and he painted something on them as well.

"Because to the Tuktu, feet are very important. To walk together through life is the symbol of both their union and their strength, for they spend their lives walking," Rika whispered to Attu.

The symbol painting finished, Spartik spoke a few words over the couple, and taking a piece of tuktu antler, placed it on Chirea's stomach, fastening it to her dress at a loop.

"A symbol of future children, and the growth of their own herd," Yural said.

Spartik handed the ends of the guiding rope to Chirea. She smiled up at her father and he kissed the top of her head, holding her face in his gnarled hands for one lingering moment. He turned and slapped the tuktu hard on the rump as he whistled a sharp sound. It took off running along the grassy edge of the beach, Chirea hanging on to the guide ropes while Kossu clung to the edges of the sledge.

The Tuktu broke out into loud cheers and an ululation cry.

"Will they be all right?" Farnook cried as the couple disappeared over the edge of the first hill. "What if they fall off?"

"They won't fall," Nealria assured her. "Chirea has driven the tuktu since she was a child."

"No bundling?" Attu looked to the spot where Kossu and Chirea had been coming up the next hill, but they were too far away to see clearly now. "No tossing?"

"No bundling. But we Tuktu love the tossing in the tuktu hide! We'll do that when they come back," one of the Tuktu hunters said, a smile spreading across his face as he looked knowingly at Attu. "If they come back…" he let his words drift off as his smile broadened.

The day after the bonding ceremony, the Tuktu left for the south with promises to return in the spring.

"Perhaps then I will get news of becoming a grandfather," Spartik teased Chirea, who hid her face behind her hands at his remark. "Take care of her," Attu heard the man say, as he took Kossu aside for some last words. Kossu nodded at the Elder, and pride swelled in Attu's spirit. Spartik had nothing to fear. Kossu would be an honorable and capable man for Chirea. Spartik had no more to worry about than they all had while at least one group of thieves still roamed.

"This winter there will be much time by the fires," Toonuk said. He clasped Attu's forearm. "On our journey south, I am going to speak with my men. We will sit around the fire, like true Nuviks. We will learn the ways of our ancestors again, one man speaking, all listening. I will work to stop the struggle for power in my own Clan first." Toonuk looked out over his Clan and herds.

Attu nodded but said nothing.

"I think the other Clan leaders will listen, when I explain how we have begun to act too much like the skittish tuktu we herd and less like the patient Nuvik hunter over the ice hole." Toonuk's lips quirked at the remembrance of some of what Attu had told him that early morning on the beach.

"You will find a way," Attu agreed. "You are a strong leader. The others will listen to you. As you have said, no Tuktu wants to continue to destroy their Clans from within. May the true Nuvik spirits go with you."

Attu stood on the hill for a long time after Toonuk walked down to join his people, until the Tuktu disappeared over the last of the hills to the south.

Sometimes I wish I were that naïve young hunter again, and all I had to do was escape the melting Expanse. Looking back, it seems much easier than what we face now. This is worse than the wait over the nuknuk hole. The nuknuk must breathe sometime. But who knows if or when the last band of thieves will sweep down on us with their sleds? Senga has said these men are determined to kill for what they want. There is no turning back for them. Attuanin, give Toonuk the strength to help his Clans stop fighting with their own people. This group of thieves must be the last to roam Nuvikuan-na.

Protect us, Attuanin. Give us strength. Give me the wisdom of the creatures of the deep, like the great killer whale fish, that I might keep my people safe as he keeps his safe from the sharks in the water of the Great Ocean and the predators, like my people, above.

Chapter 20

The next day, Attu gathered everyone together to discuss what to do. Fall was rapidly cooling toward winter, and there wasn't a moment to lose.

"We need to start filling the meat caches." Rovek said. He glanced at Senga.

"I will still give more meat back," Senga said. "I will learn to hunt the seal soon. For now, fish."

It was true. The man had fished continuously since he could walk again, both repaying Rovek for the meat he'd stolen and bringing home so much to Veshria it was as if two hunters were fishing for her. Even Kossu had been grudgingly pleased with his mother's new man. Kossu was busy hunting for Chirea now, and he was relieved his mother, younger brother, and sister were being well cared for. Fortunately, the women had their own system to handle the food and Veshria could trade for other meat, so they ate more than fish.

"Father, I need you to consider other options for our defense," Attu continued. "Take Soantek with you. Have Soantek fly over the areas with a bird before you search them, to save you time. He can report back to you what he's seen, and you can decide if you want to explore the area on foot as a second hiding place for the women and children, or a place we might be able to lure the enemy to their deaths, like Martu did with the tuktu when the thieves attacked his Clan near the fire mountains."

"How many such places should we look for?" Ubantu asked, and then answered his own question. "As many as we can find, to the north, south, and east..." he paused, thinking again.

"Yes, because we won't know which direction the thieves will come from."

"I will help them also," Suka said.

Attu had wanted Suka with him, hunting and building up weapons with Kossu, since Suka had proven as good at making bows and arrows as he was with building skin boats. But Suka also had a unique way of looking at things. Sneaky wasn't the right word for the way Suka thought, but like his story telling, with its elaborations making it better than life, Suka could see possibilities and solutions where others could not. Having him with Ubantu and Soantek was the best use of his skills.

"Good," Attu said.

"What do the rest of us hunters do?" one of the men asked.

"Hunt as much as possible." Attu turned to include the women in the group. "Your hunters will bring in as much meat as they can. We need you to dry as much as you have time to, as well as gathering as many nuts and late seeds and roots as you can, and we need you to clean and preserve every stomach and intestine. We'll fill them with water and store them in the caves, also."

"I'll take charge of that," Yural said. "We already work hard to gather stores for winter. But we'll work even harder." She drew the other women off to the side of the group, where they began planning. Attu heard something about taking turns watching children while some went out gathering. He knew his mother would help the women do their best to prepare. As he watched, Yural looked to Nuka, but the Elder had turned away from the group. She began coughing, and Yural put an arm around her to support her thin frame as the two walked away with the other women.

Chonik poked Ganik in the ribs with his elbow. Ganik glared at his friend, but stepped forward as Chonik continued to encourage him by pushing his shoulder. "What about wood?" Ganik asked, shrugging Chonik's hand off. "We will need much wood."

Attu couldn't help but grin at Ganik's concern. Ganik had learned the lesson of how much wood his Clan burned the hard way. "And?" Attu hoped he knew Ganik's answer, but he wanted the boy to voice it for himself.

Ganik turned to Chonik, and Chonik nodded. "Chonik and I will take charge of the wood gathering. We'll get the little ones to gather kindling, and Chonik and I will pile wood on old nuknuk hides to be dragged to the caves." Ganik looked to Attu.

"Grey Wolf will help us pull. All right?" Ganik was eager to get his approval of the plan.

Could it be this boy is starting to grow up into a true Nuvik? Attu looked around and realized everyone, including the two boys, was waiting for his reply.

"Excellent idea," Attu said. "You can begin at once, and I will check on your progress each sun." Ganik and Chonik grinned and headed away from the group to start gathering wood. Tingiyok joined them. The boys listened to the Elder, then Chonik ran off to his mother's shelter, and Ganik ran toward Tingiyok's. Attu knew the Elder had offered his use of the iron stone ax he'd gotten from the Nukeena.

"Don't worry," Tingiyok said to Attu as he returned to the group. "They'll be careful with it, and it will make their work go much faster. Besides, being able to carry around an iron stone ax will keep Ganik interested in gathering wood for several days."

Attu chuckled. He could see Ganik strutting around camp, ordering the little ones about, iron stone ax in its hide sheath tied around his waist. He'd have to tell the women to keep an eye on Ganik. The boy could be bossy with the littler children.

"And I told him I'd work with all the dogs. I'll rig up some harnesses like the Tuktu use on their animals. It's time Warm Fur and Dog learned to pull like Grey Wolf."

"Good."

"What if they don't come?" Veshria spoke the Clan's fervent wish aloud. "They didn't attack us last winter."

"Then we will all thank the spirits!" one of the women called from the back of the group.

"And we'll have the most well-stocked food caches and the most prepared Clan to ever meet a winter," Ubantu said. "We'll have nothing to do and will all grow lazy and fat next spring."

Some lips popped and many chuckled at Ubantu's joke, but several also reached for their spirit necklaces, praying the thieves wouldn't come.

I can't believe I'm thinking this, but I hope they do come this winter, Attu thought as he walked over to speak with Keanu. *At least we will have faced them then, and it will be over, one way or the other.*

That evening around the fire, Attu saw Senga and Soantek deep in conversation with Bashoo and a few others. He joined them.

"I was just telling Senga what happened to the Nukeena and how they were able to get Raven women to become part of their Clan."

"Did the Nukeena take all the women?" Senga asked.

"No," Soantek laughed. "There are many more Raven women where those came from. Far to the south. But they are hidden, in a bay like this one, to stay safe."

"The Tuktu never go that far south," Senga said. He seemed disappointed.

Attu and Keanu worked out a plan to continue training Tishria in mind blending with the animals. Keanu and Soantek would work with all of the dogs, and Tishria and Soantek would both learn more about the acceptable way of entering an animal's mind and having it work for them. Attu encouraged them to plan for as many possibilities as they could, and soon, whenever the dogs weren't hauling wood, they could be seen running from camp, turning, moving up hill or downhill, and then returning. Soon they were bringing back objects as well. Attu could tell the dogs were enjoying the training as much as the humans. "They get dried meat or a nuknuk bone when they follow our directions," Tishria told Attu.

"It's all about trust and control," Keanu explained one evening as she sat with Rika and Attu at their fire. "The dogs trust Tishria most. She has a way of entering their minds almost like she is another dog. She can think like them. I've never seen such a complete bond like this before without the person going too far, like you did with birds and then with the whale fish. But then again, I only knew one person who could mind blend with animals before you, Attu, and that was me." Keanu grinned at Attu. "But if the thieves' dogs are willing, we will be able to turn them when they come. And Tishria seems to know just how to make that happen, at least with our three."

"Senga is missing." Ubantu met Attu as he and Suka were rounding the bay back from the next day's hunt.

"Who saw him last?"

"Veshria. She said he was going out in his skin boat to fish early this sun and said he'd be back shortly after sun high. I was just going out to search when I saw you."

"And now it's almost sunset."

"I'll stay here and direct the other men so we all don't search in the same area of the bay."

"Suka and I will head to the area by the rocks, to the north of the bay, where we've been catching fish lately."

"There's his skin boat," Suka said as they neared the rocks. A damaged boat was wedged among some of the rocks clustered in the deeper water.

Attu and Suka searched the rocks but found nothing else. "Let's cut back toward shore," Attu said, and they paddled toward the beach, taking the most direct route, as Senga would do if he'd been thrown from his craft and had swum for shore.

Attu leaped from his skin boat, lifting it above the waves at the shoreline. His heart sank as he saw a broken paddle moving in and out with the waves.

"It's Senga's. I helped him make it," Suka said.

"If he made it to shore alive, there should be tracks," Attu said. "It's low tide.

Tingiyok, we need the dogs to track for Senga. North shore of the bay.

Attu and Suka walked up and down the beach, looking for tracks.

"I don't see anything," Suka said. He scanned the grassy area above the beach and into the trees.

"Let's search the water by the rocks again," Attu said. "In this fading light we might have missed him. He could be floating in the water still. Tingiyok will search this area with the dogs."

Attu turned back to his skin boat, his heart sinking.

"We took the dogs to track, but they just kept running east into the grass by the river," Tingiyok said as the others gathered later around the fire. "I think they were picking up the old scent of our last hunt together."

"I just kept seeing a rabbit in their minds," Soantek said. "So did Tishria."

"We searched the caves and the rocks to the north, too, just in case Senga made it out of the water but was injured, and fell unconscious there," Tingiyok said. "If he couldn't walk far, we thought he might try to reach the caves, to get food and water, and start a fire to signal us. But he wasn't there."

"I hate to say it, but Senga must have gotten too close to the rocks and fallen out when his skin boat crashed into them," Ubantu said. "Maybe he hit his head or got sucked under."

Veshria moaned and covered her face. The women rushed to her side, spirit necklaces in hand, and began the wailing chant for those drowned.

Attu walked to where Veshria sat with the other woman. She stood and motioned for him to follow her away from the others.

"Veshria, I am so sorry," Attu began. "We looked everywhere, I-"

"Senga is drowned," Veshria said. "He couldn't swim well yet, and in the near-freezing water his knee would have gotten stiff and…" her voice trailed away. Then Veshria's body stiffened and the look she gave Attu made his flesh crawl. "I am bad luck, a bringer of death," Veshria said, her voice now a mere whisper. Attu started to protest, but Veshria stopped him. "And now no man will have me," she continued. "The poolik I lost will never have the chance to be born to me again."

Veshria turned from Attu, and before he could stop her, she ripped her face with her fingernails, leaving trails of blood following her hands to her sides. Then Veshria turned back to the other women. Someone gasped as they saw what Veshria had done to herself. But Veshria said nothing. Yural looked at Veshria's blank stare and then to Attu before turning to sit beside the grieving woman. The pain in his mother's eyes was almost as deep as Veshria's. Attu turned away, his heart so filled with anguish he couldn't breathe.

"What's wrong?" Rika asked Attu later that evening as Attu twisted in his furs, unable to sleep.

"I just don't understand," Attu said, turning to face his woman in the dark. "I heard Attuanin. I saved Senga. But why? Only to have him drown and break Veshria's heart again?"

"I've been wondering that, too."

Attu slid closer and held Rika in the darkness for a long time. Still, even after her whiffling breath brushed his cheek, Attu lay awake. And when his thoughts turned by habit to Attuanin to seek guidance, he turned them away again. He felt angry at his name spirit for allowing Senga to drown, for allowing such pain to come to Veshria. *I was counting on Senga's help. I was hoping we could turn the thieves using the dogs, and then Senga could try to reason with them while we kept them at a safe distance. I was hoping not to have to kill more men...*

But now Senga was gone, and they had no alternative but to fight. And Attu felt certain that if they did, some of his own men would die.

Chapter 21

The first snow fell. It was a heavy snow, and cold settled in around the Clan. Winter came much earlier than it had their first year in their new home, and the bay froze solid in only a few days. Little wind blew as the deep cold came, so the bay turned into a solid block of smooth ice. Attu and the other hunters pulled out long-unused bone clips, restringing them onto new sinew and strapping them to the bottom of their foot miks to keep from slipping on the ice.

"This ice is so thick, we'll surely have good hunting," Rovek said as he, Suka, and Attu finished the hole they were making, widening it so the body of a full size nuknuk could be pulled out.

"The nuknuks would never be able to break through this ice," Suka agreed. "With the ice this thick, they'll be tempted to use these holes instead of swimming all the way back to the open bay to get a breath."

"Look how the ocean moves so restlessly outside the bay," Attu remarked. "It's like a giant poolik trying to sleep, tossing and turning and fussing, never settling down." He looked out over the bay and felt his own thoughts, just as restless. Senga was gone. Attu still couldn't believe it.

Suka must have seen the look on Attu's face, because he began his teasing. "You sound like an old woman, Attu," Suka said. His voice rose to a higher pitch. "That ocean's mother should not feed it dried berries," he whined, sounding remarkably like Elder Nuka, only peevish like she never was.

"How do you always know when I need cheering up?"

Suka raised his eyebrows. "I don't know what you're talking about." He paused, looking out over the ocean beyond the bay. "But you're right. I can't get used to the ocean not freezing even in this cold." He turned back to his work chipping away the ice, but not before he glanced at Attu to see if his joking had helped. Attu let his smile convey his thanks, but then he grew thoughtful. "I am worried about Elder Nuka."

"We all are." Suka stopped chipping and settled down by the hole, adjusting his spear and rope. "Rika said Nuka's cough is getting worse."

Attu moved to ready his gear for the long wait beside the hole. Suka said nothing more, but his look told Attu he was also thinking of Elder Tovut and Elder Nuanu. Both had succumbed after sickness entered their lungs.

Rovek moved to set himself up beside them. "The Nukeena showing us this bay was a blessing from the spirits," Rovek said. He piled his ice chipping gear into a hide bag, folded it up, and sat on it, pulling out water and a piece of dried meat to chew on from inside his parka. "The rocks keep the ocean waves from disturbing the bay ice. How could we have hunted the nuknuk if we'd tried to settle along the coast and assumed the ocean would freeze in winter like the Expanse used to?"

"We'd have had to move farther north by now," Suka said. "This bay is the best place for us."

"Even with the threat of the thieves?" Attu asked. "Sometimes I think we should have turned south instead of north off the ice, or even followed the others to hunt tuskies."

"Tuskies? Never. No. It's best..." Suka cut himself off as they all caught a flicker of movement in the water of the hole.

"So soon?" Rovek whispered.

Attu shook his head in the slight hunter's movement, signaling for quiet. He'd been tying his spear rope to his side when the water rippled, and now he moved his spear up to the striking position in a slow movement, imitating the shadow of a small cloud passing over the sun, or a sweep of thick snow moving across the ice.

Suka gave the tiny hand signal for "steady," and Attu flicked his eyes at his cousin. They all waited, breathing slowly and quietly, bodies still. The ocean groaned in the distance as the ice chunks moved. A sharp wind picked up, blowing loose snow across the bay and ruffling the fur around Attu's parka hood.

They waited.

Attu watched the sun sparkle on the open water in the hole. He reminded himself to look under the water, deeper, to watch for movement. And as he did so he became aware of little details at the edges of his vision. Rovek blinked, a snow swirl formed behind Suka. Attu held his hands steady on the spear, his raised arm firm and strong. He concentrated on each breath. His tendency to wander in his thoughts could mean he'd miss his only chance. Attu pushed himself to be in the Here and Now, to continue to see all, hear all, and to be prepared to move quickly to spear the nuknuk if it decided to use this breathing hole. The hole had miraculously appeared so conveniently where it was now hunting. That should arouse the nuknuk's suspicion. *Will it use the hole, anyway?*

Attu kept his thoughts tightly under control. He knew better than to allow them to slip, or they would go to the animal and either warn it or spark its curiosity. Neither was permitted. The Gift was never to be used to call animals to be killed in the hunt. Attu studied the water in the hole, thought only of the pattern of the water, watching for a change in the pattern signaling a rising nuknuk.

Attu's heartbeat quickened as he thought he saw a shadow moving under the ice near the hole. He steadied himself, flexing his hand muscles slightly to make sure his fingers hadn't gone numb. They hadn't. He was ready.

The water broke as a nuknuk's whiskery snout poked out, its nostrils flaring.

Attu's arm flew forward with his spear, plunging it into the water at the precise angle to take the nuknuk in its meaty side. Suka and Rovek jumped to assist him, and the three of them pulled the thrashing nuknuk out of the hole.

Attu struck the killing blow with his club, and the three stood, marveling at such a fast kill after the hole was made.

"Usually the sound of our chipping scares the game away for half a day," Rovek remarked. "I've never seen this happen."

"It is smaller than most. Perhaps it was too young to know to be afraid of the sound of men chipping the ice."

"I think the sound of the water crashing into the ice and rocks at the mouth of the bay probably blended with our sound, and it didn't have warning of the danger." Attu looked at the animal. It was small, but they would all enjoy the more tender meat of the kill. The first nuknuk taken out of a fresh hole belonged to all who had helped in the strenuous and dangerous work of chipping it out. "Young one," Attu spoke the words over the animal, "I am sorry your life was cut short, but know your body will feed many, and many of our women feed their own young as your mother fed you. Your meat will provide their milk. You have died with honor. May your spirit rest now, to be born next spring in the body of another nuknuk."

The other group of hunters out on the ice gave a shout, and Attu, Suka, and Rovek moved with Attu's kill to join them as they pulled a nuknuk from the water, dead by Soantek's first strike.

Ubantu grinned at Soantek's large kill.

"We eat well tonight, my brothers," Soantek said.

The sun was resting on the ocean's ice-jumbled horizon as the men grabbed one of the two ropes tied to the nuknuks. "Soantek has an idea for trapping the thieves in the ravine to the south of camp, if they attack from that direction," Ubantu said. "He told me about it as we carved out our ice hole." The others listened to Soantek's plan as they walked in single file back to camp.

"It's a good idea," Attu agreed after Soantek had outlined his plan to use small landslides of rocks from the top of the ravine to the south to create a way to block the thieves, trap them if they tried to sneak close to camp through the pass. "It would be like them to come that way, like Toonuk thought they used the caves to get as close to the Tuktu as they could before they attacked."

The men sat around the fire later that evening, discussing the best ways to set the rocks so a few tree limbs levered in could be moved and cause enough rocks and debris to fall.

"The ravine is really the only clear path to our camp from the south, except for the shoreline. And I can't see the thieves maneuvering their sleds along that ice jumble." *And we were on the point in my vision. I didn't see the thieves coming along the shore.*

"What do we do if they come from the east or north?" Rovek asked.

"The forest is thick to the north. They'd need to come on foot," Ubantu said. "We'll post extra guards there, but if I were a thief, I would use the speed of the sleds. And that's what Attu and Keanu saw."

The others nodded.

"If they come from the east," Ubantu continued, "I was thinking of using the large rock pen the Tuktu hunters built to keep their tuktu herd together, the one up against that steep wall of rock?"

"With some extra rocks placed at the south opening to hold the thieves in, it might give us enough time to surround them." Tingiyok's eyes lit up at the plan.

"Some of us need to hunt again, next day, but the rest can start on the traps," Attu said. "Take the bigger boys and girls with you. They can carry small rocks and tree limbs, too."

"Attu?" Yural walked up to where the men were sitting. "Where is Rika?"

"With Meavu in her shelter. Why?"

"Elder Nuka is asking for her." Yural turned away, but not before Attu caught the look of concern in his mother's eyes.

"The nuknuk are swimming into the bay in large numbers," Tingiyok said a few days later as the men walked out to the holes to hunt. The traps had been set, and there was little else they could do besides keeping guards posted all the time and continuing to stock more meat in the caves.

"Your idea of making the holes over the deep rocky part of the bay worked well," Soantek said. "The sunset fish like to hide in the rocks, and the nuknuks come to hunt them." He looked to Ubantu, who nodded briefly but said nothing.

Attu could see nuknuks sunning themselves on the ice chunks in the ocean beyond the bay. They were taking advantage of the late morning sun shining low in the sky. He'd killed seven of them in the last three days using the same breathing hole.

Attu had thought to pray about how he'd been feeling; taking so many nuknuks seemed wrong, even if they did need to stock the caves. But when he quieted his spirit, he found himself still angry with Attuanin – and with himself for his anger. He'd never felt this way before, unsure at such a deep level about listening to the spirits and relying on Attuanin for guidance, something he'd been so sure of just a moon ago. It was like how Attu had felt on the Expanse when he realized it was no longer solid beneath him. And Attu hated that feeling.

"You are quiet today, Cousin," Suka said, interrupting Attu's thoughts. "What's wrong?"

"The nuknuk hunting has been too easy lately," Attu said to Suka as they neared the first hole. "Do we need to store up this much food? What if the thieves don't come?"

Attu slowed his pace so the two could talk without being overheard. He couldn't share his anger at the spirits with Suka. It was too personal and would be too dangerous to speak of. *But I can share my doubts about what feels like excessive hunting.* "Each time I take a nuknuk my family doesn't need for food, something stirs in my spirit," Attu said, looking to his cousin to see if he understood.

"You feel guilty," Suka said.

"You too?" Attu searched his cousin's face. Suka wasn't joking. "I explain to each dead animal why we're taking extra food, and I know it's the right thing to do, but-"

"We are Nuvik and Nuviks believe a true hunter never makes extra kills just to store more food than he might need for the next moon, even if the game is plentiful. It's the right way to believe, most of the time," Suka said, "but this is an unusual time for us. We don't have any choice."

"But that doesn't help the way I feel."

"I would be disappointed in you if you felt any other way." Suka grabbed Attu's shoulder in a brief grasp of encouragement.

"There's no alternative. We have to build the snow houses." Attu picked up the block he'd cut and placed it at the edge of the circle they'd brushed to the bare earth.

"Not to build them would be more than foolish. It would be dangerous. We can't live all winter in hide shelters." Rika slid the ice block knife along the edge of the packed snow. "But I understand how you feel. It seems childish to think that way, but part of me wants to believe that since the thieves attack us when we're living in snow houses, if we don't build them, they won't come."

"The only alternative is to move into the caves, and we need to keep their location a secret."

"Can you imagine the paths we'd make to and from those caves if we moved into them now?" Rika carved the last side of a snow block and Attu moved to lift it into place, one more piece in the curving base of the circular snow house.

"They are ready if we need them. No one is venturing into them again, except Rovek and Tingiyok to check on the supplies. And they both know how to cover their tracks. No, I'll lift that," Attu said, moving to stop Rika from lifting a large block. As Rika bent over, small bright eyes met his. Nuanu smiled from her snug spot riding in her mother's hood. Attu grinned back at her, making a funny face. Nuanu laughed, her arms flailing up and down with delight.

Attu turned so Rika could see Gantuk. "Is he still well covered?" Attu asked. The women always knew if their pooliks were snugly in place in their hoods, standing or sitting in the carry pouch built inside. But Attu struggled with not being able to see Gantuk or Nuanu when he carried them.

"You worry like an old woman," Rika teased. "He's fine."

"Suka says I think like an old woman," Attu mumbled.

Rika shot him a glance.

"I'm glad to carry our children, even if Suka does tease me incessantly about it," Attu added and he lifted another block as Gantuk laughed at his sister, who was waving the hide string of her mother's hood back and forth and babbling about it, "but I find I start walking with my back bent forward to make sure they don't slip out."

"Oh, don't do that," Rika said. "You'll make your scar hurt from the added weight of the baby."

Attu said nothing, but turned away to cut another block, keeping his thoughts tightly to himself. Rika didn't need to know the scars from the ice bear attack hurt every time he carried one of their pooliks on his back, bent forward or not.

"Attu," Ubantu called from across the camp. "Making progress?"

"Yes," Attu said.

Ubantu walked over to them. "Yural is finishing up the inside of ours. She likes to arrange things herself." Attu's father grinned at Gantuk, stuck his tongue out at the boy, and crossed his eyes. Gantuk laughed and kicked his feet inside Attu's parka hood. Attu winced, but said nothing.

"Here, let me take him." Ubantu pulled Gantuk out of Attu's hood and settled him in the front of his own parka, face out, tying his belt around his waist more firmly, so Gantuk could stand inside his grandfather's warm garment and watch what was going on.

Attu sighed with relief at having the weight off his back. Rika glanced at him, but said nothing.

Together, Ubantu and Attu stacked the blocks, building up the slanting walls of the snow house while Gantuk jumped up and down, reaching out his small mik-covered hands and patting the blocks in imitation of his grandfather.

Attu tried to enjoy what was normally a special time for his Clan, building new snow houses. But with every block he put in place, Attu found the dread in his spirit building as well.

Chapter 22

Attu sat beside Meavu that evening in the newly built group snow house. Meavu had Tovut on her lap, and the poolik was watching the nuknuk lamp flames, putting his hands in front of his face and looking through his fingers at the way the light changed.

"I feel like we should be doing something more to prepare ourselves, but I can't think of anything else we can do," Attu said.

"This waiting is hard on all of us," Meavu agreed. Her face looked drawn in the lamplight.

"Are you all right?"

She nodded but didn't speak.

"Waiting to see if the thieves will attack us feels worse to me than when the ice bear was following our Clan across the Expanse," Attu admitted. "I was still suffering from the

Rememberings and the pain of my wounds from when the ice bear attacked us. And we all knew it was only a matter of time before the one following us would attack and probably kill at least one of us before we could kill it."

"I remember." Meavu shifted. "This waiting feels as bad to me as when I was held captive by the Ravens, waiting to be their totem sacrifice." She looked at her boy. "Almost," she added, picking Tovut up and hugging him. "But now there's even more at stake." Tovut squirmed to get out of her arms. "He's a wriggly little fish."

"Tovut grows strong," Attu said, sensing his sister's need to change the subject. Tovut pulled himself up by Meavu's hands and began bouncing on her legs. She let go of him with one hand and brushed his hair back from his face. Tovut balanced well with just one hand, babbling and reaching for his mother's other hand again.

"He said his first word today," Meavu said, her face brightening as she met Attu's eyes.

"He spoke? You mean he was playing with sounds and something came out that sounded like a word?"

"No. He spoke." Meavu looked away from Tovut toward the fire, a small smile on her face as she remembered.

"But he's still too young to-"

"I was with Suanu, and Brovik was playing with Dog," Meavu interrupted. "Tovut kept crawling toward them, and I kept picking him up and getting him out of the way of their wrestling. Tovut was frustrated and wiggled to get out of my arms. He squirmed and leaned toward them, reaching both his hands out to them and grasping with his fingers, you know, the way pooliks do when they're crawling toward something and it's still too far away, but they grab for it anyway?"

Attu nodded. "And?"

"He said, 'Dog.'"

"Surely he was just imitating-"

"He said it several times," Meavu insisted. "And when I let him touch Dog, he grabbed the dog's fur and wouldn't let go. He kept saying it over and over again. 'Dog,' just like that."

Tovut's knees bent and he collapsed onto his mother's lap. He looked up at her, and his little brows drew together. "Dog," he said. "Dog, dog, dog." And he looked around expectantly, as if his words would make Dog appear.

"That is remarkable," Attu said, and the two of them stared at Tovut as if he had just displayed the most incredible Gift. Then Attu had an idea.

"Elder Tingiyok," Attu called across the snow house. "Could you bring Warm Fur over here?" The dog had been sleeping under some furs near Tingiyok and stirred at her name. Tingiyok stood, and Warm Fur followed him across the snow house. When the light from the nuknuk lamp showed them both clearly, Tovut began jumping up and down on his mother's lap again.

"Dog!" he cried. "Dog, dog, dog!"

Lips popped all around them as the others heard Tovut's cries.

"Well, toss me to the tooth fish," Suka said, bouncing Nipka in his arms as he joined Attu and Meavu with Tovut, who had grasped Warm Fur's ruff in his hands and pulled her to his face where he was drooling all over her. Warm Fur stood still, but did not look pleased with this poolik's behavior.

Steady, Attu mind spoke to the pup.

"She's fine," Tingiyok said. "She won't hurt him."

Meavu gently removed Tovut's hands from the dog, and Tingiyok led Warm Fur away from the poolik's reach.

"Dog, dog, dog!" Tovut hollered, frustrated by having Warm Fur taken from him. He began crying.

Nipka added a lusty cry to the moment, drowning out any sound Tovut was making. "Now why couldn't you talk like Tovut, instead of bellowing like a moose?" Suka made his apologies and left with Nipka before she made them all deaf.

The next evening, the Clan sat around the nuknuk lamps in the group snow house. Chirea sat beside Kossu, and Attu watched the two of them as the others talked, thinking about the time when he and Rika were newly bonded. Soantek was answering a question Yural had asked him about his old life and how the whale meat was dried and the oil rendered for later use. The Clan listened. Babies were jostled and shared around the group. Chirea took her turn at holding Nipka. The young woman brightened when she held the little poolik, who was trying to pick off some of the colorful ornaments Chirea wore on her woman's garment.

"I wonder if Chirea misses her Tuktu Clan," Attu mused aloud.

"Of course she does," Rika said. "But she loves Kossu more. And in the fall, she will have a child. Her homesickness will subside."

"Another baby?" Attu's thoughts slipped to a dark place where he, and he alone, was responsible for the safety of every man, woman, and child in the Clan. *So many babies...* He sighed and pulled himself back. Wrong thinking got him nowhere.

"Good," Rika said. "You stopped yourself from thinking it's all on you." She slipped her arm through Attu's and looked up at him. "Besides," she added, "you will be busy worrying about the birth of your next child."

"My next child…" Attu turned to Rika, pulling her to him and searching her eyes. He found his answer there. "Another child. Attuanin has blessed us with another child? And our twins will be less than two years old when he or she is born? Elder Nuanu spoke true. I will be the father of many sons and daughters…"

Rika tightened her hold on Attu and Attu held her, his heart a swirl of emotions like trysta spirits on the Expanse, dancing in the blowing snow.

"Keanu is having her baby," Meavu called to Rika from the entrance tunnel of their snow house. Rika grabbed her things and left.

A short while later, Soantek ducked in. "I bring no evil," he said. "I've been kicked out of my snow house. Yours is farthest from ours, and the women said I must wait here."

Soantek looked mournful.

Attu put another hide near the nuknuk lamp. "Have a seat." Soantek sat for a short time; then, restless, he stood and began walking in a circle around the nuknuk lamp.

"Let's go to Farnook and Suka's snow house," Attu suggested. "Maybe his stories can help the time pass faster."

Soantek looked his thanks at Attu.

Farnook sat beside Attu with their pooliks while Suka was doing his best to keep Soantek involved in a bone tossing game. It was like the children's game, but involved betting. It seemed to be working, at least for the moment. Soantek was winning.

Farnook laid her hand on Attu's arm. "You look preoccupied."

"I am. I was thinking about Senga again."

"It just doesn't seem right. I was sure he would help us when the thieves came."

"I felt it in my spirit. I sensed it when Attuanin spoke to me and said to save him. Now I see Veshria, and I wish we hadn't saved the man. That makes me feel guilty."

Attu searched Farnook's face. "Did I hear Attuanin wrong? Is this my fault? Saving Senga and then having him drown has caused Veshria even more pain. She has not spoken since the day of his death. She said she believed she must bond with Senga because the spirits wanted her to. Did she hear wrong, also?"

"Attu, you can't know what she heard or why she made her decision."

"I know she said Rusik died because she had taken the root that killed her unborn child. And I know that is not what the Nuvik believe. But for whatever reason, Veshria bonded with Senga, and look what happened. How much grief can one woman take?"

"Veshria will heal, given enough time. A person can withstand much heartache, if necessary." Farnook looked at Attu, her eyes filled with compassion. Attu realized if anyone understood living through heartache, it would be Farnook.

"You are probably right. I just feel conflicted about all of this. It used to be I simply listened and did what I believed Attuanin and the other spirits desired of me. That's what it means to be Nuvik, isn't it? But now…" Attu let his words trail away. He didn't know what to think.

Keanu gave birth to a large boy. He looked so much like Soantek that even Attu could see the resemblance. It was as if Soantek had been given a baby's body with his own head still attached. The poolik had Keanu's light hair, which to Attu made the infant look even more unusual.

Keanu thought him beautiful, of course.

"Mothers always do," Rika assured Attu as he left from his first visit with the baby and new parents. Attu remarked on the looks of the child as soon as they were out of earshot of Keanu and Soantek.

"His eyes are so large; he looks like a startled owl with that shock of wild light hair standing straight up on his head."

Rika giggled. "But, it is a handsome face. The poolik just needs to grow into it."

Meavu stepped up beside Rika and walked with them back to their snow houses. They'd all braved the outside air today since it was sunny. The pooliks were in Yural's care, and the young parents could enjoy the quiet and the sunshine.

"I need you to look in on Elder Nuka," Meavu said as they neared the old woman's snow house. "Her cough is getting worse."

"All right. I have my healer's bag. I'll come now. Attu?"

"I'm coming, too."

Elder Tingiyok had volunteered to take Elder Nuka into his snow house this winter, and in spite of a few of the women's opinions about the two of them being unbonded and living together, Elder Nuka had said yes.

"Look at the two of us," the old woman had laughed, before succumbing to another bout of the coughing she'd been doing for many moons now. "Do you think there will be pooliks in our future?"

"Warm Fur will not let me share my bed with anyone else." Tingiyok winked at Nuka.

"Who said anything about sharing a bed?" Nuka pretended to scowl at him. "You need someone to tend your nuknuk lamp, and that's the only fire I plan on keeping bright."

The others had laughed uproariously at her remark, and Ubantu had slapped his thigh as Elder Nuka walked away to gather her things from her shelter and move into Tingiyok's. "Spoken like a true Nuvik woman," Ubantu had said.

Meavu, Rika, and Attu stopped outside Elder Nuka and Elder Tingiyok's snow house. "Come in," Tingiyok called before they could call out a greeting. "She's getting worse."

"Oh, you are a fussy old man," Elder Nuka wheezed, and tried to laugh. But her cough erupted, and the spasms took her back down into the furs she was lying on, gasping for air.

"Let me brew you some tea," Rika said, and grabbed a pouch out of her bag. "This is stronger than the potion I've been giving you. It will help with the cough."

"She can't sleep," Tingiyok said, keeping his voice low. "The cough is draining all her energy."

"I hear you," Nuka rasped and coughed again.

"Don't try to talk," Meavu said. "Let Rika give you the drink first."

Rika blew on the potion steeping in the water Tingiyok had already heated. When it was cool enough, Attu helped Rika sit Elder Nuka up so she could drink. The old woman took a long swallow, then another.

"That feels good on this sore throat," she said. The effort to drink exhausted her. She lay back on the furs and closed her eyes.

Rika looked to the others and shook her head. She laid her open palm on Nuka's chest. The Elder was so thin, Attu knew Rika could feel Nuka's heart beating her lifeblood, even through her hide clothing.

"Your heart is struggling in your chest like a bird caught in a trap," Rika said. "You need to rest."

"The bird wishes its freedom from this body. And so do I," Nuka said.

"Soon you will be feeling-" Meavu began.

"No, child. Soon I will join my ancestors in the Between," Elder Nuka said.

"You need to sleep," Rika said, moving to cover Elder Nuka with more sleeping furs, for the old woman had begun trembling.

The nuknuk lamplight wavered, and Meavu adjusted the flame so it burned steadily again.

"I know I am going to die."

"You are not-" Rika began.

"It's all right," Nuka interrupted her and turned her head to Meavu. "You can... tell them. I'm dying. I know you've Seen it. I won't last much... longer." Her breath was coming in rasps now, making it hard to speak.

"I'll go tell the others," Attu said.

"I'll get Farnook to help me feed your children." Meavu moved to the snow house entrance with Attu.

"Thank you," Rika said as they slipped out of the snow house. "Have Yural come soon," Rika added.

Chapter 23

"She passed to the Between in the middle of the night," Elder Tingiyok told Attu the next morning. "Yural was able to speak with her until just moments before she passed. It was an easy death in the end." The old man looked away, brushing at his face. "I was afraid, because of her cough…"

Both men had seen those dying of the lung sickness, and for some it was a horrible death. "I knew if anyone could keep Elder Nuka comfortable in her passing, it would be Rika," Attu said.

"Your woman is truly a gifted healer," Elder Tingiyok said. "When it comes to be my time, I pray to the spirits she is with me." The men moved to prepare the burial mound. Attu thought the Elder could have given him no greater compliment than to think highly of Rika. "I pray you will be with us for a long time still, Elder Tingiyok. Elder Nuka will be missed. Such wisdom as she had is vital for   our Clan, as is yours."

Elder Tingiyok turned and smiled at Attu before resuming their walk to alert the others and begin the burial preparations.

Attu stepped into the snow house later that day to pay his respects to Elder Nuka's spirit and the other women who were preparing her body. He was surprised to see Elder Tingiyok holding Nuka's head in his lap, but he said nothing. The two had been close.

"Did Elder Nuka dream before she passed to the Between?" Attu asked his mother.

"If she did, she didn't tell anyone." Yural looked up from her preparations, her eyes full of concern. "Sometimes a dying person will dream; sometimes, not."

"I know." Attu turned back toward the entrance to the snow house. "I'd just hoped she would have had a word for me. Something to…" his words drifted off, and he left the snow house, his mind in turmoil.

"What had I been hoping for?" Attu asked himself aloud as he walked back to his own snow house.

Something to help me in my struggle, he realized. *I wanted Elder Nuka to reassure me, to tell me I hadn't heard the sprits wrongly. But the spirits didn't even have a dream for me. I feel like I can't count on anything, anymore.*

"I almost hope those last thieves come soon," Ubantu spoke Attu's own thoughts around the nuknuk lamp that evening.

"Why do you say that?" Rovek asked. At the mention of the thieves, he'd wrapped his arm around Meavu and Tovut, who was nestled in Meavu's arms.

"Because knowing it will happen and not knowing when is torturing his spirit," Meavu said. She was looking at her father, but her words pierced Attu's heart.

"Our men are hunters," Yural said. "Give them a target they can hit and they will hit it, an animal or an enemy and they will kill it."

"It's driving me mad to be prepared, and then to wait, not knowing when the attack will come. I'm beginning to doubt it will come at all," Attu said.

Yural looked at her son, but Attu looked away.

Tingiyok and Attu walked back from the river, where they'd spent the day fishing through the ice. "Veshria will stay with me the rest of this winter," Tingiyok said.

"Some of the women won't approve, but Yural will and she'll convince the others."

"Nuka is gone. Veshria has begun speaking again, but she's still grieving deeply. Someone needs to be there for the children."

"Tishria will feel better with you there to keep an eye on Ganik."

"The boy has been kinder to his sister since Grey Wolf's return, but he still resents her Gifts. I think he realizes his sister won't try to take Grey Wolf for her own, though. She trains with all the dogs, but when they're not training, Grey Wolf never leaves the boy's side.

"Are you sure you shouldn't be training with them as well?" Tingiyok asked Attu, pausing on the trail.

"When the thieves come, I need to be able to lead our hunters. The three of them are more than capable of directing the dogs – ours and the thieves' – if that's possible. And there's no reason to believe they won't be able to.

"Thank you for taking care of Veshria and her family," Attu said as they entered camp. Attu grasped Tingiyok's arm briefly, then the men each headed back to their own snow houses.

"A few of the rocks have fallen from this side, but the others we piled are still there," Ubantu said. He and Attu and a few others had walked out to inspect the traps they'd set above the ravine. "Here is the best place now for us to hide and watch this path." Ubantu pointed toward the highest point in the ravine, between the two traps. "With the overhang above, our hunters can hide there as well."

"Once the thieves are trapped between the landslides, we can shoot them from above."

"I think we should add a pit trap at the end closest to the camp," Rovek said, looking back toward their snow houses. "If we can't get to the logs to set off the landslide in time, at least the first of the thieves' sleds will fall in, and that will slow them down."

"A good idea. But how do we dig there?" Soantek asked. "The ground is frozen."

"Use fire to thaw the ground, then dig down to where it's frozen again and build another fire, like the Ravens did to hollow out their giant canoes," Ubantu said.

Attu groaned with the rest of the men. It was going to take a lot of wood and a lot of digging.

But looking around, Attu saw determination growing on his hunters' faces. Anything they could do to protect themselves was worth the effort. And Rovek's idea had been a good one.

"I am hearing animals communicating," Tishria said. She had come to Attu's snow house as the eastern sky lightened behind the mountains. Attu and Rika sat with her around the nuknuk lamp while Gantuk and Nuanu played on the sleeping furs.

"Tell us more. What do you hear?" Rika asked.

Tishria shivered. It was warm in the snow house, but Rika gave her a fur to wrap around herself. "Thank you," Tishria said. She smiled briefly then looked back at the light of the nuknuk lamp. She stared at it, apparently gathering her thoughts.

"It started in the night. The thoughts feel like Warm Fur's, but they're not hers or any of our dogs. I know their thoughts, their minds. At first it was just feelings. Hunger. Cold. A sore shoulder. A cut foot pad. But then it became more. Eagerness. A journey. The scent of pine, the roughness of rocks on cold feet. Many thoughts. Tired, but happy. And the thoughts are getting stronger. I can sense them clearly now."

"Do you think it's the thieves, and you are hearing their dogs' thoughts?" Attu studied   Tishria's face.

"What else could it be?"

"But Keanu has seen nothing."

"I know. But I also know what I'm hearing."

"You were right to tell us," Rika assured the girl.

"I don't know how she's doing it," Keanu said to Attu later that day as they sat in Keanu's snow house. "Because Tishria insisted she was hearing something, I had Farnook watch my son while I searched farther than I usually do, many days' journey on foot to the east. I looked for rocks and pine trees. I searched lower in the sky. I even rested in the trees, something I rarely do, but the bird I was flying with had gone so far, he needed the rest. And I saw them. Tishria was right. Thieves south and east of us, coming north and west." Keanu turned her face away from Attu, her shoulders drooping.

"What else?" Attu asked. "You saw something else, didn't you?"

"Yes." Keanu met Attu's eyes, the pain in hers overflowing with tears. "I saw Senga. Senga is with them."

"No!" Veshria shouted. "I won't believe it. Senga was a good man. A good man. Like my Rusik. He drowned. He is not evil like the others. He can't be with them."

"But Keanu-" Yural began.

"Keanu. Always Keanu!" Veshria glared at Yural. "She is wrong. She didn't see Senga. He wouldn't leave me, wouldn't go back to them." Her words trailed off into choked crying sounds that tore at Attu's heart.

"Such grief, such loss for one woman, and now this," Rika whispered. Her fingers were clenched so tightly around Attu's forearm he thought she would bruise him. But he said nothing.

Veshria tore away from them and ran for her snow house.

"Why did Attuanin tell me to save Senga, only to let us think he'd drowned when in truth he was plotting to turn on us? He used us to get better, fooled us all, then went back to his friends once he was fully recovered, before the snow came again."

Attu stood in his parents' snow house. His whole body trembled with anger.

"We don't know why, Attu. All we know is Senga is alive, and he's coming with the thieves to attack us," Yural said. She reached for her spirit necklace.

"I will kill them," Attu said as a dark rage rose up in his spirit, a need for revenge like he had never felt before. "This needs to end. We will kill them all."

"You want them to come?" Tishria looked confused.

"Yes. So we meet them when we're prepared to fight and we're not taken by surprise." Attu clenched his teeth, working to control his anger.

Attu had stayed with Yural and Ubantu until he felt in control of himself again. Then he went looking for Tishria and found her out playing with some of the other children. He'd taken her aside and as soon as he began speaking to her, the anger rose in him, again.

Get control of yourself, Attu berated himself, breathing deeply.

Tishria took a step back from Attu, her eyes wide, but she said nothing about his turbulent emotions. "What do you want me to do?" she asked, instead.

"Now that you're hearing the thieves' dogs, do you have an idea about controlling them?"

Tishria swallowed reflexively before speaking. "I will begin telling their dogs our camp is a good place, with meat and warmth. It's the truth. They'll believe me. They can see Warm Fur, Grey Wolf, and Dog in my mind. They can see how happy they are to be with us, how well we treat them. It will make the thieves' dogs eager to come quickly."

"You can communicate with them? I know you thought you could hear them, but they can hear you from this distance?" Attu was shocked out of his anger. "And it doesn't tire you to mind speak with them?"

"Tire me? Why should it make me tired? I'm not running or jumping; I'm just talking to them in my head."

"If you can, please talk to them. Let them get to know you and want to come."

"I will." Tishria smiled at him briefly before turning back toward her shelter.

Attu stared after her.

"They are still two days away?" Attu asked Soantek after he'd flown the day's watch flight.

"Yes. They might make more or less progress depending on how much it snows. It's hard to tell."

Nowhere to run. Attu lay in his furs that evening and struggled, as he had for so many nights, to think of more ways to protect his Clan. *How can we face them, but keep our women and children safe? There must be a better way than hiding in caves. But caves are all we have, aren't they?*

At first light, Attu gathered a few men to walk to the point of the bay, where they could see the farthest. Attu stood on the point, looking back at the ice with Ubantu and Suka. With the severe cold they'd had for the past few days, he had thought they might be able to walk out onto the ice, move far enough out where they could hide the women and children on one of the bay's islands, making it look like both their camp and the caves had been deserted.

"We can't do it," Suka said. "Look there and over there." He pointed to two dark patches where ice had frozen, broken, and then frozen again. Just the surface was solid.

"It will take days of this bitter cold to make the ice safe enough to walk all the way to the islands," Ubantu agreed. "Even if we walk to the point and then across. It's just too dangerous right now."

Attu scanned the ice one more time. His body stiffened as the rocks and snow around him came into greater focus. The groaning ice grew silent. Attu no longer felt the wind. His mind raced back to the river's edge, to Keanu, and the vision. Everything around him looked exactly like it had that day. Except this time he was not surprised when Rika mind spoke.

They're coming, she said. *Do what you must. I will keep our children safe.*

Chapter 24

"How did they make it here so fast?" Ubantu asked as the men raced back to camp.

"Keanu says they must have travelled nonstop through last night," Rovek said. "She says it's her fault. She didn't think to fly at night, too. Just to be sure."

"It's not her fault," Attu said. "Once we knew they were traveling by day, I didn't think they would risk their animals by pushing them to pull through the night, too. This is my fault."

We're heading for the landslide traps, Tingiyok mind spoke to Attu.

Attu relayed the information to the others. "You go ahead. I'll be right there. I need to speak with Keanu, Soantek, and Tishria." Attu veered off.

Attu crawled into the snow house on the edge of camp. Keanu came back to herself for a moment as Attu arrived.

"Soantek said the thieves are hitting the dogs with the ropes on poles like I saw in your vision. Whips, I think Senga called them. Tishria keeps telling them she will make the men stop hitting them, and they will get much meat and a warm place to sleep like she's been showing them for the last few days. She says Grey Wolf, Warm Fur, and Dog are encouraging the other dogs to chase after them to get the meat. The thieves are furious, but their dogs won't stop. They're nearing the ravine."

"She's encouraging the dogs and leading Grey Wolf?" Attu asked. "And she's talking to the others? How can she do all that at once?"

"I'm fine," Tishria said. She opened her eyes for a moment, smiled at him, and closed them again.

Attu reeled at her words, but there was no more time to consider the immensity of what Tishria was doing.

"How many sleds?" he asked Keanu.

"Six."

"And Senga?"

"He's leading the way," Keanu said.

Anger flared as Attu thought of the traitor and the voice that had told him to save the man.

Keanu closed her eyes. "I've got to get back to Warm Fur." And she was gone.

Attu pushed his mind out toward the thieves. A wall of anger and frustration hit him from the combined minds of the attackers. He pulled back, his own anger flaring even higher.

Call our dogs back, Attu directed Tishria as he scrambled out of the snow house and started running toward the ravine. *Have them bark and head back to the snow houses, as if to warn us there, as if everyone is still in them. Then guide the thieves' dogs into the ravine. Senga knows nothing of the landslides or pit trap we've set.*

I won't lead their dogs into the pit trap. They might get hurt. Attu felt the anger in Tishria's voice. *I'll lead them far enough so they get caught in the ravine. You need to be ready to set off the landslides.*

Attu wanted to argue with Tishria, but if she felt it was wrong to lead the dogs where they would fall in the pit traps, he couldn't ask her to do it. He ran up the hill, dropping at its brow where the others were crouched. "It's working. Tishria is leading their dogs into the ravine."

"Then we've got them," Suka said. He turned gleaming eyes on Attu.

They stayed hidden behind the boulders at the top of the ravine, half the hunters with Attu on one side, the others with Tingiyok on the other side. A few of the men were set to release the landslides. Bows were strung.

Below Attu, a dog sled materialized like a spirit out of the snow that had begun to fall. It raced toward them along the bottom of the ravine. The lead dog barked and scrambled to stop as it neared the pit trap. Either it had smelled the trap or Tishria had warned it. But the dog couldn't stop. The driver cracked his whip, and the other dogs lurched forward. The lead dog was pushed onto the snow-covered mat of dried grass and twigs, breaking it. The dog slid into the pit, dragging several of the other dogs behind it.

A spear throw in front of the hole, rocks and debris tumbled down. Attu's hunters had set off the first landslide.

A thief cried out, pointing to the now-blocked pass ahead of them.

The first sled had stopped just two spear lengths from the edge of the pit. The driver and the two thieves sitting on it ran to the edge of the hole. One grabbed a knife and began cutting the dangling dogs free, but another one stopped him. They moved back to the sled and pushed it backward. The dogs pulled backward on their tie ropes.

But more sleds were coming, fast. The second sled careened into the first. Thieves jumped out of the way, and the dog on the edge of the hole yelped as the sled was dragged over. The others squealed and squirmed as they dangled in the hole, trying to free themselves of their restraints.

The man with the knife shouted at the others as the rest of the sleds ground to a stop in front of the hole. Then Attu's men released the landslide behind them as the first sled's rope broke and the rest of the dogs fell to the bottom of the trap.

"Their only way out now is to climb up," Ubantu whispered. "Isn't that Senga?"

The man with the knife had pulled back his hood and was looking up at the surrounding rocks, shielding his eyes from the snow and trying to see past the swirling whiteness.

"That's him," Suka whispered from Attu's other side. "He gets my first arrow." Suka stood and shot an arrow, missing Senga by a hand's breadth. Attu gasped as Senga ignored the shot and grabbed the man nearest him by the neck and flung him into the pit trap. Then he turned back toward where the shot had come from.

"Wait!" Senga yelled up toward Attu. "Don't shoot!"

A nearby thief grabbed Senga and held him in front of himself, like a shield, a knife at Senga's throat.

"If you shoot at us, I'll kill him!" the man shouted. He looked around wildly, trying to find where Attu and his men were hiding.

Suka drew his bow again.

"Wait," Attu said. "Something's wrong. Why is Senga-"

Senga threw his head backward, hitting the man holding him in the nose. The man reeled back, the knife no longer at Senga's throat. Senga shouted again. "Not all of us want to fight. Only the men in the last sled and this one are your enemies."

The thief had recovered from the blow and raised his knife to stab Senga in the back. Grey Wolf came flying out from behind the rocks near the pit and flung himself on the thief. He clamped down on the man's wrist. The thief screamed and tried to wrench away from Grey Wolf, but the dog held on, pulling the man away from Senga. The thief stumbled, and Grey Wolf released him as the man fell into the pit on top of the other man and the dogs.

Senga yelled something to one of the men in the back of the group. Eight thieves leaped off their sleds, yelling and cursing at Senga and the other men just like they had the Tuktu.

"You traitor," one of the men yelled. "How dare you-"

But the man's words were cut off when one of the other thieves with Senga drew back his bow and shot the man in the chest.

"Kill them!" Senga cried, and the rest of the thieves standing with Senga launched arrows at the now seven remaining thieves.

"Is he telling the truth?" Suka yelled at Attu. "Is he on our side?"

Attu knew there was only one way he could tell for sure. He cringed, remembering his adamant instructions to Tishria about reading others' thoughts against their permission, then he threw his mind at Senga, drilling into the man's thoughts for the kernel of truth or lie that must be there.

Attu felt Senga's mind reel in shock. But as it did, a clear thought struck Attu.

"You heard Senga. Shoot them," Attu said as he pulled his mind back and released his arrow. The closest of the men fell. Senga had grabbed his head in his hands at Attu's mental attack, but he straightened now and began shooting again.

The next two fell to his hunters' shots, multiple arrows piercing their bodies. Then the thieves closed in on each other and Attu was afraid to shoot again. He dropped his bow and ran down the hill.

"What do we do?" Suka asked as they reached the bottom.

"If someone comes after you, kill them," Attu yelled to his hunters. "If they don't, leave them alone. For now."

A thief leaped at Ubantu, and Ubantu's spear pierced the man's chest. Another grabbed for Senga, and one of the other thieves clubbed him with the end of his spear before slitting the man's throat.

Bashoo picked up the thief who came at him and dashed the man against the rocks on the side of the ravine. Another of Senga's men stabbed him as he tried to rise.

And then it was over. Five thieves, including Senga, stood before them, weapons at the ready but making no move to attack. Senga dropped his knife and motioned for the other thieves to drop their weapons as well. They all looked terrified, but followed Senga, dropping their weapons. Each lowered his right arm and beat three times on his chest, the Nuvik sign of greeting and respect. And then they smiled broadly, showing their teeth. "We bring no evil," they chanted in unison.

"Why did you make it look like you'd drowned?" Ubantu asked Senga as the men moved into the group snow house out of the increasing wind and snow. Attu had mind spoken to Rika, and the women and children were staying in the caves until he could sort out what had happened and make sure they were now safe.

"I didn't know if I could find the others. I didn't know if I could convince them to take me back. I thought they'd probably kill me. It would be better for Veshria to think I drowned here," Senga said, "then to never know what happened to me."

"I didn't want you to live in fear of when these thieves would find you and come for you," Senga added. He glanced at where the other four thieves were sitting under the watchful eye of several hunters.

The group grew quiet.

"I knew you'd be prepared. I knew you would be able to control our dogs. I know you speak in your heads and See the future. I knew you'd be ready when I brought the thieves." Senga smiled at them. "And my friends who didn't want to fight anymore."

"But you could have been killed before you were able to tell us you weren't betraying us, but them." Suka looked dumbfounded. "That was a big chance to take. I shot at you."

"It was worth it to eliminate the last group of thieves. I did it for Veshria. I did it so your Clan and the Tuktu Clans won't have to spend your lives waiting and watching for another thief attack. This was my chance to stop the killing." Senga's voice was sure. "It was worth the risk."

Attu turned to Senga. "I need to apologize for-"

"No," Senga interrupted. "You did what you had to do. But I'd like to know what you saw in my mind that convinced you I was telling the truth."

Attu hesitated. "Now?"

Senga nodded. "I have nothing to hide."

"I saw you, sitting beside Veshria. She was holding a poolik in her lap. And I knew the poolik was yours."

"You Saw his future?" Ubantu asked. "And that convinced you?"

Senga turned to the others. "No. He saw the dream I have for Veshria and myself. The reason I risked everything to make it happen. I've seen how you live. I want that for my woman and me. But I want it also for my people. And I knew it couldn't happen when Tuktu leaders like Toonuk felt constantly threatened by thieves."

"And were constantly reminded of how those thieves were a result of their own inability to lead without violence," Attu said. "So you pretended to be one of them when they decided to attack us?"

"Oh, they knew nothing of you," Senga grinned. "They let me back into the group because I said I could tell them where to find a rich Clan on the coast with much food and many women. I told them where you were, and I led the attack."

Attu stared at Senga. He felt as if his whole world were flipping over like a giant ice chunk.

Chapter 25

Attu's people sat at the evening fire talking of the thieves' send off that morning and watching the waves move on the bay in the late spring evening. The four thieves Senga had convinced not to fight had left with Tingiyok, headed by skin boat for the Nukeena. There they would plan a strategy to go to the Raven's camp and find women of their own to start a real Clan.

"Tingiyok said he'd try to convince some of the Nukeena to come back with him for a visit once they do what they can for the Tuktu men."

"I would love to see my Nukeena brothers again," Soantek said. He put his arm around Keanu, who was holding their son.

Suka joked about the thieves, who'd been so eager to go with Tingiyok, even though some could still barely keep their skin boats steady in the water.

Bashoo was sitting across from them. He looked fondly at Suanu. Each held a child, Brovik in his mother's lap, and his new little sister, born just a few days ago, snuggled in the great man's arms. "These men are wise to go find women. Women fix everything," he said.

Lips popped all around.

"But Raven women?" Rovek asked. Everyone cringed.

"Tuktu like strong women," Senga said. He smiled broadly. Veshria glared at him and he grinned at her.

"Some of the Raven women may think your friends are not too ugly. We shall see." Bashoo added.

Everyone laughed.

"And finally, we can live in peace in Broken Rock Bay," Meavu said as the group quieted.

Nuanu turned and pulled at the small fur Gantuk was holding. "No," Gantuk said and pulled it back. Nuanu moved closer to him and Gantuk let her snuggle into his side, sharing the fur.

Attu touched Rika's hand, then looked to his mother and stood, needing a moment alone with her. Yural followed him to walk along the beach.

Attu gazed at the stars. He reached for his spirit necklace. "I almost stopped believing."

"I know."

Attu turned to her in surprise, and then his shoulders slumped. "I should have known. Nothing I feel goes unnoticed by you."

Yural cupped her hand around Attu's cheek. He leaned into its warmth as he'd done as a child. "But you did not," she whispered. "Attuanin knew you would follow the spirits. You did what you believed was right, what you believed the spirits wanted you to do, and now all are safe from the threat of the thieves."

The stars sparkled and the waves lapped the shore. Attu drew in a breath of the spring air, full of new life. "Attuanin and the spirits of this world have guided our people since before any of us can know. Attuanin was with me across the Expanse, with the Ravens, heading north, and with the Nukeena. He guided us to this place and to this time, even with the thieves. He gave me the vision of what the future would be. When I saved Senga, I thought he might help me stop that vision from coming to pass. But instead, Senga had been sent by the spirits to make it come to pass. Attuanin guided me true. I just couldn't see it."

Yural searched his eyes in the starlight. "What else is troubling you, my son?"

"I still feel like I failed."

"Failed us?"

"No. Failed Attuanin. Failed by doubting, by being angry when I thought I had either heard the spirits wrong or when I thought they'd abandoned us. I'm ashamed of that now."

"You have not failed, my son, but you have learned a very important lesson." Yural stood on tiptoe to kiss Attu's cheek. "Release your feeling of failure now. It is just pride gone sour. Let it go."

Attu felt the truth of his mother's words sinking deep into his spirit. He turned to the water and felt the breeze on his face, the cool sand beneath his feet, and a rush of love toward this woman who had been as much of a leader as he or his father had ever been, and was stronger and wiser than any of them.

"I am proud to be your son," Attu felt tears in his eyes. He did not hold them back.

Yural smiled at him. "You will lead us into the future here, Attu. As People of the Waters, our children will grow and thrive, and their children after them. This is where we belong."

"This is where we will stay." Attu wrapped his arms around Yural. The last vestiges of the weight he'd been feeling faded away as Attu rested his chin on the top of his mother's head. Then he picked her up and spun her once, as he'd done with Meavu as a child. "It is good to be Nuvik!" Attu exclaimed.

Yural laughed. She wrapped an arm around Attu's waist, and they headed back to the fire where Rika and Ubantu, Meavu and Rovek, and all their people with all the children they'd been blessed with waited for them.

Where Gantuk and Nuanu and the little one yet to be born wait for me.

Epilogue

"Nuanu," Rika called, darting to grab Nuanu, who was toddling away from the group of women working on the beach as fast as her chubby legs would carry her. "Water," the poolik said as she saw the ocean sparkling in the sun. "Water pretty. Go water."

"Later," Rika said as Nuanu tried to let go of her mother's hand and run into the freezing ocean water. "It is fall now. The water is too cold to play in." She kept a firm grasp on Nuanu, balancing their new daughter in her other arm. Gantuk sat in Rika's back strap carrier.

Attu set his boat building tools down and walked over to Rika. He held out his hand for his daughter, and she ran to him. Rika pulled the infant to herself with relief, smiling her thanks to Attu.

"Here, let me take Gantuk, too. I'll walk them both to the water. Once they feel how cold it has become, they won't try to run down to it every chance they get."

Rika looked doubtful.

Attu took his children's small hands. "I want to see and touch the water, too." He grinned at his woman.

"Don't let them get drenched. The sickness spirits-"

But Attu didn't hear the rest of what Rika said. He'd turned away and was walking the two little ones down the beach. "Mother worries too much," he said to the twins. "We will just walk down to the water and you can touch it. I will hold you. I will keep you safe." Attu knew his son and daughter didn't understand what he was saying. But he'd needed to say it. It felt good to say it, as by saying it, he was telling the spirits of his intentions, making it true. Attu said it again. "Father will keep you safe. I will always keep you safe. Both of you, your mother, and your new baby sister."

They reached the water and Attu held each child around the stomach so their hands were free. He swooped them down like little birds. Just their fingers brushed the cold water of the gentle waves. Both pooliks squealed.

"More," Gantuk said. "More water."

Attu skimmed them across the surface of the water again. "Not too many times more," he said. "I'm up to my knees and my feet are starting to go numb." But he laughed at the cries of delight and the bubbling laughter of his children as they touched the water, spraying themselves in the face and getting the front of their clothing wet.

"We will get in trouble for that," Attu said. He swooped them down once more.

Rovek came running down the beach. "Tingiyok's coming into the bay. I saw him when I walked down to the point. Some of the Nukeena are with him."

"How many?"

"Several canoes. I could hear them laughing. They waved and shouted at me. Something about making a lot of food for hungry people. They have women and children with them."

"It will be a feast tonight." Attu grinned, even as he stepped out of the water to the disappointed cries of Nuanu and Gantuk.

"Don't be sad," Attu told them. "Elder Tingiyok is back, and our Nukeena friends are coming."

Attu scooped his children up in his arms and hurried up the beach with Rovek to tell the others.

THE END

Made in the USA
Lexington, KY
31 July 2016